Back

to

Lakewood Med

Book Two of the Lakewood Series

TJ Amberson

BACK TO LAKEWOOD MED
Book 2 of the Lakewood Series
by TJ Amberson

Text by TJ Amberson 2020
Cover art, design, and layout by Maria Spada and TJ Amberson 2020

Copyright Claimant
ENGLISH TRAILS PUBLISHING, LLC
Text © 2020 English Trails Publishing, LLC
Cover art, design, and layout © 2020 English Trails Publishing, LLC
All rights reserved

Paperback ISBN 978-0-9892999-9-2

This is a work of fiction. Names, characters, entities, places, events, objects, and products are the product of the author's imagination and/or used in a completely fictitious manner. Any other resemblance to actual persons (living or dead), names, characters, entities, places, events, objects, or products is entirely coincidental. Nothing in this manuscript is intended to be used or construed as medical advice.

While every reasonable effort was made to ensure a product of the highest quality, minor errors in the manuscript or cover may remain. If you have comments, please email englishtrailspublishing@gmail.com.

For my readers
Your support means everything

Books by TJ Amberson

Love at Lakewood Med
Back to Lakewood Med
New in Lakewood Med
Change for Lakewood Med
Gone from Lakewood Med

Fusion
Between
The Kingdom of Nereth
The Council of Nereth
The Keeper of Nereth

One

This is a trap.

Dr. Tammy Sanders has just asked me a question, and now she's waiting for my answer. Seated in her rightful place at the attendings' desk, Dr. Sanders is leaning back casually in her chair as she observes me. Despite the chaos of Lakewood Medical Center's emergency department swirling around us, Dr. Sanders has a calm, totally unruffled expression on her face.

But I'm not fooled.

Though Dr. Sanders is maintaining a laid-back façade, I'm not going to be lured into a false sense of security by her attending-physician mind tricks. I may only be a fourth-year medical student, but I've studied the medical education system extensively, and I know how this works. I know it's crucial that I answer her question correctly. If not, Dr. Sanders may decide I don't have what it takes, and if she decides I don't have what it takes, my entire career in emergency medicine will be over before it even starts. Poof. Gone. Eleven years of private school (I graduated early), four years of undergraduate work with dual majors in organic chemistry and biology, two summers volunteering in research labs, SATs, ACTs, the MCAT, USMLEs, the first three years of medical school, and the first rotation of fourth year (last month's emergency medicine rotation, which was also here at Lakewood) will all go up in smoke. Just like that. Because that's how it works. The medical education system is cut-throat. It's every-woman-for-herself.

In other words, everything hinges on answering her question correctly. The response I give will set the stage for this entire month of August, because Dr. Sanders is the attending physician with whom I've been assigned to work for the next four weeks. And with this being my second emergency medicine rotation here at Lakewood, the stakes are even higher than last month. Dr. Sanders knows I want to specialize in emergency medicine. She knows I'm applying for Lakewood's emergency medicine residency program. She knows I have last month's honors grade to live up to. And she knows that I know that she knows all of this.

Basically, my entire life has been building up to this moment. My answer has to be perfect. That's why I need more time to think through what I'm going to say.

"Could you please repeat the question?" I say in my most professional-sounding voice.

Dr. Sanders raises her eyebrows for a fleeting moment. "Sure: how are you doing this morning, Rachel?"

I peer back at her, still searching her face for subtle clues on how she's expecting me to answer. Dr. Sanders gives away nothing, however, as she tucks a loose strand of her long, salt-and-pepper hair into her low ponytail while waiting for my reply.

I shift in my seat, weighing my options. If I tell her I'm *good* or *fine* or *all right*, will it sound too generic? If I say I'm *fabulous* or *stoked*, will that come across as over-the-top?

It's like trying to navigate a minefield.

One thing's for sure, though: I have to hand it to Dr. Sanders. This is only her first question of our first shift together, and she's already messing with my head like the attending physician guru she is.

Well played, Dr. Sanders. Well played.

More seconds pass while I continue to calculate my move. Dr. Sanders adjusts the stethoscope around her neck and pushes her round glasses higher up on the bridge of her nose. Her eyes dart across the department before she puts her attention back on me. If I didn't know better, I would say she's starting to look a little freaked out.

Maybe I actually need to say something.

"I'm doing well, thank you," I state carefully.

I cringe as soon as the words leave my mouth. Was that too much? Not enough? Too generic? Too personal? I wouldn't be surprised if Dr. Sanders tells me I might as well give up on emergency medicine right now and try—

"Great. We've been looking forward to having you in the department for another month." Her relaxed smile returns. "Since you're already oriented to the place, I'm assuming you're ready to get busy seeing patients?"

Yikes. Another question already. I had no idea Dr. Sanders was this ruthless.

"Yes." I motion briskly to the nearby workstation where I've set out my things. I arrived an hour before our shift to ensure I had adequate time to get prepared. "I'm ready to go."

"Wonderful. How about you go see the new patient they just put in Hallway Six. Meanwhile, I'll go see the new patient in Room Nine. Once you're done, let me know what you want to do for your patient, and we'll talk it over."

I spring to my feet, resisting the urge to give her a respectful salute. "Absolutely, Doctor Sanders."

Spinning on my heels, I hurry over to my workstation. I remove my short white coat from the back of the chair and slip it on. (I ironed it last night so it would look as crisp as possible.) I smooth down my navy-blue scrubs, making sure there's not a wrinkle in sight. I then go through my usual routine of putting my stethoscope around my neck, a couple pens into the breast pocket of my coat, and a folded piece of paper into the pocket over my right hip. I finish by tucking my chin-length, dark blonde hair behind my ears.

Once I'm set, I look at the computer monitor to check the patient tracking board. The patient who was put in Hallway Six is listed as a nineteen-year-old male with a chief complaint of

"*Bilateral thumb pain.*" He's triaged as a Level Five, the lowest acuity level.

I sigh with disappointment. Level Five? It's going to be hard to impress Dr. Sanders with such a patient, since a Level Five shouldn't require complex medical decision making . . . or much of anything, for that matter. In fact, if this same patient had arrived only forty-five minutes later, he would have been triaged over to the Fast Track area of the department, which opens at seven o' clock every morning.

Around here, Fast Track gets used every day for low-acuity patients, since the main emergency department is always overcrowded with people who are critically ill. And even with the diversion of non-emergent patients to Fast Track, the overcrowding in the main department remains so severe that many sick patients still wind up being cared for from hallway stretchers. There's nowhere else for them to go.

Thankfully, things are going to change. Mark Prescott, the president of Lakewood Medical Center, recently announced they'll be breaking ground on an entirely new, much larger, and vastly more up-to-date emergency department. I was thrilled when I heard the news. A new department will be so much better for patients and staff. And on a personal level, it makes me hope even more that, one day, after graduating from residency, I'll be able to work in Lakewood's emergency department as an attending physician myself.

In his same announcement, Mr. Prescott also said construction will be overseen by one of

Lakewood's current emergency medicine attendings, Dr. Wesley Kent. That was more great news and no surprise, since Dr. Kent has spent years diligently campaigning to get the emergency department renovated. Meanwhile, in addition to acting as a consultant on the design of the new department, Dr. Kent will continue working as the director of the med student emergency medicine rotation here at Lakewood, which means he's the other attending I absolutely must impress this month. He may have approved an honors grade for me in July, but there's no guarantee he'll do it again.

Speaking of Dr. Kent, I've been meaning to call Savannah Drake, a fellow med student who also did the emergency medicine rotation here last month. Rumor has it there's something romantic brewing between Savannah and Dr. Kent now, and I've been extremely curious to know if the gossip is true. If Savannah is really dating Dr. Kent, I'm absolutely thrilled for her. But I have no idea how she (or any medical student, for that matter) could possibly have time for romance.

I know I don't.

I put my attention back on the tracking board and re-read the information for the patient in Hallway Six. The nurse has finished getting him settled in, and the patient is still listed as a Level Five. I sigh again. I'm guess I'm just going to have to make the best of it.

Rolling back my shoulders, I stand up as tall as I can, which is still not very tall, since I'm only five-three. However, I've read in several self-help books that carrying oneself with a commanding presence increases the respect one will receive. And as a rather petite female, I've learned I need all the help with looking commanding that I can get.

I turn away from the desk and give myself a silent pep talk. I can do this. I can impress Dr. Sanders with the care I'm about to provide this patient, even if it's a low-acuity complaint. I will obtain a focused-but-thorough history, perform excellent musculoskeletal and neurologic examinations of the patient's thumbs, come up with a comprehensive treatment plan, and determine the appropriate disposition.

Feeling ready, I begin striding across the busy department. The "room" designated as Hallway Six is actually a stretcher pushed up against a water-stained wall beside a cart of clean linens. Currently, a young man is sitting on the stretcher, dangling his legs over the side. He begins watching me as I approach, and his face takes on an expression of unmasked skepticism.

I exhale hard. I've seen that look from countless patients before. It's the look that says I can't possibly know what I'm doing. After all, in addition to having on a short white coat that lets everyone know I'm still a med student, I'm small and a little younger than my colleagues (I'm twenty-five). So it's hard to convince patients I might actually know what I'm talking about. Since the day I began pursuing a career in medicine, in fact, it has been a constant battle to prove myself to patients, attendings, colleagues . . . my family . . . and myself.

I swallow, sensing an all-too-familiar feeling of self-doubt threatening to creep in. Still, I manage to maintain my outwardly confident demeanor—something I've become well-practiced at over the years—and study the young man in return. He's dressed in a black t-shirt and jeans, and he has on a straight-billed baseball cap that partially covers his straggly red hair. There's darkness under his eyes, as if he hasn't slept. He looks upset, yet it doesn't strike me that he's in any sort of acute medical danger.

As I draw closer, my attention shifts to a woman who's seated on a rickety folding chair next to the stretcher. I'm guessing she's in her sixties, though her coarse, wrinkled skin ages her by at least another decade. She has a small bag at her feet.

Reaching the stretcher, I focus on my patient once more. I begin speaking to him in crisp tones. "Good morning. My name is Rachel Nelson. I'm a fourth-year medical student, and I'll be caring for you today."

"Hey," he mutters, scratching his nose and barely bothering to look my way.

I can't stop my attention from drifting back to the woman on the chair. She's leaning forward slightly, and I can see her chest rising and falling with effort as she breathes. I take a step toward her.

"Ma'am, are you okay?"

The woman nods and speaks between her raspy breaths. "Oh, yes, honey, I'm okay. I don't need anything. Thanks for asking, though. I have COPD from smoking, so I'm always a little short of breath, especially in the mornings." She puts on a smile and motions from herself to the young man. "My name is Linda. This is my grandson, Josh. He lives with me. He's the one who wanted to come see you this morning."

I press my lips together as I continue watching her. She's clearly having a COPD exacerbation, yet she's not interested in receiving medical care. Meanwhile, I still have to churn through this Level Five visit quickly. If I take too long with such a low-acuity visit, Dr. Sanders will make a note about it on her evaluation of me after the shift, which will lower my overall grade for the rotation.

I force myself to pull my eyes from the woman and concentrate again on Josh. "I reviewed the nurse's triage note, which indicated you're having thumb pain?"

"Yeah, it totally sucks." He holds up his hands. There's nothing wrong with his hands. "I was playing *Wizard Kingdom* on my gaming station overnight, but around five in the morning, my thumbs started getting sore, and so I had to stop." His eyes get wider, and his nasally voice begins to rise. "But I need to get back to my game. My online gaming group has a scheduled attack on a rival tribe later this morning. We'll be battling the Dwarfs and Goblins Tribe to take back the Flaming Sword of Death." He stops only to catch his breath before going on. "I really need to be able to play because I have the sacred levitation powers my tribe relies on. So you have to give me some pain pills, okay? My thumbs have to feel better before the battle."

I stare at him, my expression deadpan. There's a lot I want to say to Josh. I'm just trying to decide if a medical student is allowed to say it.

When I finally open my mouth to reply, my gaze instead moves back to Linda. The area around her mouth is getting pale, and I can hear a faint wheeze each time she exhales. I deliberate a moment longer and then face Linda squarely.

"I'm sorry to keep bothering you, Linda, but may I ask: are you supposed to be on supplemental oxygen?"

Appearing increasingly out-of-breath, Linda reaches down and pats the bag at her feet. "Yes. I'm usually at two liters. I brought my portable oxygen concentrator along with me to use while I was here."

"Well, perhaps it would be a good idea if you started using it." I crouch down on my haunches in front of her. "You're having a pretty significant COPD exacerbation."

"I know. And I actually tried turning on my concentrator after we arrived here, but the battery was dead." Linda coughs up some phlegm as she unzips her bag to reveal the small device stowed inside. She glances Josh's way. "Apparently, my oxygen concentrator didn't get charged overnight."

"Gosh, Grandma, stop acting so mad about it! I already told you, like, a hundred times that I needed the electrical outlet, okay?" Josh throws up his hands. "It was the only outlet that was close enough to the computer so I could plug in my gaming console and still sit in the recliner!"

My posture stiffens. I get back to my feet, spin toward Josh, and point a finger in his face. "You unplugged your grandmother's oxygen concentrator so you could play a *video game*?"

Josh recoils. "I, um, well . . . yeah. I mean, the game is really important. There's an evil grand-master wizard threatening to conquer all the tribes in the kingdom, and if my tribe doesn't stop the poisoned vegetables from growing—"

"Okay, that's it," I interrupt. "Get off the stretcher, Josh. Off. Now. Right now." I reach over to Linda and gently wrap a hand around her upper arm. She's having such a hard time breathing I almost have to pull her to her feet. I give Josh another chastising look. "Magic vegetables and flaming swords or not, your grandmother needs that stretcher more than you do."

Josh mutters something about not being able to help his tribe withstand the onslaught of the sparkling tornado, but he does as he's told and steps aside. While I assist Linda onto the stretcher, I glance over my shoulder. Through the crowd of patients, doctors, nurses, secretaries, techs, and EMS personnel filling the hallway, I spot one of the veteran nurses, Pete, coming out of a nearby exam room. I call to him over the ambient noise:

"Hey, Pete, I need your help over here."

He does a double take when he spots me and starts jogging over, surveying Linda with his brows drawn together. "Hi, Rachel. What's up?"

"COPD exacerbation, and she hasn't been able to use her home oxygen today." I help Linda get situated more comfortably on the stretcher, and then I use my stethoscope to ascultate her lungs. As anticipated, she's hardly moving air at all. Her lungs are tight, and her wheezing is diffuse. I continue talking to Pete. "Please get a Duoneb going, a portable monitor set up, and an IV placed. Have registration enter Linda into the computer system. Once she's registered, I'll put in orders for everything else."

"You got it." Pete darts off.

"Rachel, is everything all right over here?"

I look behind me. Dr. Sanders is approaching. Her expression is calm, as always, but I can see her eyes carefully taking in the scene. Instantly, my confidence disappears and I'm hit with a pulse of anxiety. Have I screwed up? Will Dr. Sanders disapprove of what I've done? Should I have finished caring for Josh first? Am I managing Linda's care incorrectly?

As my stomach twists with apprehension, I move to allow Dr. Sanders to reach Linda's stretcher. Keeping my voice steady to mask my nerves, I start to explain:

"Doctor Sanders, this is Linda. She was accompanying her grandson here this morning, but she was experiencing a COPD exacerbation, and I determined she needed the stretcher more than he did." I tilt my head in Josh's direction.

He's currently sitting on the chair, bouncing one leg and watching me with an expression of disdain. "I also believe this young man could be triaged over to Fast Track once it opens."

Dr. Sanders flicks her gaze from Linda to Josh and then to me. "Agreed."

The tension in my muscles releases. Dr. Sanders hasn't decided I'm not good enough yet. However, there are seven more hours to go before this shift is over. I could be deemed a failure at any moment.

Dr. Sanders introduces herself to Linda and proceeds to listen to her lungs. Meanwhile, Pete returns, starts the patient on a Duoneb, and begins preparing to place an IV. At some point, the gal from registration comes by to obtain Linda's information and then hurries off to return to her desk.

"The patient should be in the computer system soon. I'll go put in orders," I tell Dr. Sanders.

Without waiting for a reply, I whip around and rush to my workstation. Sitting down in front of the computer, I log into Linda's newly created chart and put in orders for the IV, the Duoneb treatment, and cardiac monitoring. I go on to add orders for a dose of IV steroids, blood work, an ECG, and a chest x-ray.

I pause, taking a second to review the orders while I rack my brain. Am I forgetting anything? I don't think so, but I want to be absolutely certain. I have to get this exactly right. Otherwise, Dr. Sanders will conclude I'm not good enough, and then I'll never have a chance to get accepted into next year's emergency medicine residency class here at Lakewood. The residency program is nationally renowned and extremely competitive, and only the very best med student applicants get in. Frankly, it will be a miracle if they even offer me an interview.

Once I finally decide the orders are ready, I use the computer mouse to click the *enter* button. I then raise my head to check on my patient. From where I'm seated, I can see Pete is done placing the IV in Linda's left arm. Dr. Sanders is speaking to Linda, who is finishing her first breathing treatment. Even from across the department, I can tell Linda is going to need at least one more breathing treatment—likely several more—before her symptoms improve. She may also require further testing to search for an identifiable, treatable cause of her COPD exacerbation. Amidst it all, there's a high likelihood she's going to need to be admitted to the hospital, and in a busy facility like this, the sooner patients can be put in the queue for an inpatient bed, the better. Otherwise, she could be waiting hours down here before a bed becomes available.

Taking the initiative, I enter an order for Linda to receive an albuterol breathing treatment, and then I pick up the receiver of the phone at my desk, press the *zero* button, and ask the hospital operator to page the admitting medicine resident to my workstation. Not long after I hang up, the phone rings. I pick up the receiver again and put it back to my ear.

"Hello, this is Rachel Nelson, fourth-year medical student in the emergency department."

There's a pause.

"Hi, Rachel," a guy says in a tone that's devoid of emotion. "I'm calling on behalf of the admitting medicine resident."

I close my eyes and groan silently as the familiar voice hits my ear. It's Austin. Austin Cahill.

Austin is another fourth-year medical student. He and I have known each other since the first day of med school, when we met after being assigned to the same discussion group. The small-group discussions were supposed to provide an opportunity for the two hundred new med students to start getting to know one another. Instead of a warm-and-fuzzy discussion, however, Austin and I clashed almost immediately. When I mentioned I had used wood glue while assembling a bookcase for my apartment, Austin insisted wood glue was meaningless. Things took off from there, and it wasn't long before the afternoon of small-group discussions had been hijacked by our fierce debate over the utility of wood glue. By the end of it, the whole class had split into two camps to cheer us on. The "incident" has become something of a legend among our classmates, and it's still talked about to this day. The fact remains, though, that Austin's mockery was a deliberate attempt to publically humiliate me, and I haven't forgiven him since.

After that first clash, Austin and I tried steering clear of each other, but our paths always seemed to keep crossing. A week later, we were put in the same anatomy dissection group for the rest of the year, where we spent more time arguing about the pterygopalatine fossa than actually dissecting anything even close to it. During second year, we wound up on the same team for practice rounds at University Hospital. So every Friday, between the hours of eight and eleven in the morning, I had to endure Austin correcting me any time I said a medication's brand name instead of the generic name. I know Austin only did it to show me up in front of the others. I mean, who wants to bother saying *tisagenlecleucel* even if they actually know how to pronounce it?

Austin. That's who.

Then came last year, our third year, when I had the misfortune of being on back-to-back inpatient rotations with Austin: a month of OBGYN followed by eight long weeks of internal medicine. By the time we were doing internal medicine, Austin had decided it was the specialty he wanted to go into. So, of course, he strutted around for the entire two months in an attempt to impress our attendings and outdo me for the best grade. He always took the most complicated patients. He was constantly trying to study and research more than me. We even got into an unspoken battle over who could get to the hospital first in the mornings to start pre-rounding—at one point, we both showed up at two thirty am, which was before the overnight team had even finished rounding on their shift.

And most aggravatingly of all was the smug way Austin spoke to me whenever we disagreed over treatment plans for patients.

In other words, everything Austin did made my blood boil. It also made me even more determined to prove myself.

Finally, the chance to prove myself came. Last month, Austin was also on the emergency medicine rotation here at Lakewood. But I wasn't about to let him show me up that time around. Emergency medicine was *my* chosen specialty. The emergency department was my territory. My turf. Though I nearly killed myself doing it, I earned an honors grade. I don't know what grade Austin received, but the fact that he never gloated about it makes me think I got a better grade than he did.

And that was extremely satisfying.

Anyway, Austin must now be on another internal medicine rotation, getting additional experience for his chosen specialty. Normally, I couldn't care less what Austin Cahill might be doing, but the fact that he's on the admitting medicine team this month will make what's already a daunting four weeks for me even more stressful. Since he's on the medicine service, Austin is part of the gate-keeping team I'll need to speak with every time I want to admit a patient to the hospital. Having to interact with him over and over again throughout the month is going to be a mild form of torture.

Austin Cahill is a curse.

But I'm not going to let Austin wreck this month for me. Besides, we're technically on different rotations, so it's not as though we're competing with each other this time. Therefore, as much as I'll loathe talking to him, he and I should be able to maintain our professionalism . . . and hopefully not want to kill each other by the time these four weeks are over.

"Good morning, Austin," I say into the phone, keeping my tone indifferent yet dignified. "I have a patient who needs to be admitted for a COPD exacerbation."

"Name?" he asks.

"Linda." I glance at the patient's info on the tracking board. "Linda Yates."

"Age?"

I roll my eyes at his rapid-fire questioning. He's acting as though he's a senior resident or something. "Sixty-four."

"Room?"

"Hallway Six." I peek over the top of the monitor to check on Linda, who's currently getting her new albuterol treatment while the radiology tech is setting her up for a portable chest x-ray. I then refocus on the call and start my patient presentation. "Ms. Yates is a sixty-four-year-old woman with COPD who presented to the emergency department this morning for—"

"I've pulled her up on the computer. I can see the information I need," Austin interrupts flatly.

I freeze with my mouth still partly open, stung by his not-so-subtle dismissal. Austin doesn't think it's necessary to hear the patient's history or exam findings from me? Considering I'm the patient's emergency department provider, that's a low blow. A really low blow. Yet I refuse to give Austin the satisfaction of knowing how much he's bothering me. Clearing my throat, I maintain my businesslike air and go on:

"Very well. Will you or someone from the admitting team be—"

"We'll be down."

The dial tone reaches my ear. I growl as I hang up the receiver while Austin's patronizing words replay in my mind. Austin doesn't think my input is helpful? Well, somehow I'll show him—I'll show everyone—I know what I'm talking about.

At least, I *think* I know what I'm talking about.

I hope I do.

Do I?

Pricked again by familiar feelings of inadequacy, I compulsively open Linda's chart and start reviewing her past medical history until I've committed every detail to memory. I then pull up her chest x-ray and look it over. Unfortunately, she has a left lower lobe pneumonia. All the more reason it's good we're admitting her. I do a quick check of her allergies and then add IV antibiotics to Linda's treatment regimen. Next, I review her lab results and ECG, which are also available in the computer.

Once I'm done, I push back from my desk and cross the department to return to Hallway Six. Josh is no longer around. He must have gone to Fast Track to get assessed. Or maybe he went home to bravely suffer through his bilateral thumb pain while his tribe launched their attack to obtain the Flaming Sword of Death.

"Hi, Linda." I reach the stretcher. "How are you feeling?"

"Better," she tell me. "Those breathing treatments helped, I think."

Using my stethoscope, I take another listen to her lungs. She's moving more air than before, thankfully, though she still sounds extremely wheezy. A glance at the portable monitor that Pete set up beside her stretcher shows Linda's saturation level is only ninety percent on supplemental oxygen, which is lower than her documented baseline.

I put my stethoscope into the pocket of my white coat. "Based on your x-ray, it appears you have pneumonia, so I'd like to get antibiotics started. Also, I think it's advisable to admit you to the hospital. You're going to need a lot of respiratory care. We want to keep a close watch on you and make sure your symptoms improve."

Linda's brow furrows. "But what about Josh? There won't be anyone to make his meals for him, and he's very particular about how he likes his food."

I put a hand on her shoulder. "Josh will be able to take care of himself. Remember: you need to take care of yourself, too."

She looks away for a time, and then she nods. "You're right. As much as I'd prefer to go home, I really don't feel well at all." She gives me an appreciative smile. "Thank you."

"You're welcome." I lower my arm back to my side. "In the meantime, how about we get you started on another breathing treatment?"

"That would be great."

After giving her a nod, I turn away from the stretcher. With the sounds of overhead announcements, conversations, crying babies, ringing phones, and the screams of a belligerently intoxicated patient filling the air, I start making a path back to my work station, weaving past EMS crews who are wheeling in new arrivals on stretchers, nurses taking reports, attending physicians and residents speaking with patients, and techs rushing by with ECG machines.

When I finally reach my desk, I re-open Linda's chart and place the order for her next albuterol treatment. I then attempt to start an electronic chart note. This is my first day using computer-based notation here, since we were still using paper charts in the ED last month. Thankfully, the ED computers were finally upgraded, and I can already tell having legible notes and orders, rather than handwritten scribbles, is going to be a welcome improvement.

As I'm typing, out of the corner of my eye, I notice Dr. Sanders emerge from another patient's exam room. When she spots me, she begins walking my way. I gulp, my calmness swiftly changing into my usual mixture of nerves and anxiousness to please.

Dr. Sanders reaches my side. "So what's your overall impression of Ms. Yates, and what would you like to do for her?"

Though my insides are squirming, I try to appear as calm and intelligently doctor-ish as possible. "Her chest x-ray shows a left lower lobe pneumonia, so after reviewing her allergies, I put in orders for Rocephin and azithromycin. Her ECG is stable with priors, and her labs thus far are within normal limits." I pause to do a hurried mental review of all the details I stuffed into my head, making sure I haven't forgotten anything, and then I continue. "Given her underlying COPD, her pneumonia, the hypoxia, and her need for further breathing treatments, I believe Ms. Yates warrants inpatient care. I took the liberty of calling the admitting team about her."

"Great." Dr. Sanders is about to say more when her attention is caught by something behind me. "And it looks like the medicine team is already here to evaluate her."

Following her gaze, I turn in my chair and look across the department. I see Pete starting Linda on her next breathing treatment. Standing beside Pete are two other people. One of them is a gal who's dressed in light blue scrubs and a long white coat. She has her auburn hair pulled back in a bun. I recognize her as one of the second-year internal medicine residents.

The other person is Austin.

I frown at the sight of him. However, though I have no desire to be within a hundred yards of Austin, it's my responsibility to make sure the admitting team has everything they need. And I will not let my aversion to Austin stop me from doing my job. Especially not when I'm trying to earn an honors grade on this rotation.

I get to my feet. "I'll go confirm the admitting team doesn't have any other questions," I tell Dr. Sanders before stepping away.

Maneuvering once again through the increasingly crowded department, I venture toward Hallway Six. Through the fray, I can see the internal medicine resident talking to Linda. Linda is listening attentively, and she appears to be handling her latest breathing treatment well. Meanwhile, silently watching the exchange, and standing taller than everyone around him because he has got to be six-four, is Austin.

Dressed in blue hospital scrubs and a short white coat like mine, Austin has his arms crossed over his chest while he observes the resident and Linda conversing. Austin's light brown hair is slightly disheveled, and there's a hint of facial scruff above his upper lip and on his chin, so I'm guessing he was on-call here in the hospital last night, which means he and the resident are now finishing morning rounds and seeing new admits before going home after their twenty-four-hour shift.

Austin's eyes flick my direction. He does a double take when he notices me approaching and drops his arms to his sides. I tip up my chin and fix my gaze straight ahead. Even though

Austin towers above everyone—especially me—I pretend not to notice him.

Reaching the stretcher, I place myself on the resident's other side and wait while she finishes explaining to Linda the plan for admission and what her anticipated inpatient care will entail. Once the resident concludes what she's saying, she turns my direction and smiles.

"Hi, there."

"Good morning," I say, trying to sound as though I know what I'm doing. "I'm Rachel Nelson, the fourth-year med student who has been helping to care for Ms. Yates."

"I'm Tara Hess." The resident gives me another warm smile. "It's really nice to meet you."

"It's nice to meet you, too." I venture a hint of a smile in return, but I don't overdo it. After all, I'm speaking to a resident. An actual doctor. So I can't be presumptuous and act too chummy. Still ignoring Austin, who's standing behind Tara and watching me with his ever-critical eye, I clear my throat and continue. "Are there any questions I can answer for you, Doctor Hess? Or is there anything else you'd like me to get ordered from down here while awaiting Ms. Yates's inpatient bed to become available?"

Tara is about to reply when a shrill sound erupts from one of the pagers she has clipped to the waistband of her scrub pants. She casts me an apologetic look before she slides the culprit pager from its holder and holds it up to read the message.

"A nurse on the fourth floor has a question about a discharge." Tara turns to Austin while sliding the pager back into its holder. "Do you mind finishing up here with Rachel? When you're done, meet me back up on the fourth floor, and we'll resume rounding with the team."

Austin pulls his eyes from me and adopts a more amiable expression as he nods to Tara. "Okay."

Tara smiles at him, shifts back to Linda and apologizes for needing to depart, and then steps away from the stretcher and walks quickly out the back exit of the emergency department.

I take in a long, slow breath as I watch Tara—the last remaining buffer between Austin and me—disappear from view. I then make myself face Austin and raise my eyes to his.

"Is there anything else I can do to help you and your team from down here?" I inquire with exaggerated politeness.

His hazel eyes are sharp as they meet mine. "Have you started her on antibiotics?"

"Yes." I show him a fleeting, victorious grin. Try as he might, Austin isn't going to find fault with the care I've provided. Not this time. Not here. This is the emergency department. This is my realm. "I've already placed orders for azithromycin and Rocephin."

"Ceftriaxone," he immediately corrects me.

I pause, my jaw clenching a little. "Rocephin," I repeat, deliberately emphasizing each syllable of the medication's brand name.

"Ceftriaxone," he repeats without missing a beat.

I narrow my brown eyes at him for only an instant. Austin is doing this on purpose. He's just trying to show me up.

"Rocephin," I say again, and before he can retaliate, I shift my attention back to Linda. She's still got the nebulizer mask over her nose and mouth, and her eyes are darting back-and-forth between Austin and me like she's watching a ping pong match.

"We're discussing your antibiotic regimen," I explain, adopting a pleasant tone. "Rocephin and ceftriaxone are the brand and generic names for *the same medication.*" Turning to Austin once more, I go on with a forced smile. "Would you like to step over to my workstation to continue our conversation?"

"No." Austin's gaze remains steady. "I have everything I need."

Yet again, Austin is brushing me off. He's making it clear he thinks what I have to say isn't helpful or important. Frankly, I'm not sure what hurts more: Austin's insult or the fact that he may be right.

Don't let him get to you, I tell myself. *There's an honors grade you need to achieve on this rotation, and an emergency medicine residency program you're dreaming of being accepted into.*

Mustering all my willpower to remain collegial, I open my mouth to reply to him. However, Austin doesn't give me the chance. Instead, he looks to Linda and says:

"They'll get ceftriaxone going while you're waiting down here. Your inpatient bed should be ready shortly. I'll chat with you some more as soon as you're brought upstairs."

Linda's voice is muffled as she speaks through her mask. "Thank you."

Austin finishes by giving me a last look—a smirk, really—and then he strides out of the department. My lips smash together as I watch him go. After he's gone from view, I shift to Linda and address her again.

"Is there anything I can get you at the moment?"

"No, thank you. I'm feeling a lot better already." Linda seems to pause before she motions to where Austin was standing. "So is he a friend of yours?"

I adamantly shake my head. "No. He's just a classmate."

"Ah." She tips her head, studying me for a second or two. If I didn't know better, I would say she's trying not to smile behind her mask. She then settles back on her stretcher. "Thank you again for your help today, Rachel. I'm really grateful for what you've done."

"You're welcome. It's my pleasure."

I recheck Linda's vitals, glad to see they're improving, and then retrace the route back to my workstation. Sitting down, I try to resume working on Linda's chart note, but I find myself distractedly drumming my fingers on the keyboard.

I cannot believe Austin is on the admitting medicine service this month. He's the most antagonizing person I've ever known, and now I'll have to deal with him on a regular basis for another four weeks. How did I get so unlucky as to overlap with him on rotations *again*? Frankly, graduation next June can't come soon enough; that's when Austin and I will finally go our separate ways and head to our respective residency programs (wherever they may be). Finally, I won't have to put up with his antics anymore.

In the meantime, though, I am resolved not to allow Austin to interfere with my goals. I'm going to work as hard as I can to impress Dr. Sanders and earn another honors grade on this rotation. It's the only way I'll ever have a chance of even being considered for Lakewood's emergency medicine residency program next year.

Returning my attention to the chart note, I start typing with renewed determination. Despite my resolve, however, I can't ignore a little voice that's whispering in my head. It's the voice that always makes me doubt myself. Austin and all the other medical students seem so confident. So sure. So knowledgeable. So skilled at what they do. It's like I'm the only one who worries she's not good enough.

I stop typing. Maybe the truth is that I'm really just not good enough. Maybe I don't have what it takes to do this.

Will I ever be good enough?

Two

I'm woken from a deep sleep by the alarm on my cell phone. As my heavy eyelids open halfway and my weary mind starts coming into focus, I find that I'm lying on my bed in a strangely contorted position with one arm hanging off the side and my face smashed against the pillow.

The perky alarm song gets louder. With a groan, I reach over to my nightstand and feel around to locate my phone. The song continues while I blindly tap the phone's screen until, at last, I manage to hit the spot that shuts off the music. Silence mercifully takes over the room once more. I roll exhaustedly onto my back, making a mental note to change my alarm to something a bit more subdued next time.

I lie there another minute or two before I force my eyes to open fully. My body is begging to go back to sleep, but I don't give in. It's six in the morning, and I need to get going. So I push myself up into a sitting position and brush my hair from my face while starting a mental review of my to-do list for the day.

Today is one of the days this month when I don't have a shift in the emergency department or a didactic to attend. That doesn't mean I'm going to slack off, though. In fact, my self-assigned agenda is pretty packed. I'm going to start by reviewing Lakewood's online emergency medicine syllabus. Created by Dr. Kent, the syllabus is a wealth of information intended for the twelve medical students who are on the rotation each month. There's an immense amount of info to help with both patient care and preparing for the end-of-rotation written exam. Granted, I could probably recite the entire syllabus from start to finish already—I committed it to memory during the rotation last month—nonetheless, I intend to reread the whole thing today. I want to ensure I'm totally prepared for whenever Dr. Sanders or any of the other attendings asks me a question. Because I have an honors grade and a chance to get into Lakewood's residency program on the line.

After my morning study session, I'll go to the gym here in my apartment complex to work out. Don't get me wrong, I'm no athlete. Working out regularly is a fairly new thing for me in my adult life. I only started doing it on a consistent basis after one of the med school counselors suggested I try exercise as a way to "burn off some extra energy."

As for why I was meeting with a counselor in the first place, that goes back about three years. During the first month of med school, all the new students were assigned to meet with the school's counselors. This was intended to allow students to familiarize themselves with the counseling center as a resource, which we were encouraged to use as we faced the stresses med school would inevitably bring.

I went to a few counseling sessions, as did my classmates. Though the counselors were knowledgeable and well-intentioned, I found they didn't tell me anything I didn't already know about myself. I already knew I was gripped with self-doubt. And I definitely knew I always felt pressure to perform perfectly. I've been that way my entire life. So, ironically, counseling sessions wound up being more discouraging than helpful, since repeatedly being reminded about what was wrong with my way of thinking didn't exactly prove beneficial for my psyche.

What the counselors would have had a much more interesting time exploring is *why* I'm wired the way I am. Not that I needed a counselor to help me sort through that, either. I've had it figured out since I was a teenager. It's not complicated. The short version is that I'm the middle child in a family of super-high achievers. My father is Chief of Neurosurgery for a huge hospital on the east coast. My mother earned a PhD in physics and is a professor at the major university that's affiliated with my father's hospital. My older brother, Jacob, is already board certified in internal medicine, and now he's in the middle of his three-year hematology-oncology fellowship. Meanwhile, my younger sister, Julie, has recently aced her MCAT and is currently applying to medical school herself.

Needless to say, the expectation of success in my family is . . . high. While my family members don't sit around and brag about their achievements to one another, the unspoken pressure is there, and as an impressionable kid, I quickly internalized that I had to be an early high school graduate, class valedictorian, *summa cum laude*, and a doctor in order to keep up. I believed anything less would be a massive disappoint.

Luckily, I genuinely loved academics and absolutely fell in love with medicine—especially emergency medicine, which became my own little niche in the medical world. I'm forever thankful things worked out so well in that regard, since I'm not sure I would have been brave enough to pursue anything other than a career in medicine even if I hadn't loved it. I would have been too afraid of my family thinking a different career path wasn't good enough.

Anyway, after attending those obligatory counseling sessions during the first month of med school, I decided the one good piece of advice I gleaned was to find an outlet for my angst. That was when I started going to the gym. Initially, it was intimidating to be around all the cutely dressed, tan, selfie-taking-in-the-mirror gym types, since I hadn't done any serious working out for years (I loved gymnastics when I was young, but my parents pulled me out in junior high so I could concentrate on academics). It didn't take long, though, for me to discover that breaking a sweat on an elliptical, especially when pairing it with watching *Gilmore Girls* reruns, was extremely therapeutic. I've been doing it ever since.

I glance at the clock on my phone. It's now six-ten in the morning. I need to get going. Throwing aside my comforter, I get to my feet, shuffle over to the window, and open the blinds, letting the early morning sunshine pour into the bedroom. I blink as my eyes adjust to the brightness and then peer out at the city skyline.

My apartment is located in a new, hipster area of town. There are plenty of restaurants, cafés, shops, and grocery stores within walking distance—most of them proudly proclaiming their products are *organic, gluten-free, ethically sourced, fair-trade, indie, artisanal, vintage*, or something along those same lines. Frankly, until moving here for med school, I had no idea people put so much coordinated effort into being "unconventional" or that living a lifestyle "outside the social mainstream" meant groceries had to be so expensive.

Most of the people living in my area are in their mid-twenties to late-thirties, so there are a lot of popular nightclubs and bars around, too. Not that I ever make time to socialize, but if I did, I'm sure this would be a great place for it.

I sigh. The truth is, I don't socialize at all anymore. What makes it worse is knowing that while I'm focusing all my time and energy on my medical education, I'm missing out on lots of other things life has to offer. Though I believe the sacrifice will ultimately be worth it, it's still hard to wonder how much is passing me by in the meantime. At the very least, it's lonely. *I'm* lonely. None of my close friends live around here. I haven't had a boyfriend since my sophomore year in high school. I haven't even gone on a date since college—and, to be honest, those college dates could barely be considered "dates" at all.

While doing my undergrad work at Stanford, my parents were constantly setting me up with wealthy sons of their professional acquaintances. It wasn't that my parents were trying to rush me into marriage. Rather, they wanted me dating guys who came from reputable, rich families because, in my parents' opinions, that was part of the package. It was part of the image they felt a pre-med student should uphold. In my parents' minds, how I carried myself and what circles I moved in were extremely important, and dating the sons of rich, successful people was a way to set the standard.

I don't remember the names of most of the guys I went out with or even what half of them looked like. They were all pretty much the same: fairly handsome, well-dressed, rich, prone to partying, and paying lip service to becoming doctors, attorneys, or CEOs. In truth, most of them didn't need to be at college, since they would be inheriting their parents' businesses fortunes. Rather, for them, it was about having the status symbol of a degree from a prestigious university, even if they spent most of their time partying while they were there.

So the cringe-worthy dates came and went almost every weekend. They were really more like forced attempts at business mergers than anything even remotely romantic. Usually, the guy would take me to a fancy restaurant and then suggest we go out for drinks afterward. It didn't take me long to perfect the art of thanking the guy for dinner and politely bailing on the rest of the night. Instead of drinks and partying, I would return home, relay to my roommates my latest dating horror story, and retreat to my room to resume studying. Needless to say, love never blossomed on any of those dates, and I wound up a little tainted about the whole dating thing in general. Once I got into med school, I vowed to forgo further attempts at romance until residency was over. I knew that I would be too busy for love until then, anyway.

However, even with my complete lack of socializing these past few years, I've still enjoyed living in this part of the city. Access to public transportation is easy and abundant. It's a clean, safe area of town. And my apartment is an easy bus ride away from Lakewood Medical Center. (When I moved here, Dad insisted I choose an area close to one of the hospitals I would be rotating at so I could more easily stay late and arrive early for my shifts.) Overall, I certainly can't complain.

I shoot another glance at the time on my phone as I break from my thoughts. Spinning away from the window, I make my bed, being sure to fluff up my thick, white comforter and matching pillows like I always do. I then cross the room, open the door, and step out into the main living area of my apartment. I live alone, so my place is always quiet and tidy—a much-needed contrast to the loud, hectic atmosphere of a hospital. Admittedly, though, living by myself can make the loneliness worse at times. I miss my high school and college friends, who have gone on to do awesome things like start a small business, graduate from law school, marry, or get a high-level position in the State Department. My friends and I keep in touch, of course, but it's not quite the same when I only get to see them while I'm home for Christmas.

Nonetheless, though I knew it would be lonely, I still made the decision to live alone when I moved out here. Since I didn't know a soul, I figured living by myself was safer than potentially getting stuck with some psychopath roommate who puts on a toilet paper roll the wrong way. While solitude has, at times, been a downside, being in control of my home environment has at least allowed me to make it the retreat I've needed. I decorated the apartment in a simple, modern décor with subdued, soothing colors, and I made sure to put a cozy, thick rug over the hardwood floors in every room.

With a yawn, I head into the kitchen and get a cup of hot chocolate brewing. Unlike the other ninety-nine-point-nine percent of med students in the world, I don't do coffee. I discovered a long time ago that caffeine and I aren't a good mix. The first (and last) time I had a *grande* drip, I was so wired I wound up staying awake for over forty-eight hours straight.

While the aroma of chocolate begins filling the air, I pull open the fridge and survey what I've got inside. Unfortunately, it isn't much: a couple apples, cans of sparkling water, a nearly empty jar of cream cheese, and a bowl of pasta that's at least a week old. I grimace and shut the fridge. Moving on to the cupboards, I scan the shelves while my stomach growls. All I have are protein bars, a few packets of instant oatmeal, and a small thing of peanut butter.

I shut the last cupboard with another sigh. I guess I need to add a trip to the grocery store to my list of things to take care of today.

Picking up my hot chocolate, I make my way into the other bedroom, which I use as a home office. Settling into the chair behind my desk, I reach forward to open the blinds and pull the window ajar. Placing my mug on my desk, I take in a deep breath of the refreshing morning air.

Outside, the summertime sun is rising higher in the blue, cloudless sky, and the city streets are growing busy with the usual weekday bustle. From my vantage point several stories up, I can see pedestrians and bike riders maneuvering the sidewalks and darting along the crosswalks. I hear the roar of bus engines and the chaos of car horns being honked. Delicious smells of pastries from nearby cafés are being carried by the breeze, making my stomach growl again. Maybe, in a little while, I'll take a break from studying and go grab a late breakfast somewhere.

Pulling my gaze from the window, I reach for the computer mouse and wake up my PC. I get on the Internet and navigate to the log-in page for Lakewood's emergency department attendings, residents, and med students. In what has become a very well-practiced routine, I enter my user name and password, and I click over to the med student syllabus. I'm just about to begin reading a chapter when I hear my phone start to ring. It's the ringtone I've specifically set for my mom.

Hopping up from my chair, I scurry back into the bedroom and put the phone to my ear.

"Hello?"

"Hi, hon, how are you doing?" My mother's voice is as calm and steady as ever.

I begin meandering back toward the office while casting a glance at the clock hanging on the wall. I shake my head. Only my mom or dad would call for a non-emergency before seven in the morning. Either they think everyone is always as on-the-go as they are, or they forget about the time zone difference between us.

"I'm doing fine." I get settled again in my desk chair and resume watching out the window. "I'm about to get some studying done, and then I'll be heading out to run errands."

Mom makes a humming sound of approval. "Is your new emergency medicine rotation going well?"

"Well, it only started yesterday, but the attending physician I've been assigned to is really good." I push off the floor with the ball of one foot, causing my chair to start turning slowly in a circle. "How are things at home?"

"That's what I'm calling about. Have you heard the news about your sister?"

"No." I bring my chair to an abrupt stop. "Is Julie okay?"

"Oh, yes. She's doing wonderfully, in fact. She submitted her medical school application a few days ago." Mom pauses before adding, "You may not know, but she committed to the early decision program."

"Oh." I immediately feel the full impact of my mother's remark.

Several years ago, back when my brother applied for med school, he chose to do the early decision program. Basically, it meant he applied a few months earlier than other applicants, and he applied only to one med school. It's a way applicants can show particular interest in a certain program, and by demonstrating such commitment, applicants hope to increase the likelihood their desired med school will accept them. The strategy worked for my brother; not long after applying, Jacob got accepted to the med school of his choice.

So, apparently, Julie has also committed to the early decision route, which my mother is obviously pleased about. No doubt Dad is equally satisfied. And I'm sure they'll make their approval of Julie's choice abundantly clear to me for years to come, which will become yet another reason for me to feel inadequate compared to my siblings since I'm the only one who didn't do the early acceptance program.

When I applied to med school, there were three programs I was interested in, so I wanted to keep my options open. I therefore applied on the regular timeline. Though my parents never said anything about my decision, I knew doing the "normal" med school application process was akin to failure in their eyes. It didn't matter that I still wound up getting accepted quite early, receiving an acceptance letter only days after I interviewed. It also didn't matter that I got into the med school I was most interested in. The fact remained that I had applied via the "normal" route, and in my family "normal" is not good enough.

"I'm glad to hear Julie has her application done. That's a big step," I say, having to make a conscious effort not to fall into the trap of saying a bunch of overly gushy things to please Mom. It's something I still do at times, if I'm not careful, whenever I sense Mom or Dad is dissatisfied with me.

"Yes, we're extremely proud of her and expect she'll be receiving an invitation to interview soon." Mom pauses for emphasis. "And did you hear her other exciting news?"

"No." My eyebrows rise. "I actually haven't talked with Julie for a few days. I've been pretty swamped with wrapping up last month's rotation and starting a new one."

"Well, I normally wouldn't spoil her surprise, but Julie is *so busy* volunteering at the children's hospital and in the biochemistry lab, I'm sure she won't mind if I tell you."

I sigh yet again. Neither Mom nor Dad ever acted impressed about anything I did as a pre-med student. Yet now that Julie is essentially doing all the same things I did at her stage, Mom and Dad constantly rave about her. It was the same way when Jacob was pre-med—he could do no wrong.

What's wrong with me?

"Okay," I prompt. "What's Julie's other news?"

Mom takes in a breath. "Julie is going out on a date this Saturday."

Long pause.

"A date?" I manage not to snicker. This is the big news Mom called at six forty-five in the morning to tell me about? "That's nice. Who's the lucky guy?"

"His name is Lars. He's the son of one of your father's colleagues, and—"

"Hang on, Mom. Is this the same Lars you and Dad set me up with, like, four years ago?"

Now it's her turn to pause.

"My goodness, what do you know? It certainly is." My mother lets out a titter of laughter. "What are the odds of that?"

Pretty high, considering there can't be too many guys Dad knows who happen to have a son named Lars, I think to myself.

While I don't remember a lot of the guys I went out with over the years—the whole Saturday night dating thing during college is mostly a blur—I do remember Lars. Blond and handsome, he had the car and the looks to match his ego. However, he most certainly did *not* have intelligence or manners.

"If Lars is still hanging around Stanford and prowling the undergrad dating scene, I take it he hasn't yet found his soulmate?" I nearly giggle aloud. "I'm shocked to hear it."

"Don't be snippy. The poor young man recently broke up with his latest girlfriend." My mother has adopted her chastising tone. She's clearly not happy that I'm not in total awe of her choice of a date for Julie. "I heard from Lars's own mother that the girl he was with was excessively demanding. Thank goodness Lars got out of that relationship so quickly."

I blow a strand of hair from my face. "So what makes you think Lars is a good match for Julie?"

"I'm not saying they're necessarily a perfect match, Rachel. I'm not trying to get Julie married. I'm simply saying Lars is the *type* of man who an intelligent, beautiful woman like Julie should be dating. After all, she is going to be a *physician*. She should set her standards high and be selective."

I literally bite my tongue to stop myself from saying anything else. Mom and Dad have mingled in what I would deem rather snobby social circles for so long that I don't think they realize how out-of-touch they sound sometimes.

Yet even though Mom is being ridiculous, I'm still starting to feel anxious. Anxious to please her. Anxious for my mom to praise me the way she praises Julie. I can't help it. My impulse is to bring up the fact that I'm also going to be a physician—that I'm going to be graduating from med school and earning my medical degree in less than a year, in fact. But it's not like Mom has forgotten.

Still, though, it sometimes feels like I'm forgotten.

I decide to change the topic slightly. "What does Julie think about going out with Lars?"

"I believe she's looking forward to it," Mom replies matter-of-factly.

Until she meets him, I think with another suppressed laugh. "When did Julie start agreeing to blind dates? I thought she was dating Marcus."

"She and Marcus broke up recently." Mom sounds triumphant. I don't think she ever liked Marcus, not because he wasn't a good guy but because Mom hadn't hand-selected him herself.

I feel a real pang of sadness for my sister. No wonder Julie hasn't been answering the texts I've sent her lately. She's probably an emotional wreck. She and Marcus were together for over a year. I actually liked him a lot, and I thought they were good for each other. I wonder what happened between them?

I mentally add calling Julie to my day's to-do items, and I put it at the top of the priority list.

Shifting in my chair, I go on. "So is Julie okay with you setting her up on a date with someone else already? Does she really want you doing that to, I mean, *for* her?"

"Whether she realizes it or not, Julie needs someone to take her mind off Marcus," Mom asserts. "Both she and Lars have recently gone through breakups, so they'll be able to relate well to one another. It's a perfect opportunity for Julie to see there are other fish in the sea."

"Perhaps she doesn't want to go out with someone new yet, though."

"Julie agreed to go. At least your sister is *trying* to continue socializing rather than shutting herself off from the world."

Her comment zings me right in the heart. She has a point, of course. I certainly never encouraged any of the guys I went out with during college to call for a second date. And for the last three-plus years, I haven't gone out at all.

I can't ever do anything right.

"Hey, Mom, I'm sorry to break this off, but I need to get back to studying." I swallow past the lump that's forming in my throat. "I'll talk to you later, all right? Please give my love to Dad."

I end the call before she can say anything more and drop my phone onto the desk. A few tears escape and roll down my cheeks as I stare out the window.

The truth is, I wish I had more going on my life. I miss having close friends around. I miss going out. I miss having free time to relax. I miss romance. But I'm so busy with my medical training and education, and with trying to excel at all of it, I don't have time for anything else.

One day, though, I hope to meet a wonderful guy and fall in love. I even want to get married. I want that special connection with someone who loves me for who I am—and someone I love as completely in return. I can't think of anything more beautiful than that. For now, though, I'm simply too busy. Love will have to wait.

Exhaling hard, I spin my chair so I'm facing my computer once more. I click on the tab to open the syllabus and get to the first page. Cupping my hot chocolate in my hands, I focus on the words on the screen. This is something I can control. This is something I can do well. It might be all I have at the moment, but at least it's something.

And I begin to study.

Three

"Mr. Egbert is a forty-six-year-old male we were called about when law enforcement requested for him to be transported to the nearest emergency department for medical evaluation."

I'm standing just inside the exam room, listening with full concentration as the lead member of the ambulance crew provides report. This is my first time taking an EMS report independently, and so my stomach is tangled in a giant knot. I have to make sure I do everything right, since interacting well with EMS crews is another way I can show Dr. Sanders I would be a great addition to next year's emergency medicine residency class here at Lakewood.

The patient I'm receiving report about was brought in by ambulance only a few minutes ago. When Dr. Sanders invited me to start the case on my own, I dashed into the exam room before a nurse even got assigned to the patient. So it's currently just the two-person ambulance crew, the patient, and me.

While his partner assists the patient with transferring from their stretcher over to the stretcher that's in the room, the lead EMT continues with his report:

"The patient was being driven to jail for booking when he disclosed that he had possibly swallowed the head of a Dixie Doll."

I do a double take. "Excuse me? As in the popular children's toy?"

The lead EMT glances at the tablet in his hand to reference his note. "Yes, while en route to the jail, the patient notified the arresting officer that he had possibly swallowed the head of a Dixie Doll. The police officer called for ambulance transport so the patient could be medically evaluated."

I shift my widening eyes to the patient, who is now situated on the exam room's stretcher. He's sitting up and appears quite comfortable. He's of average build. His blond hair is messy but not unclean. His tanned skin is marked with what appears to be a bunny rabbit tattoo on the right side of his neck. And he's wearing a black tank top, orange athletic shorts, and superhero-patterned socks.

Recovering my professional demeanor, I step closer to the stretcher. "Good morning, Mr. Egbert. My name is Rachel Nelson. I'm a fourth-year medical student, and I'll be taking care of you while you're in the emergency department today."

The patient stares back at me but doesn't reply. Awkward silence settles upon the room. I clear my throat and glance at the EMTs. The one who transferred the patient just gives me a slight shrug before she wheels their stretcher out of the room. The lead EMT scans his note again.

"I guess that's all the info we have. Transport was short, so we didn't obtain any further details. The police officer who called to get help for the patient is right outside, though. Maybe he can provide you with more information."

The lead EMT gives me an apologetic look before he slips out. Suddenly, I find myself alone with Mr. Egbert. The alleged Dixie Doll head swallower. Somehow, I still manage to maintain my in-charge air as I move up to the foot of the stretcher.

"So, Mr. Egbert," I begin, drawing out the words while trying to figure out exactly what to say. "Why don't you tell me a little more about what brings you into the emergency department today."

"I swallowed Dixie's head," he replies in a gravelly voice.

"And do you . . . swallow Dixie's head often?"

He blinks several times and reverts back to saying nothing.

I sigh to myself. Unless this man is blinking in Morse Code, I doubt he'll be engaging in much nuanced conversation . . . or much conversation at all, for that matter. I think it's time for yes-or-no questions.

"Sir, are you having any pain?"
"No."
"Are you having *any* symptoms or concerns right now?"

Two blinks.

"Do you have any medical history, Mr. Egbert?"

He peers upward, appearing to think. "I once got a rash from a toilet seat."

I opt to move on to the next topic. "Do you take any medication?"

"No, but I used to take a medication for the toilet seat rash."

"Do you have any allergies?"

"I was allergic to the medication I took for my toilet seat rash."

"Does anyone in your family have serious medical problems?"

"I think my brother had the same toilet seat rash."

I give up and remove the stethoscope from around my neck. "Sir, do you mind if I examine you?"

Blink.

Taking that as permission, I go to the patient's left side to begin my exam, but not before I pull open the room's curtain so the police officer who is waiting outside can keep an eye on things. I figure if this patient has a propensity to eat the little head off a Dixie doll, it's better to be safe than sorry.

The exam goes quickly, and I don't find anything unusual. When I'm done, I sling my stethoscope back around my neck and retreat a few paces from the stretcher.

"Sir, please excuse me for a few minutes. I'm going to speak with the attending physician and place orders. I'll be back to update you on results."

Blink.

I blink back at him and depart the room, leaving the curtain ajar, and approach the policeman who has been watching from outside.

"Officer, may I ask what information you've gleaned about Mr. Egbert?"

"Certainly." The officer reaches to the side of his vest and turns down the volume on his radio, which has been emitting a constant stream of background dispatch chatter. "I responded to a disturbance call at a local ShopMart. Staff reported finding this man in the store's toy section. Based on eye-witness reports and what was captured on security camera footage, Mr. Egbert appeared to be ripping open numerous boxes of Dixie Dolls and tearing off the dolls' heads with his teeth."

I do my best to appear unruffled. Like nothing rattles me since I work in an ED. Like I care for Dixie head swallowers every day. "I see."

The officer continues in an equally no-nonsense way, making me wonder if he really *does* deal with Dixie head swallowers on a regular basis. "While transporting Mr. Egbert to the jail, he notified me that he had possibly swallowed one of the Dixie Doll's heads. I therefore requested medical transport to bring the patient to the nearest hospital for further assessment."

I grab a pen from my coat's breast pocket, and I remove the paper from the pocket on my hip. I jot down a couple notes about what the officer said and then look up at him again.

"Thanks. I'll be back shortly."

As the officer heads into the patient's room, I go the other way, maneuvering through the usual ruckus of the main emergency department. After a glance at the patient tracking board, I stop, stand on tiptoe, and scan the chaos. I soon spot the nurse, Hadi, at a nearby computer. I'm always glad to see Hadi here; though he's only about my age, I think he's one of the best nurses in the department. I quickly stride over to him.

"Hi, Hadi."

He looks up from his computer with his usual friendly grin. "Hey, Rachel. How's it going?"

"Well, my shift just began, but it's already off to a rather interesting start." I tip my head in the direction of the Dixie Doll room. "I saw your initials are now on the tracking board for Room Eleven. Will you be the primary nurse in there?"

"Yup. I just got assigned." Hadi faces me and leans in a relaxed pose against the counter. "How can I help?"

"I would like to make the patient NPO, start IV fluid, and get some labs drawn. I'll also be ordering an abdominal x-ray."

Hadi nods. "I'll get going on everything right now. I haven't had a chance to read the patient's chart yet. What are you working him up for?"

"Funny you should ask." I can't help grinning. "The patient doesn't give the most comprehensive history, but he allegedly bit off the heads of several Dixie Dolls and possibly swallowed one."

Hadi snorts a laugh. "Are you serious? Now that's a chief complaint I haven't heard before."

"I'm serious." I laugh quietly along with him. Hadi is one of the few people around here with whom I feel like I can let down my guard. I've considered him a friend since I began working in this department. "I'm gonna go update Doctor Sanders and put in orders."

"Sounds good." Hadi is still chuckling as he strides off toward the patient's room.

I walk the opposite direction and make a path through the fray to reach the workstation where I set up for the shift. Dr. Sanders and I are doing a swing shift today, which covers the hours of eleven am to seven pm (I arrived an hour early, though, to get fully settled in and do more syllabus review). Swing shifts are my favorite. They don't start too early, and they don't wrap up too late. Smack in the middle of the day, swing shifts go by fast because they're busy, partly due to a predictable late-morning and early-evening rush of patients. From start to finish, swing shifts are filled with challenging and interesting cases. As a bonus, swing shifts allow me to interact with both the day and the evening nursing crews, which I enjoy.

From the looks of things around here, today's shift will be particularly hectic. This isn't surprising, though, since it's Monday, which is typically the busiest day in an emergency department. In fact, in anticipation of the crazy, I wore sneakers with my scrubs. Admittedly, sneakers aren't nearly as cute as the clog-style shoes most female med students and residents wear, but they do make it much more comfortable to run around the department for eight hours straight. Not to mention, I particularly need the cushioning these sneakers provide at the moment. I have impressively large blisters on the bottoms of both big toes, thanks to a three-hour hike I did over this past weekend.

Like last month, Dr. Kent organized a wilderness retreat for the twelve med students who are currently on the emergency medicine rotation here at Lakewood. We went to the same mountain cabin where the retreat was held in July. The other med students and I carpooled up there this past Friday, and over the course of Saturday and yesterday, several of the ED attendings taught us about wilderness medicine and other cool topics. Though I really wanted to demonstrate to the attendings how much extra time I had put into studying wilderness medicine since the last retreat, I made sure not to answer *all* their questions, even though it often seemed I was the only student paying attention.

As the only student who had been on the retreat the month prior, I also made sure to warn the others about Dr. Godfrey's enthusiasm as a trail guide. I think the rest of the gang appreciated the heads-up to prepare accordingly, since Dr. Godfrey took us on what proved to be an even longer and more strenuous hike than last time (hence the blisters on my toes). This month, the hike took place during the day rather than after dark, which was probably a good thing, since during last month's night hike Savannah basically fell down the side of the mountain after losing sight of the trail. Dr. Kent rescued her and got her to the hospital. Thankfully, Savannah fully recovered from her injuries.

"So, Rachel, what's going on in Room Eleven?"

The voice of Dr. Sanders brings me to attention. Looking up from my computer, my nerves quintuple when I see my attending coming my way. I sit taller, wet my lips, and promptly launch into my official patient presentation:

"Mr. Egbert is a forty-six-year-old male who was brought to the emergency department by EMS for medical clearance prior to being booked into jail. He was found at ShopMart, tearing off the heads of Dixie Dolls with his teeth. He told the officer that he might have swallowed one of the dolls' heads, and so he was brought to the ED for evaluation."

Dr. Sanders stares for a long time. "That's a rather interesting way to start the shift," she finally remarks. "So what are you going to do for the patient?"

Though I want to, I dare not crack a smile the way Dr. Sanders is now doing. The patient's story is definitely hilarious, but I'm only a med student, and I'm a med student who's currently applying for next-year's residency class. So I don't want to appear as though I'm not taking Mr. Egbert's medical care completely seriously. Dr. Sanders needs to see I'm fully dedicated to everything I do around here. Therefore, I maintain a straight face as I motion to the patient's chart, which is open on the computer monitor.

"I've made him NPO and initiated IV fluid. Labs are being drawn. I was also going to place an order for an x-ray of his abdomen." I break off, momentarily seized by fear that I've left out something important. Taking a deep breath, I force myself to fight off the panic and resume what I was saying. "Once his results are back—assuming his labs are unremarkable, his x-ray is clear, and his exam remains unchanged—I believe we can discharge him to jail."

"Sounds good." Dr. Sanders is still grinning as she scans the rest of the tracking board. "Looks like they just brought a couple patients back from the waiting room. Why don't I go see the abdominal pain and you go check out the ankle injury while you're waiting for results on Room Eleven?"

"Absolutely." My fingers fly over the computer keyboard as I place the x-ray order for Mr. Egbert. I then skim the tracking board to read the information about my next patient, who has been placed in Room Four. The board says she's an eighty-five-year-old woman with an ankle injury. "I'll go right now."

I hop to my feet and hurry across the department, trying to appear as focused and efficient as possible, just in case Dr. Sanders is still watching me. I'm rushing so fast, however, that I nearly get run over when a radiology tech comes around a corner wheeling the giant portable x-ray machine. I dart out of the way but wind up colliding into someone who's standing nearby. I let out a yelp as I lose my footing in the crash and begin to fall. A hand quickly wraps around my upper arm, catching me. I regain my balance and raise my head.

"I'm so sorry about that. I . . ."

I trail off. It's Austin. Of all the people in this entire hospital, why did I have to literally run into Austin Cahill?

Before I stumbled into him, it appears Austin was talking with one of the first-year emergency medicine residents, Elly Vincent. I haven't had a chance to really get to know Elly— I mean, Dr. Vincent—yet, but in my brief interactions with her, she has been super nice and supportive, and she seems fearless, great with patients, and absolutely brilliant. It's even more impressive considering she only started her intern year a month ago.

I silently sigh. With such incredibly skilled people like Elly Vincent being accepted into Lakewood's emergency medicine residency program, how will I ever have a chance?

I make myself shift my focus back to Austin. He still has his hand around my arm, and he's peering down at me with one eyebrow slightly arched. His hair is brushed, and he shaved today, so I gather he hasn't been on-call. He's dressed in dark blue scrubs and his short white coat. As I take in the sight of him, there's a distinct and completely unexpected punch inside my chest. My body gets warm, and my breathing quickens. Austin, I realize, looks . . . handsome.

Extremely handsome.

I practically choke when the scandalous thought crosses my mind. Since when did I start noticing that Austin is handsome? Since when did I care?

Never. And I never will.

"I'm sorry about that," I resume saying to him, adopting an indifferent expression to match his. "I was trying to get to a patient's room."

"It's all right." Austin lets go of my arm, continuing to observe me with that piercing gaze of his. "I enjoy getting plowed over while talking to someone about an admit."

I feel a rush of indignation. It's almost a reflex whenever Austin talks to me now, since he's always badgering me about something. The next moment, however, I come to the startling realization that Austin is nearly grinning. I think he was cracking a joke. My lips part in surprise. I don't think I've ever heard Austin joke around before.

Elly laughs good-naturedly, clearly catching Austin's humor. "Very true. At least getting mowed down in the middle of the ED is more interesting than the patient I'm admitting to you." She shakes her head. "Nothing exciting usually happens when caring for patients with significant fecal impaction."

I snicker, in spite of myself, but hastily bite my lip and readopt a serious façade. Dr. Sanders may not be around, but I still need to act professionally. Elly is one of the emergency medicine residents. If I come across as flippant or goofy to her, she might relay a negative opinion of me to the residency application committee, which is the group that chooses the applicants to interview for next year's residency class. I definitely don't want to give Elly the wrong impression. I can't let my guard down.

I clear my throat, my eyes darting between Elly and Austin. "I'm sorry again for interrupting. Have a good day."

Without another word, I slide around Austin and finish making my way over to Room Four. I come to a stop outside the curtain, finding I need another moment to catch my breath because I'm still thinking about Austin's strong, handsome features.

This is very strange.

Once I finally collect myself, I say into the curtain, "May I please come in?"

"Yes," a woman replies.

Straightening my white coat, I slip around the curtain and step into the room. I take in the scene in an instant. Sitting on the stretcher is a woman who appears her stated age. She's well-dressed, and her white hair is styled nicely. She's observing me with a kind smile, though I can tell she's nervous and a little uncomfortable. A glance down at her left leg reveals why: the poor woman has her leg propped up on a couple of pillows, and her ankle joint is swollen and bruised.

Standing to the right of the stretcher is another woman who appears to be about twenty years younger than the patient. She's wearing a more casual ensemble of a sweatshirt and jeans.

I give them a polite tip of my head. "Good day. I'm Rachel Nelson, the fourth-year medical student who will be helping you."

"Hello, Rachel. I'm Brenda Quigby," the woman standing beside the stretcher greets me with a hint of a southern drawl. She motions to the patient. "This is my next-door neighbor, Flora Jessop."

"Hello." Settling my concentration on the patient, I gesture to her ankle. "What happened, Ms. Jessop?"

The woman peers back at me for several seconds. Her smile falters. Her lower lip begins quivering before she covers her face with her trembling hands. "I don't remember. I don't know. I just don't know."

I take a step closer to the stretcher and observe the patient more closely. In addition to the ankle injury, the potentially more important issue is how she sustained it. An ankle injury from a simple mechanical fall, like tripping on the corner of a rug, is one thing. A fall preceded by lightheadedness, chest pain, or loss of consciousness is worrisome for a cause much more serious.

I'm about to delve into more pressing questions when Brenda chimes in:

"Flora was walking to her mailbox when she slipped on some loose gravel and fell. I was sweeping my front porch and saw it happen." Brenda puts a hand on Flora's shoulder and gives her a reassuring smile. "You got hurt when you went out to get your mail by yourself."

Flora raises her head to peer at her neighbor. "Was I? I don't remember."

Brenda pats Flora's shoulder and then goes on speaking to me. "Flora and I have been neighbors for nearly thirty years. Unfortunately, she's now dealing with rapidly advancing dementia. She doesn't remember a lot of details the way she used to."

"Oh. I see." I give Brenda an appreciative look. "Did she hit her head when she fell? Or did it appear she lost consciousness at any time?"

"No. She rolled her ankle as she slipped, and she landed on her knees. She was awake the entire time. I ran over to help her, and she told me her ankle hurt. So I went back to my house, drove over to her place, helped her get into my car, and brought her here."

"She was fortunate to have your assistance." I smile at Brenda again and then turn to Flora once more. "Ma'am, I'd like to examine you and get some x-rays of your lower leg, if that would be all right with you."

"Why?" Flora peers at me with a furrowed brow. "Why do I need x-rays?"

"Because you've hurt your ankle." I lightly touch her leg. "Brenda saw you fall down outside."

"Brenda?" Flora looks from me to her neighbor. The anxiousness in her voice increases. "Who's Brenda?"

Brenda again pats Flora's shoulder. "I'm Brenda. Brenda Quigby. I'm your next-door neighbor."

"Oh." Flora turns to me. "Are you my neighbor, too?"

I shake my head. "No, ma'am. I'm a medical student, and I'm going to help take care of your ankle."

While Brenda starts re-explaining everything to Flora, I wash my hands and then proceed to perform an exam. Though her ankle is bruised and swollen, thankfully the rest of Flora's exam is normal. Once I'm done, I take a step back from the stretcher.

"Before I excuse myself to go inform the attending physician about you and get the x-rays ordered, is there anything else I can get for you, Ms. Jessop?"

"No, I don't think so." Flora looks to Brenda. "Who's getting x-rays?"

"Thanks," Brenda quietly says to me before turning to Flora and once again telling her the plan.

While the two women converse, I back out of the room and let the curtain close behind me. As soon as I'm out of their view, the tears I've been holding back well up in my eyes. I lower my head and stride across the department to my workstation, my chest getting heavier as I continue thinking about Flora. For a woman of her age, her body is quite healthy. But her mind is terribly sick, unable to remember events or even what was said to her. She doesn't recognize longtime friends. All the experiences that made her who she is are rapidly draining from her memory. It's an agonizing situation, and it's one I understand all too well. I watched my own grandmother go through the same thing. Dementia is a cruel thing, indeed.

Reaching my workstation, I take a chair, wipe away my tears, and make myself focus on my work. I enter x-rays for Ms. Jessop and then flip over to Mr. Egbert's chart. His results are back. A check of his labs shows they're all within normal limits, which is good news though not particularly surprising. I next click on his abdominal x-ray. There's a moment's delay, and then the images fill the screen.

My mouth nearly plummets to the floor.

Mr. Egbert didn't swallow a Dixie Doll head. He swallowed . . . I'm still counting . . . thirteen Dixie Doll heads.

I keep staring at the screen, gobsmacked. Against the familiar abdominal x-ray backdrop of organs and bone in various shades of black, gray, and white, numerous foreign bodies are visible within Mr. Egbert's bowels. Bright white on x-ray and almost circular in shape, they're scattered along Mr. Egbert's intestines like a string of lights. I count the objects again. Yup. Thirteen.

Still in shock, I open the radiologist's dictated report and read it over. It concludes with the impression:

"Thirteen foreign bodies are noted throughout the patient's bowels. Given the reported history of the patient's alleged Dixie Doll head consumption, the visualized foreign bodies are likely the tragic remains of Dixie and her plastic friends. No evidence of bowel perforation. No evidence of obstruction."

I can't help giggling in appreciation of the radiologist's humor. Closing the report, I resume gawking at the x-ray images while I pick up the phone and ask the operator to page the on-call provider for gastroenterology.

It isn't long before the resident from GI calls back. I have to explain the story twice before he believes me. He then logs into his computer, reviews the x-rays, and agrees with my proposed plan for admitting the patient to the medicine service for monitoring while awaiting the heads to work their way through the patient's bowels.

To be thorough, before starting the process of admitting the patient to the medicine team, I next have the operator page the on-call resident for general surgery. Many swallowed foreign bodies can pass on their own. However, I need to make sure the surgeons don't think there should be any operative intervention, especially given the high number of Dixie Doll heads that are currently making their way through Mr. Egbert's GI tract.

My phone soon rings again. I answer and cringe when I hear Dr. Brittany Chen on the other end of the line. She's one of the general surgery interns, and she doesn't exactly have a reputation for being kind to med students—or to most people, for that matter. (Though she's always sweet to Erik Prescott, one of the orthopedic interns, so I know there's a kind human buried deep down inside of Brittany Chen somewhere.)

After I explain the patient's story to Brittany, there's a long pause. So long, in fact, I wonder if the phone has gone dead. Finally, I hear her start typing on a computer keyboard. I'm guessing she's logging into Mr. Egbert's chart to see the patient's x-rays for herself. She suddenly stops typing. There's another drawn-out silence. Then, with slightly less abrasiveness to her tone, she informs me that she's going to speak to her attending and call back.

While I wait for Brittany's call, I glance over at Room Four. I see the same radiology tech who nearly ran me over wheeling the monstrous x-ray machine into Ms. Jessop's room. Also heading into her room is a tall, wise-appearing gentleman who appears to be around Flora's age. I'm guessing he's her husband who has just arrived to join her in the ED.

Shifting in my seat, I direct my attention to Room Eleven. The curtain of Mr. Egbert's room remains drawn back. I can see the police officer standing by the stretcher, resting one hand casually on his belt while scanning the department. Meanwhile, Mr. Egbert continues to appear completely comfortable and content. Sitting on the stretcher, he's tapping one of the railings in time to whatever song he's humming to himself.

The phone rings. I pick it up, and Brittany informs me that her attending agrees Mr. Egbert doesn't require surgical intervention at this time, but the surgery team will consult on the patient during his inpatient stay and intervene if his condition changes.

Brittany ends the call. With the patient's disposition decided, I push the phone's *zero* button once more. This time, I ask the hospital operator to page the admitting resident for the medicine service. While the page is being sent, I get up and head to Room Eleven to give Mr. Egbert and the police officer an update. As I get close, I hear the patient is humming the song, "Baby Doll." Of course he is.

"How are you doing, Mr. Egbert?" I step into the room.

He stops humming. "I'm hungry."

I slide back, putting a little more distance between us. "Unfortunately, for now, we need to ask you not to eat or drink anything. Since it looks like you swallowed thirteen Dixie Doll heads, I need to admit you to the hospital for monitoring."

The police officer coughs. It's the first time I've seen him look ruffled since he got here. "I'm sorry, did you say *thirteen*?"

I nod. "That's what it looks like on x-ray, at least. So we'll be admitting him to the hospital for monitoring. He'll probably be here a couple of days."

Mr. Egbert observes the exchange and heaves a sigh. "I can never quite get up to fifteen," he notes before he shrugs and resumes humming.

The officer and I exchange a glance.

"Thanks for the update," the officer tells me. He pulls a cell phone from one of his vest pockets. "I'm going to make a few calls."

I look again at my patient, who draws his legs into a cross-legged position as he continues humming his song. I then check the monitor, which shows his vitals are stable. A re-examination of his abdomen confirms it remains benign. Considering there are a bunch of plastic doll heads slowly making their way through his intestines at the moment, I would say Mr. Egbert is doing remarkably well.

"Rachel Nelson, there's a call holding for you on line A," the secretary's voice blares out from the overhead speakers. "Rachel Nelson, there's a call holding on line A."

"Excuse me while I go answer that." I back out of the room. "That's probably the admitting medicine team."

Whipping around, I race back to my workstation and pick up the blinking line.

"This is Rachel Nelson in the emergency department."

"It's Austin."

Oddly, the sound of Austin's voice doesn't immediately trigger aggravation deep within my core like it usually does. Instead, my heart skips at the sound, and I find myself recalling how handsome he looked earlier. Then, suddenly, it's as though the clouds finish parting and the mind-boggling realization strikes me fully: Austin isn't just handsome. He's hot. Like, really hot.

How did I not notice this before?

I nearly drop the phone receiver. My breathing is getting funny. My mind is swirling. Austin? Drop-dead gorgeous? Have I really been so busy all this time that I failed to realize how strikingly handsome he is? Or have I subconsciously known Austin is hot but have been too preoccupied with other things to care? Or have I cared but didn't want to acknowledge that my nemesis was also extremely attractive?

I'm not sure. Frankly, I have no idea what's happening right now. However, there is one thing I can't deny any longer: the man I most despise is also the most handsome guy I've ever known.

I think my whole world has just been thrown a major curveball.

As I've said before, Austin Cahill is a curse.

"Rachel?" Austin's voice breaks the silence. "Are you there?"

"Yes. I'm . . . here."

My voice actually quivers, and my heart rate ticks up even higher. What is the matter with me?

I hastily suck in another breath and sit up as tall as I can. This is absurd. I need to get a grip. Handsome or not, this is still Austin. The same Austin Cahill I've clashed with since the first day of med school. The same Austin who contradicts and challenges everything I say or do. The same Austin who tries to show me up in front of patients, residents, and attendings. The same Austin who even once had the audacity to round on my patients as well as his own in a blatant effort to outdo me.

I will not let him ruffle me now.

"So . . . did you call for a specific reason or just to chat?" Austin now has a hint of amusement in his tone.

My nostrils flare. I'm actually glad he's being provoking. It makes it easier to remind myself how much he irritates me. "I'm calling because there's a patient I need to admit to the medicine service." I don't even give him a chance to start grilling me with questions before I go on. "Room Eleven. Mr. Jerry Egbert. Forty-six years old. Swallowed thirteen Dixie Doll heads. Normal exam. Normal vitals. Normal labs. X-ray negative for evidence of perforation or obstruction. NPO with IV fluid running. Cleared by GI. General surgery will consult." I finally come to a deliberate pause before asking, "Do you have any questions for me?"

When Austin doesn't reply, my lips turn up into a satisfied smile. I can almost feel him staring at me through the phone with that incredulous expression he often displays. I know Austin won't be able to find fault with how I've handled this case. There's not a single question he can drill me with. This time—

"Were they Beach-Fun Dixies or Rockstar Dixies?" I hear him ask.

I blink. "Wh-what?"

He chuckles. "I'm just kidding, Rachel. We'll be down shortly."

Austin hangs up. For a couple of seconds, I keep the receiver against my ear, replaying the conversation in my head. Then it dawns on me: Austin was being funny. That's the second time today. Impossibly, the man I have always believed to be unflappable and robotic has shown he actually has a sense of humor. A great sense of humor.

How did I not know Austin has a sense of humor?

I blow a strand of hair from my face and finally put down the phone receiver. My mind is reeling even harder than before as I try to process everything.

Austin is drop-dead gorgeous.

Austin is funny.

What else am I going to discover about him? That he has walked on the moon? That he once negotiated an international peace treaty? That he's secretly a circus performer?

I snicker at the image of him on a trapeze. Actually, though, now that I think about it, Austin could undoubtedly pull it off. He's tall, and he's thin in a really athletic, fit-and-muscular way, so he'd be able to . . .

Oh my gosh. Am I thinking about how *fit* Austin is?

My cheeks ignite.

Desperate to find something to occupy my mind, I open Ms. Jessop's x-rays, which have just resulted, and start looking them over. Unfortunately, it appears she sustained a distal fibula fracture. It's not displaced, though, so it hopefully won't necessitate surgical intervention. However, she will need a splint or cast, and given her age, even that can get quite tricky. Immobilizing an extremity can make an elderly person more prone to falling than usual, so it takes some work to determine the safest option for care. I doubt she'll be able to use crutches, but we can do a trial with a walking boot, possibly with a walker. Or perhaps a scooter. Or a wheelchair. I think I'll get the ortho team's help in determining the best treatment for her.

Lifting the phone for what feels like the millionth time this shift, I ask the operator to page orthopedics to the emergency department. I then push back from the desk, get to my feet, and return to Room Four.

"It's Rachel," I say when I reach the curtain that leads into Ms. Jessop's room. "May I come back in?"

"Yes," an elderly sounding man says in reply.

I slide around the curtain, making sure to have a reassuring smile on my face so Flora won't be worried, since she probably can't remember meeting me a few minutes ago.

I find Flora on the stretcher with her left leg still propped up on pillows. She was given an ice pack by her nurse, and it's resting over the injured ankle. Flora continues to appear nervous but less apprehensive than before. Her neighbor, Brenda, has left, and the tall gentleman I previously saw entering the room is at Flora's side.

"Hello. I'm Rachel Nelson, the fourth-year medical student," I tell them both.

"Hi, Rachel," the man replies, reaching out to shake my hand. "I'm Donald Jessop, Flora's husband."

"Nice to meet you." I shake his hand and take another moment before turning to his wife. "Flora, I've had a chance to look at your x-rays. Unfortunately, it does appear as though you broke your ankle. You have an ankle fracture."

"I do?" Flora's eyes widen. "How did I get an ankle fracture?"

Donald sits on the chair beside her stretcher and gently rubs her arm in a calming manner. I get the impression he has done this many, many times before. "Our neighbor, Brenda, saw you fall, sweetheart. She called me while I was at the grocery store and told me you slipped when you tried going to the mailbox alone."

"I did?" Fiona stares at her husband. "When did that happen?"

"This morning." Donald clearly knows the best pace and tone to use when talking with her. He makes sure to repeat, "It happened while I was at the grocery store and you were alone."

"That's so odd. I don't remember falling." Flora shakes her head. She looks away for a few moments, and then she refocuses on her spouse with an expression of genuine curiosity. "Are you the man who delivers mail to my house?"

I silently catch my breath.

An unmistakable look of pain crosses Donald's features as he continues gazing at his wife, and then his kind, patient smile returns. He cradles her hand in his. "I'm your husband, Flora. I'm Donald. We got married fifty-three years ago."

Fresh tears sting my eyes as I observe the exchange. It suddenly feels as though I'm intruding on something very private between them. Flora's polite ambivalence juxtaposed against Donald's heartbroken devotion is tragic. Flora doesn't know her husband anymore. Her companion of over fifty years has become a stranger. Long ago, these two fell in love, wed, and probably raised a family. Through the years, they undoubtedly experienced struggles— financial concerns, worries about loved ones, work difficulties—and they got through those challenges because of the love and support they gave to one another. But now Flora's recollection of their life together is gone. Even though she's seated beside him, Donald has already lost his dear companion. The memories of the life they shared are his alone to carry. Every day, he must endure the agony of caring for a beloved wife who no longer knows him.

The poignant quiet is broken by a brisk knock on the doorframe, which causes me to jump and look over my shoulder. The curtain is pulled aside, and the orthopedics intern, Erik Prescott, enters the room.

"Hello. My name is Doctor Prescott. I'm from the orthopedics team," he announces to all of us in his suave, confident way. He crosses his muscular arms over his chest and focuses his attention on me. "I was paged to the emergency department, and based on the info on the tracking board, I assumed this is where I'm needed?"

Jarred back to the task at-hand, I give Erik a nod. "Mrs. Flora Jessop suffered a mechanical fall this morning and sustained a distal left fibula fracture." I motion to her spouse. "She does suffer from dementia, and so her husband, Mr. Donald Jessop, will be a great help to you as you discuss options for care and follow up."

"Oh." Erik's self-assured demeanor falters as his eyes shift between the patient and her spouse. I recognize his look of uncertainty; it's a common and understandable reaction for those who aren't used to dealing with someone suffering from severe memory loss.

"Would you like me to ask one of the ED techs to come assist you with applying a splint, Doctor Prescott?" I prompt, steering the dialogue back on track.

Erik pulls his eyes from Flora and focuses again on me. His assertiveness restored, he gives me a nod. "Yes. Thanks."

Erik begins speaking with the Jessops, and I head toward the curtain to depart the room. I pause, though, and glance back. Seeming to sense I'm watching, Donald looks past Erik and puts his eyes on mine. There's sorrow in his gaze, but it's mixed with unwavering love. It's another look I know very, very well.

"Good luck with everything," I say softly to him.

Donald tips his head. "Thank you, Rachel."

Saying no more, I pull aside the curtain and leave the room. Doing my best to push my emotions aside, I locate one of the ED techs and tell her about Flora's injury. The tech heads off to gather the necessary splinting supplies, which she'll take to Erik in Room Four. Next, I find Dr. Sanders and start to update her on the plans for both Mr. Egbert and Mrs. Jessop. However, my conversation with Dr. Sanders gets cut short when she is called away to assess a critical patient. So I return to my workstation, drop down onto my chair, and type up as much of Flora's discharge instructions as I can; Erik will do the rest, including the information about her outpatient follow up appointments in ortho clinic.

Only once I'm done do I allow myself a chance to stop and breathe. The image of my grandmother returns to my mind. My father's mother was even tinier than I am, but she was far more feisty, brave, and determined. She lived the longest of my grandparents, so I got to know her the best. Our bond grew even stronger when she moved in with us after my grandpa passed away. But it wasn't long before dementia took its hold. The terrible irony of my father—a physician and neurosurgeon—being unable to "fix" his mother's condition haunted him as she got worse. Like my father and the rest of my family, I watched helplessly as the grandmother I loved forgot everything. In a way, it was a blessing when she finally passed; at least she was no longer tormented by constant confusion and fear.

It's not until a tear hits my desk that I realize I'm crying again. I lower my head and discreetly begin wiping the tears from my cheeks.

"Hey, Rachel," I hear someone say in a friendly voice. "We've met with Mr. Egbert."

I whip up my head. Tara Hess, the admitting medicine resident, is approaching my workstation. In contrast to her more casual look when she was on-call the other day, Tara has her hair styled half-up, and she has put on mascara and lip gloss.

I then realize Austin is right behind her. I think he looks even hotter now than he did earlier in the day.

How is this possible?

I frown, sternly reminding myself yet again that whether or not he's immensely attractive, Austin Cahill is still one of the most frustrating, aggravating people I've ever known.

Thankfully, Tara comes to a stop in front of my workstation so she essentially positioned herself as a demilitarized zone between Austin and me. It's a good thing, too, otherwise I'm sure Austin would have already launched into a critique of something I did or didn't do for Mr. Egbert. And though I vowed to act professionally toward Austin this month, given the emotions that are currently coursing through me, I'm not certain I would be able to politely put up with his antics at the moment.

I get to my feet, concentrating all my attention on Tara. "Is there anything else you'd like me to do for Mr. Egbert while he's down here?"

"Thanks, but no. You've done a great job working him up, and I can't think of anything else he needs before going upstairs." She giggles and looks over her shoulder at Austin. "The patient certainly has quite the story, though."

Hang on. Did Tara just *bat her eyes* at Austin? I peer at her more closely. She's now gazing up at him with a cute little smile on her face.

She's *flirting* with him!

Instantly, my body gets hot, and a strange sensation begins brewing within me. It's a sensation that makes me a little bit restless, a whole lot protective, and extremely grumpy. A sensation, I realize, that feels a lot like jealousy.

No. There's no way. I am not jealous of Tara Hess. Austin can banter, flirt, and exchange googly eyes with Tara or any other girl he wants. I don't care. I'm not bothered in the slightest if the resident Austin will be closely working with this entire month happens to be smart, pretty, and syrupy sweet. If Austin is attracted to Tara, it doesn't matter to me.

So why are my eyes narrowing and my teeth grinding as I watch Tara totally send Austin the vibe?

I clear my throat and also turn to Austin. For the first time in my life, I find myself wishing he would initiate some sort of criticism just so we could argue.

Austin pulls his attention from Tara and focuses on me. Instead of critiquing me, though, he asks, "What's wrong?"

I cringe as my cheeks get even warmer. Has Austin somehow figured out what I'm thinking? Am I being that obvious?

"Um, nothing." I quickly avert my gaze. "I'm fine."

Out of the corner of my eye, I see him shake his head. He pulls a tissue from the box that's sitting on the corner of my workstation and holds it out to me. "You're not fine. You've been crying."

I relax a little when I realize what he's referring to, and I face him again. I take the tissue from his hand. Austin is right, of course. I'm not fine. The bittersweet memories of my grandmother are still pulling at my heartstrings. However, I can't admit how much I'm hurting. I can't show weakness. Not in the emergency department. Not in front of Tara. And definitely not in front of Austin.

"I have a patient with a sad story." I try to sound unaffected. "She has dementia, and . . . she reminds me of my grandmother."

I break off when my voice catches, and I avert my gaze again, cursing the fact that I said anything at all.

"I'm sorry," I hear Austin tell me, and he sounds as though he means it.

"Thanks." I dare to peer up at him once more. "I guess this has been a bit of a rocky morning."

"Afternoon," he says.

I stop blotting my eyes with the tissue. "What?"

He motions to the clock. "It's noon. It's the afternoon."

I also look at the clock. It's about forty-five seconds past twelve o'clock. I spear Austin with an exasperated look. "It was literally the morning less than sixty seconds ago, Austin. It's still acceptable to say it's the morning."

Austin shrugs. "Not if it's actually the afternoon."

I open my mouth to counter him, but I pause when I hear Tara cough softly. Both Austin and I look her way. Her eyes are shifting between us.

"So, um, Austin and I should probably head back up to the floor." Tara seems to be studying me more intently now. "We have some rounding left to do."

I collect myself and nod. "Please let me know if you decide there's anything else you'd like us to do for Mr. Egbert before his room is ready."

"I will. Thanks. And I'm sorry about the tough patient you're dealing with. I hope it goes well," Tara tells me. She then spins toward Austin, and that flirtatious smile reappears on her face. "So how about we finish rounding and then go grab some lunch in the cafeteria?"

Austin's expression relaxes. "Sounds good."

Tara and Austin walk away together, leaving me behind. I turn to watch them go. Tara starts giggling as she says something to him, and Austin breaks into a broad smile and replies. Tipping back her head, Tara laughs with apparent amusement at whatever Austin said to her. The sound of her laughter fades away as they round a corner and disappear from my view. I slowly crush the tissue that's still in my hand and toss it into the garbage. There's no question about it: Tara and Austin are getting along well.

Extremely well.

Developing-a-relationship well.

I drop down onto my chair with a huff. I stare straight ahead for a moment or two, and then my eyes shift back to the door that Tara and Austin exited through.

Okay, so Austin is hooking up with Tara. It's no big deal. I don't care.

Oddly, though, it feels like I care.

"Code Blue. ETA seven minutes. Code Blue. ETA seven minutes."

The loud announcement that blasts out from the overhead speakers jolts me back into work mode. I spring up from my seat and jog toward the resuscitation bay, joining Dr. Sanders, Hadi, and several other members of the ED staff who start preparing for the arrival of a patient in cardiac arrest. Moving fast, I don a gown and gloves and move deeper into the fray, grateful to have something to channel my restless energy toward. At least I won't have to think about Austin Cahill anymore.

Four

"So who can tell us some of the contraindications to using succinylcholine as a paralytic agent for rapid-sequence intubation?"

There's a delay before I realize Dr. Kent has just asked a question. Shaking myself from my daze, I sit up in my chair and glance around. I'm seated at the big table in the middle of the Discovery Conference Room with the eleven other med students who are on the rotation this month. Today marks the first of our Wednesday-morning didactic sessions, which are taught by the emergency medicine attendings.

Dr. Kent has kicked off the morning with a lesson about rapid-sequence intubation in the ED. Normally, I would be riveted. For one thing, Dr. Kent always gives fantastic lessons; they're informative, interesting, and infused with humor. Plus, today's topic of emergency airway management is arguably the foundation of emergency medicine.

Yet I'm having an uncharacteristically difficult time focusing this morning. Actually, I've been rather distracted for the past two days. Julie called late Monday night after I got home from my shift, and we finally had a chance to talk. She filled me in on her quasi-blind date with Lars. From what I gathered between her exasperated sighs and slightly maniacal bouts of laughter, the date proved to be as much of an ego-stroking session for Lars as the date I had with him a few years ago. Needless to say, Julie wasn't interested in him, and I was impressed to learn Julie made it clear to Lars and also to our parents that there wasn't going to be a second date. I admired Julie for being so bold. She has always been more confident than me.

After discussing the date, Julie and I talked about how her med school application process is coming along (fantastically, of course) and how my emergency medicine rotation is going. I bided my time as we talked, sensing Julie would eventually want to open up about her breakup with Marcus. She did, and we spent another hour-and-a-half exploring what happened between them. Sounds like Marcus didn't like the prospect of being "dragged around" with Julie for the next several years while she does medical school, a subsequent residency program, and possibly even more training if she chooses to do a fellowship. Marcus wanted more stability and certainty, and so he also wasn't keen on a prolonged, long-distance relationship. Ultimately, he made the tough decision to break up with her.

Poor Julie. My heart ached as she tearfully relayed to me how devastated she was about it. Admirably, she didn't blame Marcus, and she wasn't angry with him either. In fact, she said she could understand his aversion to tagging along with her for the next several years while she does her intense, time-consuming medical training.

Though she could understand Marcus's perspective, however, it didn't change the fact that Julie was devastated about the relationship ending. She shared with me how much she loves Marcus and how she really believed he was her soulmate. She said she couldn't imagine ever wanting to be with anyone else, and she admitted it was hard for her to think of Marcus happily dating another woman one day. It was late into the night by the time our phone call was over, but I didn't sleep much afterward. Julie's words about love and relationships kept playing in my mind on constant loop. I decided her experience only reaffirmed that I'm making the right decision to put off romance until after my medical training is over.

I snap out of my drifting thoughts and find silence still has its hold on the conference room. The other med students are exchanging uncertain glances or averting their gazes, their body language making it clear they're hoping Dr. Kent won't ask them to answer his question. I sigh to myself. Didn't *anyone* else study the syllabus before today's lectures?

Apparently not.

I shove my hand into the air.

Standing by the whiteboard at the front of the room, Dr. Kent grins when he notices me. "Go ahead, Rachel."

In my mind's eye, I can perfectly recall the chart from the syllabus that I reviewed this morning. It compares in detail all the various RSI medications, including their pros and cons, contraindications, dosages, times to take effect, and durations of action.

"Contraindications to utilizing succinylcholine include hyperkalemia, old burns, old crush injuries, and a patient history of malignant hyperthermia."

"Great. Thanks, Rachel." Dr. Kent flips the whiteboard pen in his hand and then starts casually rolling back the long sleeves of his shirt. He looks around the rest of the group. "And what are some benefits to using succinylcholine over rocuronium?"

Other than the sound of a couple people clearing their throats, the same nervous quiet takes over the room. I peer to my left and then to my right. Everyone is staring at the tabletop or sliding a little lower in their chairs. I shake my head, extremely unimpressed with my fellow med students' lack of preparedness. I realize I'm the only one in this group who's planning to go into emergency medicine as a career, but don't the others find this topic *fascinating*? I mean, it's emergency medicine! It's airway management! It's literally life-and-death stuff! This is way more interesting than chronic skin rashes, finger x-rays, or pathology tissue samples. I don't understand how anyone in the medical profession wouldn't want to learn about this topic. Astonishingly, though, it appears I'm the only one here who thinks there's far more to be gleaned from the syllabus than what you can cram the night before the rotation's written final.

I make another pass of pointed stares at the others, giving them one last chance. No one says anything. So, once again, I raise my hand.

Dr. Kent's dark eyes seem to flicker with amusement as he gives me a nod. "What do you think?"

"Most proponents of utilizing succinylcholine for rapid-sequence intubation would argue the medication's rapid onset and short half-life are its biggest advantages."

"Exactly." Dr. Kent shows his ruggedly dashing smile. He has been smiling a lot these past few days, I've noticed. With a laid-back air, he goes on, "Meanwhile, those who advocate for using rocuronium would say succinylcholine's short half-life is its biggest disadvantage."

I sit back in my chair, letting Dr. Kent's point sink in. I hadn't thought of it that way before. I feel a little pulse of excitement about this new tidbit of understanding. Like I said, this stuff is absolutely fascinating.

"Excuse me, Doctor Kent?" someone says from the doorway.

Dr. Kent turns toward the source of the voice. The rest of us follow his gaze.

Lynn Prentis is entering the room. Lynn is the coordinator for the emergency department and the med student rotation. She's basically Dr. Kent's right-hand woman. Lynn is extremely sweet and kind, and she can somehow fix every problem that's brought to her attention. More than once, I've heard Dr. Kent and other attendings say they wouldn't be able to do their jobs without her support. I know the med students are also profoundly grateful she's around to help with everything from correcting scheduling glitches to finding hydrogen peroxide to remove a blood stain from a white coat.

"I'm sorry for interrupting," Lynn continues speaking to Dr. Kent while casting us all a warm smile. "Mark Prescott is calling again. He's holding on your office line. I assumed you would want to speak with him."

"Thanks, Lynn. Yes, I definitely want to take that. I'll be right there." Dr. Kent glances at the clock and then faces us. "I apologize for needing to step out. How about we break early and reconvene in fifteen minutes?"

There's a round of murmured replies from the group, which is apparently enough to convey everyone is in agreement with the plan. Dr. Kent gives us a casual salute and then strides out of the room alongside Lynn.

As soon as they're gone, the guy with brown, wavy hair who's seated next to me—I recall he introduced himself at the weekend retreat as Zach O'Cain—starts to chuckle. "Geez, it's only ten in the morning and I already feel like my brain is about to explode with information."

Everyone else laughs appreciatively.

When Zach notices I'm not laughing with the others, he shifts my way. Fixing his gray eyes on mine, he studies me curiously. "What do you think?"

"I think this lecture has been fantastic." I tuck my hair behind my ears. "In fact, I can't think of a more important topic for us to cover during our first didactic. Airway management is, after all, the foundation of emergency medicine."

His eyebrows rise. "You're pretty passionate about this."

I sense my cheeks get warm. "I am. I love emergency medicine."

"I figured as much, based on the way you were answering all of Doctor Kent's questions." Zach's smile broadens. "You're like a walking syllabus."

My cheeks get hotter, and I turn away. Zach obviously thinks I'm a total nerd.

Am I a total nerd?

"Hey, I wasn't making fun of you." Zach reaches out and nudges me. "I was just pointing out that you know the information really well."

He sounds genuine enough, so I turn his way once more.

"Well, I should," I reply. "I'm going into emergency medicine. Not to mention, I actually reviewed the syllabus before coming to didactics this morning." I finish with a hard glance around the table at everyone else.

Zach chuckles again. "Is it that obvious I didn't study?"

"Yes." In spite of myself, now I'm grinning, too. "No one stares at carpet for that long unless he really doesn't want the attending to ask him a question."

Zach tips back his head and laughs loudly. "Fair enough. You called me out. Nice one." He looks at me again. "Your name is Rachel, right?"

"Rachel Nelson."

He tips his head slightly to one side. "So, Rachel Nelson, you're applying to emergency medicine residencies?"

I nod nervously. Applying to emergency medicine residencies is certainly no guarantee I'll get accepted anywhere, and it almost feels as though I'll jinx myself if I talk about it too much.

Zach, however, clearly has no such concerns about jinxing things. He continues, speaking louder than I wish he would. "Is there a particular residency program you're hoping to get into?"

I hesitate, checking around us to make sure no one else is listening. I then lean closer to him and lower my voice. "Here. At Lakewood. This would be my number-one choice."

Zach leans my way, bringing our faces even closer together, and whispers back. "Is that some sort of secret?"

"N-no," I sputter, sitting up again. "But I don't want to announce it to everyone, either. It will be . . . embarrassing if I don't get in."

"Don't worry. You'll get in somewhere." Zach runs a hand through his hair. "With how much you know, you could probably skip residency and be an attending already."

He's grossly mistaken, of course, but I realize Zach is trying to give me a compliment. So I give him an appreciative smile before I turn away. My mind is swiftly becoming distracted once again, this time with thoughts of the current class of first-year emergency medicine residents here at Lakewood. There's Elly Vincent, who is all-around amazing. And Grant Reed, who let me watch as he drilled an intraosseous line into the tibia of a septic patient the other day. He was totally calm and cool the entire time, despite the high-stakes situation, and he clearly knew his stuff.

As more and more of the residents' faces go through my head, I sigh. I'm not like them. I'm not like any of the ED residents around here. I'm not that good.

The question is: am I good enough for any program to want me?

"Hey, Rachel!" I hear someone say.

I look up. To my pleasant surprise, Savannah Drake is standing in the doorway of the conference room. She gives me a friendly wave.

"Hi, Sav!" I hop out of my seat and scurry over to meet her. "What are you doing here?"

"I brought over some food for Wes." She holds up a small bag. I see a couple Keurig cups, fruit, and what I'm pretty sure is a blueberry scone inside. "Apparently, he had business calls all morning and didn't get a chance to eat breakfast before didactics started."

I look from the bag back to Savannah's face, which is glowing with happiness. *Wes.* Savannah called him Wes. She's referring to Dr. Kent by his first name now, which is definitely something she didn't do last month. And she's bringing him breakfast. And she knows the details of how Dr. Kent spent his morning.

Well, I think that pretty much clears up any questions about whether or not the rumors are true. Savannah and Dr. Kent are definitely a couple.

Wow.

Not that I'm surprised someone would be dating Dr. Kent. Though he's not my type, I would definitely agree he's the classic tall, dark, and handsome man. Not to mention, he's extremely smart, he's funny, and he has a great job. There's no question he's a catch.

Savannah is equally incredible and definitely deserves a top-notch guy like Dr. Kent. She's kind, intelligent, athletic, pretty, and has a fantastic sense of humor. Dr. Kent undoubtedly considers himself extremely lucky that he won her over.

What puzzles me, though, is the fact that Savannah is also a med student and currently applying for emergency medicine residency programs, just like I am. So how in the world has Savannah found time for love? It doesn't seem even remotely feasible at this stage in my life.

I realize Savannah is now watching me with a confused expression. Go figure. I'm just staring at her.

"He's in his office," I quickly pipe up. "Doctor Kent had to go to his office for a few minutes. Sounds like Mark Prescott called."

"Ah. That makes sense." Savannah nods. "They're having meetings with the investors tomorrow about some details of the ED build, so Wes and Mr. Prescott are spending today getting a bunch of info together."

I nod, too. It's taking all my willpower not to pry more into her love life. I decide to change the topic. "So how's your ED rotation at University Hospital going?"

"It's great." Savannah's face lights up again, her blue eyes shining with an enthusiasm I completely understand. It's the same way I feel about emergency medicine. "Tyler Warren is doing his second ED rotation there, too, so it's nice having at least one familiar face around. And the work is really interesting. Lots of complicated patients, including transplant recipients and people with rare neurological disorders." She pauses, and then she shows another smile. "Of course, there are also plenty of patients like the ones we managed in the hallways here at Lakewood."

I smile in response. "Things are still as wild and crazy at Lakewood as ever. The other day, I took care of a guy who was brought in by ambulance after someone spotted him standing in a lasagna tin in the middle of the road."

Savannah starts to laugh but abruptly stops with a double take. "Wait. Short guy? About sixty? Beard?"

My eyes get bigger. "Do you know him?"

"He was brought to University Hospital last night for the same thing. No, I take that back. Last night, he was found standing in a macaroni and cheese pan." She shrugs. "Anyway,

I saw a note in the computer system that said he had been seen at Lakewood a few days before for something similar. Apparently, he simply enjoys standing in food tins. He wasn't too happy that the EMS crew spoiled his fun." She adjusts her grip on the bag she's holding. "The good news is that he did well. His workup was unremarkable again, and like the day you saw him, his son's family elected to take him home for follow up with his regular care team."

"That's good." I'm really trying not to be nosy, but curiosity finally gets the better of me. "Hey, Sav, I have a question for you: are you and Doctor Kent . . . dating?"

Color tinges her cheeks. Her eyes sparkle even more brightly. "Yes. We realized how we felt about each other after last month's rotation ended. So our relationship is still pretty new, but it's . . ." she trails off with a wistfully happy sigh. "It's wonderful."

I feel a flicker of something inside me. It's not envy, exactly. It's not bitterness, either. I'm genuinely thrilled for Savannah; she deserves all the happiness in the world. Rather, I think what I'm feeling are hints of emotions I've kept bottled up for a really long time. Feelings that are starting to surface and remind me of how much I hope to fall in love one day, too.

I know it would be impossible to date right now, though, even if I wanted to. I don't have time. I've got to stay focused on my medical training. Everything I've worked and sacrificed for is on the line. I can't get distracted now.

A soft chime pulls me from my thoughts. The noise came from Savannah's cell phone, which she's pulling out from the back pocket of her jeans. As she reads a text, and an unmistakably love-struck smile appears on her face.

"Looks like Wes got my message that I came," Savannah explains to me. "I should probably take breakfast to him, so he can stash it in his office and eat after didactics are over." She puts her phone away. "It's awesome seeing you, Rachel."

"You, too," I reply sincerely.

Sav takes a step to leave but stops, seeming struck by an idea. "Hey, we should go grab dinner in a couple of weeks. We could celebrate finishing another ED rotation."

"I'd really like that." I can't even remember the last time I went out with friends. I would love a chance to do so.

"Awesome. I'll text you later today so we can pick a date. Talk to you soon." Savannah gives me a quick hug and then walks off in the direction of the attendings' offices.

Things seem to get really quiet after Savannah leaves. I glance around the empty hallway, pausing when I catch my reflection in a mirror on the wall. My eyes look tired. Stressed. Sad.

With a sigh, I rub my hands over my face. I just need to keep it together for a few more weeks. I'll work as hard as I can to get an honors grade on this rotation. I'll finish applying for residency. Then, finally, I'll have a chance to relax and rest.

As for love, I don't think anyone could get as lucky as Savannah did. As Julie's experience with Marcus proves, for the other ninety-nine percent of us, medical training simply isn't compatible with romance. That part of my life will just have to wait.

Five

"Code Blue. ETA ten minutes. Code Blue. ETA ten minutes."

I've just arrived for my shift—actually, I'm here an hour early because I planned to do some studying beforehand—when the overhead page blasts through the ED. My pulse shoots up, and my eyes scan the department. There's a sick-appearing patient on every hallway stretcher, which means each exam room is occupied by a patient who is even more critically ill. Yikes. It's only ten in the morning, and this place is already packed.

I decide to forgo studying to go see if I can help with the incoming code. I drop my bag next to a vacant workstation, throw my stethoscope around my neck, and jog across the department to the one resuscitation bay that isn't already occupied by a patient.

Stepping into the large, brightly lit resuscitation bay, I'm swept up in the tsunami of preparation for the arrival of a patient in cardiac arrest. The nurse, Pete, is setting up the monitor. Carrie, another nurse, is logging into the computer. Two ED techs rush into the room; one of them gets the ECG machine ready while the other puts the code cart into position. The inpatient pharmacist arrives and slides over to a corner to wait. A radiology tech steps in pushing the portable x-ray machine. Another nurse dashes over to assist Pete and Carrie. Dwayne, the ED social worker, heads to the opposite corner to remain on-hand in case he can be of assistance.

Making my path through the fray, I don a yellow gown and put on a pair of gloves. I then shift my attention to the middle of the room. Grant Reed, the first-year resident who let me watch him place the intraosseous line the other day, is standing at the head of the empty stretcher with Dr. Godfrey. The tray of intubation supplies is beside them. Usually, first-year residents don't manage the airway during a resuscitation; that's typically the job of the second-year resident who's working in the department at the time. However, if the second year is already busy with another critically ill patient, one of the attendings will handle the airway if a code gets brought in. I'm guessing that's the situation here: the second-year resident must be caring for another patient somewhere else in the department, so Dr. Godfrey stepped in to do airway on this code, and then Dr. Godfrey invited Grant to do the intubation under his guidance. In the few seconds I spend observing Grant, I'm once again impressed by him. He seems as cool and collected as always, even though he'll be bearing the weight of a critical procedure so early in his intern year.

Shifting my attention to the other end of the stretcher, I focus on Dr. Sanders and Elly Vincent. Given where they're standing, it signals they'll be running the code. Once again, this isn't how things are usually done; most often, the third-year resident is in charge of running codes. But again, if the third-year is wrapped up with another sick patient, the attending runs the resuscitation. In this case, it looks like Dr. Sanders is giving Elly the opportunity to manage the code, which I take as confirmation that the third year is tied up elsewhere. From my vantage point, I can see Elly's eyes darting around the resuscitation bay, taking in the scene, while she speaks to the team. Her aura is confident without being cocky. She seems to know exactly what she's doing. Even though she has only been a resident for a month or so, it's evident this code is going to be in very capable hands.

I could never be as confident as her.

Dr. Sanders notices me staring and waves me over. "Hey, Rachel. You got here early?"

I nod, suddenly timid, as I approach.

"I'm glad you did," Dr. Sanders goes on. "I just arrived myself, but I'm hearing it has been an extremely busy Saturday so far."

Elly also gives me a welcoming smile while she hurriedly tucks her long blonde hair into a tight ponytail. "Yeah, we're glad to have your help. We've had three codes this morning already, and most of the residents are tied up managing those patients' ongoing care. The ICU has been full since yesterday, so even resuscitated patients are having to board down here longer than usual."

My eyes widen. This will be the fourth code just since Elly started her shift? It definitely sounds like a particularly wild Saturday in the emergency department.

"Yup, today has been *insane*," Carrie interjects into the conversation. She begins drumming her fingernails, which are painted hot pink, on the computer keyboard. "Is it a full moon right now or something?"

Pete chuckles. "I dunno, but regardless of the phase of the moon, it always seems to get crazy whenever Doctor Reed and Doctor Vincent are working at the same time." He turns between Elly and Grant with a grin. "I think the two of you have some sort of crazy mojo together. Maybe the scheduler should make sure your shifts don't overlap anymore."

Grant looks up from what he's doing and puts his piercing blue eyes on Elly. Her gaze flicks his direction before she looks at Pete with a good-natured laugh.

"I'm afraid I've always been a black cloud in the ED, Pete. Even during med school, my shifts were consistently like this." She shrugs. "Apparently, whenever I work, I somehow manage to attract everything and anything that's wild, crazy, or sick into the ED . . . all at the same time."

Dr. Sanders snorts. "Maybe we should have taken your notorious reputation into account when you applied for residency."

"I'm glad you didn't." Elly laughs again. "You probably wouldn't have let me into the program."

I cringe, suddenly reminded about my own application. My eyes start leaping between Elly and Grant, and I can feel my stomach sink and my hope sinking right along with it. Elly and Grant are skilled, sure of themselves, and so *good* at what they do. With such high-caliber residents getting into the program here at Lakewood, I don't have a chance. It's a crushing realization because I truly love it here—the attendings and staff, the residents, the supportive and team-oriented culture, the high-acuity patients—it's exactly the type of place where I would love to train.

"Doctor Sanders?" someone calls from the doorway.

Everyone turns toward the source of the voice. It's Hadi. His expression is serious as he goes on:

"I think we need another doc in Resus Two. Both the patients who are boarding in there are teetering on becoming unstable."

Dr. Sanders nods, back to being all-business. "We'll be right in." She turns to Elly. "Why don't you go help the third year with the patients in Resus Two. Rachel and I will run the code that's coming in."

I do a double take and feel the color drain from my face. Did Dr. Sanders just say my name?

Elly nods. "You got it."

Without another word, Elly jogs across the resuscitation bay and follows Hadi out the door. There's a beat before I turn to Dr. Sanders. She's calm, but serious, as she meets my stare.

"Are you ready to run this?" she asks.

"Of course," I reply, though it's a complete lie. There's no way I'm ready. In fact, my nerves are rising so fast they're threatening to explode out the top of my head.

Dr. Sanders motions to the doorway. "Laura will be coming in to give report, so we should have more information about the incoming patient soon."

I swallow. This is for real. I'm running the resuscitation. With my heart pumping so hard it hurts, I slide into the spot where Elly stood only moments ago. Meanwhile, in my mind's eye, I'm frantically reviewing the cardiac arrest protocols from the syllabus. I've had them memorized since the first day of last month's rotation, but I need to make sure I remember everything. Every. Single. Detail. Because I'm being asked to step into Elly Vincent's shoes and run this code. And how I run this code will significantly impact the opinion Dr. Sanders has of me. And the opinion Dr. Sanders has of me will be reflected on the grade I get for this rotation. And my grade will affect what residency programs decide to grant me an interview. And any remote chance left for me to get an interview here at Lakewood is on the line.

And, above all else, a patient's life is at stake.

The door into the resuscitation bay is opened again, and a resident who has brown hair cut short, military style, pokes his head inside.

"Hey, I'm Jay Moen from trauma surgery. Any need for our team?"

Before anyone can reply, the charge nurse, Laura, steps around him and enters the resuscitation bay. Reading from a fluorescent green sticky note, she proceeds to announce the information she obtained over the phone from the EMS crew:

"Seventy-one-year-old male. Last known well about thirty minutes ago. Witnessed by his daughter to slump over onto the kitchen table and become unresponsive. 911 called. On scene, patient found by EMS to be in v-fib arrest. Status-post one shock and one dose of epinephrine. CPR ongoing en route."

"Thanks," Dr. Sanders tells Laura before looking back at Jay. "Sounds like there's no obvious indication for the trauma team, but we'll call if something changes."

Jay replies with a casual salute. "Good luck, everyone," he says before slipping out the door with Laura trailing behind him.

Dr. Sanders shifts my way once more. "Okay, Rachel. You're in charge now."

I blink. "Sure. Right."

I'm not ready, but it doesn't matter. It's time to run this code. Clenching and unclenching my hands at my sides, I survey the resuscitation bay, attempting to sort out what has already been done and what still needs to be prepared. Meanwhile, my heart continues galloping so fast I'm starting to wonder if I'm going to pass out. I sure hope I don't. I doubt becoming the ED's fifth resuscitation of the day will help my chances of getting into residency here.

I take in another breath to steady myself and look straight down the stretcher at Grant. "Doctor Reed, do you have everything you need for airway?"

Grant nods. "Airway is ready."

"And respiratory therapy is here. Sorry I'm late," a gal with bright red hair announces as she enters the bay and scurries over to Grant's other side. I can see from her badge that her name is Brenna.

I nod to Grant and Brenna, and then I turn to Pete. "You'll be pushing meds?"

"Yup," Pete replies.

"Pharmacy?"

"Present."

I look next at Carrie. "You'll be charting?"

"Uh-huh."

I motion to the techs. "The two of you will be alternating on chest compressions?"

"Yes."

"Radiology?"

"Here."

The door of the resuscitation bay is slammed open. In a sudden explosion of motion and sound, the three-person EMS crew pushes in a stretcher that has the coding patient upon it.

One crew member is bagging the patient while another member of the crew is riding on the side of the stretcher doing chest compressions.

"Seventy-one-year-old male. History of hypertension," the lead crew member declares in a loud voice as he pushes the stretcher inside. "Witnessed to become unresponsive at home. V-fib arrest. IV placed in the left AC. Status-post one shock and one dose of epinephrine."

There's another rush of activity as the EMS crew reaches the middle of the resuscitation bay and the unresponsive patient is transferred to the ED stretcher. One of the techs takes over doing compressions, allowing the EMS crew member who had been pumping on the patient's chest to step back and wipe his brow. Brenna steps in to bag the patient to supply oxygen. Pete begins attaching the defibrillator pads to the patient's chest. Carrie hangs IV fluid and gets to work placing a second IV in the patient's other arm.

Amidst the coordinated commotion, I make eye contact with Grant. "Go ahead with securing the airway, Doctor Reed."

Dr. Godfrey backs up to give Grant room. The tech pauses compressions. With steady movements and an unfazed expression, Grant quickly uses a Mac blade to get a view inside the patient's airway, slides in an endotracheal tube, and intubates the patient on his first try. As Grant takes a step back, Brenna hooks the exposed end of the endotracheal tube to the ventilator.

"Good color change," she tells me above the din.

Grant is already listening to the patient's lungs with his stethoscope. "Breath sounds present."

A glance at the monitor confirms the patient remains in ventricular fibrillation. I give the tech a nod, and chest compressions resume. I look to the pharmacist, who reads my mind and pulls out a dose of epinephrine from the code cart.

"The patient's daughter is here," Laura states, coming back into the bay.

I pull my eyes from the resuscitation to meet Laura's gaze. "Does the daughter want to come in?"

Laura shakes her head. "No. She chose to wait in the family room."

"I'll go introduce myself and help her with phone calls and anything else she may need," Dwayne offers, heading for the door.

"Great," I call after him. "Thanks."

As Dwayne exits the bay, I turn back to the stretcher. I open my mouth to give the next order but hesitate, casting an uncertain glance at Dr. Sanders. She's standing nearby, studying the scene closely. She isn't interrupting or assuming command, however, so I take that to mean I'm supposed to continue running this. Wetting my lips, I raise my voice and say:

"Hold compressions."

The tech freezes with her hands poised a couple inches above the patient's chest. Everyone falls silent and looks over at the monitor. Based on the tracing on the screen, the patient remains in v-fib, a completely disorganized cardiac rhythm where the heart is just quivering instead of pumping in a coordinated way to circulate blood and oxygen throughout the body. Every second this patient stays in v-fib increases his risk of suffering permanent damage to his organs. And if we can't get his heart to start beating normally soon, he'll be dead.

It's time to reboot his heart.

"Prepare to defibrillate at one hundred fifty joules," I say.

The other nurse responds by pushing a button on the defibrillator machine, which is sitting on top of the code cart. The machine lets out its recognizable, ear-piercing sound, which rapidly rises in pitch and then starts beeping to indicate the machine is fully charged.

"Everyone clear?" I check to make sure no one is contacting the patient or the stretcher. I then tell the nurse, "Go ahead."

The nurse presses the *shock* button on the defibrillator. The patient's body arches as electricity is administered to his heart through his chest.

"Resume compressions," I tell the other tech, who immediately starts working on the patient's chest.

I look over at Pete and the pharmacist. "One of epinephrine, please."

"One of epi going in," Pete replies as he's handed the medication by the pharmacist and pushes it into one of the patient's IVs.

I raise my eyes to the clock on the wall and anxiously start watching the bright-red second hand as it moves steadily in a circle. The two-minute interval goes by in a blink, and then I lower my eyes and call out:

"Hold compressions."

The tech stops and leans back from the stretcher. Once again, the room falls still as everyone's attention returns to the monitor. I stare at the screen, holding my breath. There's a pause, and then the line tracing across the screen takes on a new waveform. It's something that looks like a coordinated heart rhythm.

"Do we have a pulse with that?" I ask, my mouth dry and my stomach clenched.

Grant reaches forward and palpates the patient's neck. "There's a pulse."

I exhale with relief. The patient is back in a perfusing heart rhythm. We've managed to resuscitate him. What his long-term prognosis will be, no one can say at this point, but at least he has a chance for a meaningful recovery.

I wipe my clammy hands on the pants of my scrubs. "Okay, let's keep the patient at thirty-two degrees Celsius."

"You got it." Carrie scurries over to get the cooling machine, which will make sure the patient remains within therapeutic hypothermia ranges.

Laura steps closer to Dr. Sanders and me. "I'll go give the daughter an update."

"I'll be in to join the discussion shortly," Dr. Sanders replies. She then focuses on me. "I'd love to let you stay and continue managing this case, but since the ED is so busy, it would probably be best to divvy up duties. I'll stay here to manage the post-resuscitation care, and then I'll update the patient's daughter and call the intensivist." She shakes her head. "I have no idea how they're going to get another patient into the ICU, but they're going to have to figure out a way to make room." She pauses before giving me a smile. "Anyway, that's not for you to worry about. Let's have you go cover any new patients who are brought back from the waiting room. The department is so full, it's not happening often, but when they do room a new patient, it would be a huge help if you got their workups started."

"Certainly." My heart is still galloping, but I try to appear as smart and self-collected as Elly. "I'll go right now."

Backing up from the stretcher, I peel off my gloves and drop them into the trash can, and then I pull off the yellow gown and drop it into the linens bucket. Spinning on my heels, I cross the resuscitation bay toward the exit, but when I reach the door, I stop. Looking behind me, I take a moment to view the scene one last time.

The bay has fallen quiet as everyone settles in to manage the patient's post-resuscitation care. I hear the steady beeping coming from the monitor, which is tracking the patient's heartbeat, and the hiss of the ventilator as it controls the patient's respirations. Pete is hanging medication that will keep the patient comfortably sedated while he's on the vent.

Carrie is preparing another bag of IV fluid. The radiology tech is getting ready to take a chest x-ray to confirm the endotracheal tube is in the correct position.

I shift my eyes to the patient—the man—who remains motionless on the stretcher. I don't know his name, yet I feel a powerful connection with him. I played a role in this stranger's life, and though he'll never realize it, he played a significant role in mine. Being involved in someone's care is an honor, which no one takes lightly. Every patient we have the privilege of caring for educates us and makes us better at what we do. Most importantly, every time we care for someone who's critically ill, I think we're reminded not to take life for granted. Something about what we see in this line of work gives us a little better understanding of what it really means to be alive. I'll be forever thankful to this man for allowing me to learn from him. I hope he'll be able to return home to his family soon.

Facing forward once more, I pull open the door and step out of the resuscitation bay. The ED has gotten even nosier, busier, and more crowded than when I first arrived. At this rate, we're going to run out room completely. What would we do then? Treat patients outside?

As I reach my workstation and sit down, the sound of a patient's cantankerous shouting hits my ears. Looking left, I see that two stretchers have been crammed into a nook not far away. On one stretcher, there's a man shouting incoherently with drunkenly slurred speech. On the other stretcher, a guy is fast asleep, impressively unbothered by the commotion caused by his obnoxious neighbor.

A check of the patient tracking board reveals both men are in their forties. They were brought into the ED by ambulances around the same time. Their triage notes indicate they were both transported in for medical evaluation after they were found behind a local supermarket passed out and surrounded by several empty bottles of alcohol, which had been stolen from the store.

Having been tasked by Dr. Sanders to get workups started on new patients, I promptly get to my feet, slip on my white coat, and start heading toward the nook. As I get close, the combined odor of alcohol, cigarettes, and marijuana floods my nostrils. My eyes water, and I cough reflexively from the overpowering smell. Once I'm able to catch my breath, I proceed with a more thorough review of the scene before me.

The stretcher on the right is occupied by the man who appears to be sleeping comfortably. He's snoring and actually has a slight smile on his face as he dozes. His shoulder-length hair is falling out of his ponytail. There's a picture of Chuck Norris on his t-shirt. His jeans are wrinkled but appear clean. Hooked to the left railing of his stretcher is a plastic urinal, which is nearly filled to the brim. My eyebrows rise. Yes, this guy definitely had a lot to drink over the past few hours.

Also squeezed into the nook, underneath a paper towels dispenser only a couple inches to the left of the snoring guy's stretcher, is the stretcher that has the shouting man sitting upon it. His short hair appears to have been combed nicely at some point in the not-too-distant past. Like his buddy, the shouting man is also wearing a t-shirt (The A-Team) and jeans. He's contributing to the ambient noise of the department with his bellowed, drunken ramblings about Johnny Lawrence and Cobra Kai.

"Hello," I say above the shouting man's dialogue, positioning myself at the foot of his stretcher. "I'm Rachel Nelson, the medical student who will be helping you today."

The snoring guy just keeps snoring. The shouting man ignores me and starts talking about Burt Gummer killing Graboids. I blow a strand of hair from my face while my eyes shift between the two of them. Something tells me they may have more in their systems than just alcohol and marijuana.

"So what were you doing so early this morning?" I continue speaking above the commotion while I begin to exam the snoring guy.

"Isss hisss birfffday." The shouting man waves his arm in the general direction of the snoring guy's stretcher. "Heee isss my besssst friennnd."

The snoring guy suddenly snorts and opens his eyes. "Happy birthhhday to meee!" he exclaims before falling back to sleep.

I sigh. There's no way I'm going to get a coherent history from either of them, let alone get them to cooperate with a full exam. While it's likely they're just overloaded with alcohol, marijuana, and whatever else they may have ingested, injected, or smoked—and they'll eventually detox back to their normal selves— the unreliability of their condition means I can't assume they're otherwise all right. I need to make sure there are no occult head injuries, electrolyte derangements, or other serious issues contributing to their altered mental states.

I examine the snoring guy as best as I can, and then I attempt to get some sort of exam on the shouting man. By the time I'm done, I'm actually starting to get nauseated from the fragrant mixture of smells on their collective breath.

"Okay, gentlemen, I'm going to go put in some orders for you." I retreat from the stretchers. "I'll be back."

Neither of them reply. Frankly, I'm not sure they even know I'm really here. The guy on the right has rolled over and fallen back to sleep. The other man is now debating with himself about whether he would rather drive KITT or go back in time in a DeLorean.

I turn around to head back to my workstation but come to an abrupt halt when my eyes fall on Austin. He's standing outside Room Five, reading a message on his pager. I gulp as my intense, newly realized attraction to Austin starts going to war with my longstanding aversion to him. Ducking my head, I try to dart over to my workstation before Austin notices, but I see him raise his head and stand up a little straighter when he spots me. Still, I pretend not to be aware of him, even though my cheeks are now flaming in a very incriminating way.

Taking a seat in front of my workstation, I begin inhaling some calming breaths. I learned the technique from yoga classes Julie and I attended a couple summers ago. Thankfully, the breathing calms the emotional battle inside of me, and my clear head is restored. I make myself busy inputting orders for the intoxicated duo, yet I can't help also keeping watch on Austin out of the corner of my eye. His attention is pulled from me as the curtain of Room Five is moved aside and Tara exits the room. Even from where I'm seated, I can tell Tara has on more makeup today than the last time I saw her. I think she has even curled her hair. Adopting her trademark smile, Tara strolls up to Austin, standing closer to him than mere work acquaintances would. She then does that eyelash-batting thing while she starts chatting with him.

I stop typing. My nostrils flare. There's no doubt about it: Tara is crushing on Austin, for sure. But is Austin attracted to Tara in return? I discreetly observe them a while longer, trying to decide. The focused way Austin is watching her and the fact that he appears so comfortable with how closely she's standing to him certainly suggest he's as into Tara as she is into him. In fact, everything about their expressions and body language implies Austin and Tara are becoming an item.

I resume my work, and I find myself clicking the computer mouse with extra gusto as I finish entering my patients' orders. If Tara wasn't such a nice person, I don't think I'd like her at all.

Tara's soft giggle reaches my ears. In spite of myself, I peek down the hallway again. Tara is still gazing up at Austin as she talks, and Austin is grinning at her in return. Austin's grin is a subtle, slightly lopsided look of amusement . . . and it's incredibly hot.

My chest squeezes hard, and I force myself to look away while mentally reciting all the reasons why I cannot be attracted to Austin Cahill. It doesn't matter if he's hot. Or smart. Or has a sense of humor. He's still Austin. The man who has constantly aggravated me for over three years. So I don't care if he and Tara are becoming a thing.

Why, then, does it feel like I care?

"Hey, Rachel!"

Tara's friendly greeting only causes my scowl to deepen. I do my best to temper my disgruntled expression before I shift in my chair to look her direction. She and Austin are coming toward me.

"Hi, Doctor Hess." I manage a smile. "How are you?"

"I'm doing great." Tara's eyes flick Austin's way before she comes to a stop beside my workstation. "We were supposed to be off today, but we got called in to help admit patients since it's so busy."

"You got called in from home, and that's why you're doing great?" I quip before I can stop myself.

I swear I see Austin's mouth nearly turn up into another grin.

Tara giggles and shakes her head, causing her curled hair to bounce lightly on her shoulders. "No. The good part about getting called in today is that we won't have to be on-call tomorrow. We get the entire day off."

"Oh." I nod, making myself readopt my professional façade. "That is nice."

Just then, Elly emerges from another exam room. She's wearing a hair cover, a face mask with shield, gloves, a yellow procedure gown that's sprinkled with blood, and shoe covers. When she sees us, she heads over to join the conversation.

"Hi, guys." Elly's words are muffled by her mask. She remains totally calm, as if walking around in a blood-covered gown doesn't rattle her in the slightest. "How's it going?"

Tara gives her a warm smile. "We got called in to help with admissions today."

Elly's expression seems to brighten behind her mask. "Then you should come out with us later. Some of the ED residents are going out for dinner after the shift. You're welcome to join, if you're done by then." Elly looks between Tara, Austin, and me. "All of you should come."

My heart flickers with longing. I would love to go out. To socialize. To hang out with the ED residents and get to know them better. But I won't, of course. I'll be going home after my shift to study as I always do. I can't get behind on my study schedule. Besides, I must remain completely professional around the ED team. I can't hang out casually with the same people I'm trying to impress. As I keep telling myself, I can't let my guard down.

"That would be fun! I'll definitely go!" Tara's voice yanks me from my thoughts. She's beaming as she shifts Austin's way. She bats her curled eyelashes. "What about you?"

Austin's focus darts from Tara to me and then over to Elly. "Sure," he says, shrugging. "Why not?"

My mouth drops open. Did Austin just agree to go out? After work? To socialize? With other people? Voluntarily? We must have entered a space-bending vortex or something because Austin has always acted more averse to socializing than anyone I've ever known. What is going on with him?

An instant later, the answer hits me hard: Tara. Tara is the reason Austin agreed to go out.

"Awesome," Elly says to all of us, apparently assuming I'm also planning to go. She tips her head toward the other side of the department. "Well, I guess I'd better get going."

"Can I help you with anything, Doctor Vincent?" I pipe up, barely managing not to shoot a pointed look Austin's way. He may be busy flirting and making plans to go out after work, but I'm going to stay focused.

Elly shakes her head. "Thanks, but I'm all good. I just got done incising a huge axillary abscess. Lots of pus. It was rather satisfying. Now I'm searching for a place to discard my gown, since the soiled linens bin in the exam room was gone." She gives us a wave with a gloved hand, which I realize also has dried blood upon it. "I'll page you later with details, once I know where we're going. See you all tonight."

Elly walks away. I watch her go, silently hoping Tara and Austin will leave, too. I have no desire to continue watching Austin and Tara flirt in such an annoyingly cute way. Unfortunately, though, I hear Tara inquire of me:

"Do you have anyone you think might need to be admitted? We're happy to get the process started and help keep things moving down here."

Reminding myself that Tara Hess is an extremely nice person, I look back at her while shaking my head. "No, not at this point, at least. Thanks, though. Currently, I've only got two patients, and I'm working them both up for what is hopefully nothing more than polysubstance intoxication."

"Okay, but please let us know if you need anything." Tara pauses when her pager goes off, and she reads the new message. Her lips press into a line, and then she raises her head to address Austin. "It's Brittany Chen. She says the woman they asked us to admit for cholecystitis will be going to the OR and transferring to the surgical service, after all. I knew it." She sighs with a hint of exasperation. "I'll head back up to the patient's room and explain to her what's going on. Meanwhile, how about you finish rounding down here and message me when you're done?"

Austin nods, observing her closely. "Will do."

Tara replies by showing him another smile. The two of them hold eye contact for a distinctly protracted moment before she departs. Deciding I've definitely had enough of everything related to Austin, I spin away from him without another word and start heading the other direction.

"So are you going tonight?"

I halt when Austin's question reaches my ears. I take a second before turning around to face him. "No."

"Why not?" He crosses his arms over his chest. He's not wearing a white coat over his short-sleeved scrubs top today, so his pose gives me a full view of his muscular biceps and well-defined forearms. Why haven't I ever noticed his forearms before?

I snap back to attention, shifting my eyes to his face. "I'm not in the mood," I say, the words coming out with more bite than I intended.

Austin narrows his eyes with concentration. "I don't buy that excuse."

"Well, it's the truth," I lie, glancing away. "I'm just not interested in going out tonight. Especially if—"

"You've said more than once that you miss going out with your friends," Austin cuts me off.

"Why won't you take the opportunity to go out and make some new ones?"

I now stare up at him in genuine surprise. "When have I ever told you about how much I miss my friends?"

Austin uncrosses his arms. "During last month's weekend retreat, you told Tyler that you missed spending time with your high school and college friends. And one time when we were eating breakfast with our hospital rounding group during second year, you said the rigors of med school were causing you to miss out on enjoying the social scene around where you live."

I keep staring. My lips move as I try to formulate a response, but no sound comes out. Austin remembers all that?

Eventually, I gather my wits enough to reply. "It's . . . true. I miss going out and spending time with friends. I miss it a lot, actually." I pause with a sigh. "I did appreciate Elly's offer about tonight, but I've got other things I need to do."

"You mean, you're going to study." Austin continues watching me intently. "Not because you need to study, but because you think you're supposed to study."

His words hit a little too close to home. Tipping up my chin, I reply, "Or maybe I really do have other plans on my schedule. Maybe you don't know me as well as you think you do, Austin. Maybe I actually have more of a life than you realize."

He crosses his arms once more. "Okay. What other plans are on your schedule?"

I tuck my hair behind my ears, stalling for time as I flounder for a response. "Well, for starters, I . . . I . . ."

My voice fades away. The truth is, I have nothing else going on in my life. Nothing.

I avert my gaze once more, feeling utterly humiliated. I wouldn't be nearly so embarrassed if Austin wasn't the cause of this. Suddenly, I find myself frustrated and upset. Upset at Austin. Upset at my lack of a social life. Upset about the fact that no one ever thinks I'm good enough. Upset that I'm actually not good enough. Upset that I'll never get into the residency program here at Lakewood.

Austin remains silent. I still avoid looking at him. I'm not sure if he's gloating or pitying me, but it doesn't matter. Either way is mortifying. Another second or so passes before I finally hear him remark:

"I'm sorry you're not going to come out with us tonight. To be honest, I'd rather just go home after work and relax."

I take in a stuttering breath and dare to look at him again. "If you'd rather go home, why are you going out?" I can't resist adding, "Does it, perhaps, have anything to do with a certain . . ."

I trail off, my attention caught by what's happening behind Austin. From where I'm standing, I've had a full view of my two patients in the nook. A nurse just finished drawing their labs and strolled away. The snoring guy has already fallen back to sleep. The shouting guy is sitting up, and he's currently reaching for the filled urinal that's still hanging from the railing of his buddy's stretcher. Getting his hands around the urinal, the shouting man lifts it off the railing and begins putting it to his lips.

"Sir?" I dart around Austin and speed toward the nook. "Excuse me, sir? That's not a drink. That's a . . ."

Too late.

The man gulps down a swig of the snoring guy's urine, smacks his lips with satisfaction, and politely hooks the urinal back on the stretcher railing where it belongs. He does a double take when he notices me gaping at him. Breaking into a smile, he gives me a thumbs-up.

"Whhhat wasss that drink? It wasss delicioussss. Very refressshhhing." He lies down, situating himself comfortably on the stretcher and pulls up his blanket under his chin. "I'd like to have one of whatever my buddy isss having, pleassse."

I stare. For a very long time.

The snoring guy remains blissfully asleep. The shouting man gives me another thumbs-up and soon drifts off to sleep like his buddy. Before long, the alternating, buzz-saw-like sounds of their snores begin carrying through the department.

Slowly, I emerge from my stupor. I suppose one drink of urine can't kill the man. I'll let Dr. Sanders know what happened, of course, but I doubt it will change anything about our monitoring or treatment of this patient.

I watch them both for another few seconds, and then I pull my eyes from the drunk duo and turn around. Austin is still standing by my workstation. He's staring at the two guys in the nook. He shifts a questioning gaze over to me.

"Don't you dare say anything." I point at him. "I had no way of knowing that guy would think his friend's urine was some sort of frosty beverage."

Austin keeps peering at me. Only then do I realize the corners of his mouth are twitching upward. I soon begin feeling my own lips curving into a smile and a giggle rising inside me. I snicker aloud before I can stop myself and break into quiet laughter. Austin shows a smile of his own and starts chuckling, too. His laughter is warm and inviting, and the sound causes a flutter of delight within me. As our laughter slowly dies away, there's a pause as we look at each other.

"Change of plans, Austin!"

Tara's voice shakes me to awareness. Spinning around, I see her returning through the ED's back entrance. She's smiling at Austin and doesn't even seem to notice I'm here. As Austin turns to face her, his smile broadens. I immediately feel the delight fade from my body.

"Everything was taken care of for the cholecystitis patient, and she's already going to the OR." Tara reaches Austin's side and does a slow toss of her hair over her shoulder. "Meanwhile, I just got a page that there are two more admits down here, so it looks like we've got more work to do."

Austin is still gazing at her. "Sounds good."

They walk away together, leaving me behind. I stagger back a step, attempting to squelch my hollow, horrible sense of disappointment. Why am I so unhappy that Austin is getting involved with someone else?

Because you've always had romantic feelings for him yourself, the voice in my head declares.

Swallowing hard, I brush aside the idea and sit down in front of my computer. I have to keep working. I can't get distracted with thoughts of Austin Cahill. He's attracted to someone else, and I need to focus on what is undoubtedly the most important rotation of my career. I need to impress these attendings and residents. I'm fighting for a chance to be a resident here myself one day.

I do a rapid check of the tracking board, desperate for something to do. Imaging is pending and labs are in-process for the two guys who are sleeping in the nook. The department is so full we're almost on complete lockdown, but one more patient was just brought back from triage. Thankfully, this will give me something to occupy my mind.

The board says the new patient is a thirty-eight-year-old female named Gloria Tiller. Her chief complaint is listed as "*Chest Pain.*" I get up, straighten my white coat, and stride to Room Seventeen. I stop outside the curtain.

"Hi. Is it okay if I come in?"

"Yes, please," a gentle-sounding female voice replies.

I slip past the curtain. I find an overweight, well-dressed woman who appears her stated age sitting comfortably on the stretcher. Her hair has been styled in a pixie-cut and bleached blonde. She's got her cell phone in one hand and a bag of fast food in the other. Behind her, the cardiac monitor that she's hooked to shows her vital signs are within normal limits.

"Hi, Ms. Tiller." I adopt a professional smile. "I'm Rachel Nelson, the med student who'll be helping you today. I understand you're having some chest pain?"

"Are you freaking kidding me?" Gloria's serene expression disappears, replaced by one of unrestrained anger. She glares furiously while looking me up and down. Her voice rises even higher. "Do you know how long I've been waiting to be seen?"

I'm so stunned by her sudden change in demeanor that it takes me a moment to recover. "I'm sorry you had to wait. It has been an extremely busy day here in the emergency department, and—"

"Forever! I had to wait forever! I'm having chest pain and it took *forever* for someone to come see me!" She slams her bag of fast food to the floor, spilling an extra-large container of french fries and causing a huge milkshake to splatter everywhere. "And after waiting for so long, I'm only getting some dumb medical student to see me?" She vehemently shakes her head. "What are you, like, seventeen?"

My breath catches. I've been exposed to countless unreasonable, demanding, rude, angry, dishonest, drug-seeking, violent, and dangerous people in the emergency department before. Right or wrong, it's something those who work in an ED are simply expected to accept as part of the job. Yet this woman's words hurt more than most. Perhaps it's because my feelings are already raw and vulnerable from the roller coaster of emotions I've experienced since I got here. Maybe it's because her insults cut to the core of my insecurities. Or perhaps, in my anxiousness to do everything right, it's devastating to be told I'm doing things wrong.

Regardless, her spiteful, irate remarks cut deeply and feel intensely personal.

Still attempting to find my voice, I notice an ECG on the counter. It would have been done as soon as she arrived to the ED. With my hands shaking slightly, I pick up the ECG and make sure it looks okay. I then glance at the time stamp at the top of the page. It was done only eight minutes ago.

I look up from the ECG and view the patient again. She has already been properly connected to the cardiac monitor, and she has an IV in place. No doubt, the nurse also sent bloodwork to the lab so it could get processed as quickly as possible. The ECG was done, and the STAT blood test to make sure her troponin level is within normal limits is currently running in the little machine at the bedside. All of this has been done in just the few minutes since she arrived.

I focus on the patient, force down a swallow, and try again. "Could you please tell me more about your chest pain?"

"*Could you please tell me more about your chest pain?*" she mimics in a nasally voice. "Get out of here. I want someone else. Someone who actually knows what they're doing. Get out!"

I stumble backward into the curtain. "Okay. I'll, um, go get the attending."

"Get me a new lunch while you're at it." She motions to the food on the floor, which is rapidly smelling up the room with the odor of cooking grease.

I untangle myself from the curtain and exit the room. My head is light. I still can't quite catch my breath as I start to scan the department for Dr. Sanders. Anxiety swirls within me as I realize I'll have to tell her a patient kicked me out because I'm too young. Too inexperienced. Too unknowledgeable.

Because I don't have what it takes.

I spot Dr. Sanders. She's in one of the resuscitation bays, and it looks like she's helping the residents manage the ICU patients who are still boarding while awaiting inpatient beds to become available.

"Rachel? Are you all right?"

I shift my gaze and see Hadi approaching.

I shrug pathetically. "Yes and no. I just got kicked out of Room Seventeen."

Hadi comes to a stop, glances in the direction of the room, and shakes his head. "I triaged her. She's not a nice woman."

"No, she's definitely not." I have to fight to keep my voice from wavering. "She doesn't want me caring for her, Hadi. She kicked me out."

Hadi's forehead wrinkles. "Hey, don't take it personally. She's a weirdly demanding woman." He tips his head in the direction of the resuscitation bays. "I'll go tell Doctor Sanders the patient specifically requested to be evaluated by an attending physician. You go see if there's another patient and put this behind you." He smiles and rests a hand on my shoulder. "I've unfortunately seen tons of med students get treated badly by patients. It's never personal. It's not you. Trust me. Don't worry about it."

I sniff. "Thanks."

With a tip of his head, Hadi departs. I turn to go back to my workstation, but my gaze is caught by Austin, who's standing nearby and watching me while he's talking on the phone. As our eyes meet, Austin's focus shifts from me to Hadi's retreating figure and back to me. He says something more into the phone and then hangs up. At the same moment, Tara appears from the adjacent exam room and heads toward him. Austin faces her, and Tara says something that causes him to break into his handsome smile once more.

Another wave of crushing emotion hits me. Pulling my attention from Tara and Austin, I go to my workstation, sit down, and reach for a tissue. When I realize there isn't a box on my desk, I bend down and start rifling through my bag to find one. My fingers brush my phone, which shows I received a text message from my dad about an hour ago:

Your brother will be starting as an assistant professor next year. Thought you would be interested to know of his accomplishments.

I stare at the screen for a long time. I know Dad didn't mean to hurt me, yet his text is another punch to the gut. It's another reminder that I'm not as good as everyone else.

I sit back in my chair, feeling numb. Austin is attracted to Tara, not to me. That patient wanted to be seen by the attending, not by me. My parents are proud of my brother and sister, but they aren't proud of me. Lakewood Medical Center wants residents like Elly and Grant working in their emergency department, not me.

No one wants me. No one thinks I'm good enough.

I jump when my pager lets out a chirp. Reaching down to where it's clipped on the left pocket of my white coat, I slide the pager from its holder and check the new message. It's from Elly, and it's about tonight. She says everyone is going to an Irish pub after the shift is over. I know the pub she's referring to; it's not far from where I live. It's one of many places I've always wanted to go to but never made the time.

I set the pager on the desk, my emotions still heaving within me as I try to ignore yet another intense pang of loneliness. I should go home and study after work, but the thought of doing so causes something inside me to finally break. I can't go home after work. I can't study tonight. I can't sit in my apartment all alone, wallowing in misery. I can't.

With trembling hands, I reach for the computer mouse and use it to click open the hospital's paging system software. Putting Elly's name in the recipient's box, I type a message back:

I'll be there

Six

The bus doors open with a hiss, and I scurry down the steps to the sidewalk. I'm disembarking the city bus two stops earlier than I usually do, so instead of arriving near my apartment, I'm smack in the middle of the most popular nightlife area of town.

There's a palpable energy infusing the warm, August evening air. I look around, taking in the bustling scene that surrounds me. The sidewalk stretches in both directions as far as I can see, lined by an endless number of shops and restaurants. People are passing by in all directions; I see couples holding hands, packs of college students laughing as they stagger from one bar to the next, and the occasional person who, like me, is strolling alone. The charming lampposts lining the street are glowing, as are strings of white lights that hang high overhead and criss-cross from one side of the street to the other. The lights look like stars against the evening sky, which is swiftly developing the rich purple and deep blue hues of twilight.

I take in a breath, inhaling the delicious aromas that are being carried on the gentle breeze from the various restaurants. I smell everything from curry to ice cream cones to hamburgers. Also drifting through the air is a mash-up of music as a techno song playing in one bar mixes with the tune of a live band performing in another. Over the music, I can hear the conversations and laughter of folks who are eating at the restaurants' outdoor tables or meandering by.

The bus closes its doors and pulls away with a rumble, leaving me on the curb. My gaze drifts to a nearby park-style bench, where a couple is snuggling close together and sharing a humungous ice cream sundae. Despite the activity swirling around them, they seem not to notice; they only have eyes for each other. I sigh and look the other way.

Hiking up my bag on my shoulder, I check the time on my phone. It's about eight forty-five. I stayed an hour after my shift to help transition care of the ED patients to the doctors who arrived to work the late-evening and overnight shifts. I was going to stay even longer, since the ED remained insanely busy and overcrowded, but Dr. Sanders insisted I go home and rest after what she described as a "very long day."

She had no idea.

Yet despite how physically, mentally, and emotionally exhausted I was by the time I shuffled out the hospital's doors, I still couldn't bring myself to go home. My emotions were too raw, and my mind was too unsettled. I had hoped my unrest would fade as the rest of my shift went by, but it only got worse. So by the time I left the hospital and boarded the bus, even though I was utterly wiped out, I couldn't go home. I couldn't sit in the silence of my apartment with only my restless thoughts and aching emotions for company. I didn't want to have to think. I didn't want to feel.

So I got off the bus here instead.

Now, as I peer up and down the street again, I realize I'm not exactly sure where I'm supposed to go. I know the Irish pub is somewhere on this road, but I come to this area so infrequently, I can't recall exactly where it's located.

Another pang of remorse hits me. I've lived only a couple blocks from this incredible part of town for years, and I've hardly spent any time exploring it.

I turn around and check the establishments on the other side of the street. Soon, I spot what I'm looking for: O'Flanagan's Pub, with its bright-red exterior and a sign that has the pub's name written in yellow, Celtic-appearing font against a black background.

After checking up and down the road once more, I dash across the street. Reaching the opposite sidewalk, I start approaching the pub. As I get closer, the sound of someone playing traditional Irish music on a fiddle begins filling my ears. I can also hear the laughter, shouts, conversations, and cheers of the pub's patrons— the place definitely sounds busy tonight. Once I get near enough to see through the pub's huge front windows, my view of inside confirms the place is packed.

Making my way to the open doorway, I halt when I'm unexpectedly struck by a flicker of recollection. For a moment, I'm transported back to all the hilarious, silly, fun times I had with my college friends when we would go out. Admittedly, I spent nearly every weeknight and most weekends studying—I had my nose in the books far more than anyone else—yet, somehow, I still had balance in my life. So even though maintaining my four-point GPA, doing volunteer work, shadowing physicians, and attending pre-med meetings were my priorities, and that meant I often stayed home when others went out, I still managed to find time for relaxation and fun.

I haven't done much of anything fun since med school started.

I'm brought from my thoughts when someone tries to exit the pub and I have to slide out of the doorway to make room. Once my route is clear, I move inside and take a look around. Quickly, I understand why this place is so popular. The pub is one large, square-shaped room. The ambience is boisterously fun, welcoming, and authentically Irish. A bar made of dark, ornately carved wood spans nearly the entire length of the wall to my right. The shelves behind the bartenders are filled with all sorts of bottles, while most of the drinks on-tap are marked with the right-facing Guinness harp, which is recognizable even to me, and I don't drink.

The center of the pub is filled with tables and chairs for patrons, though most of the people here—who predominantly appear to be in their twenties and thirties—are on their feet and mingling with drinks in-hand. Those who are at the tables are enjoying plates piled high with burgers, fish and chips, and shepherd's pie. My stomach growls. I'm famished. I haven't eaten since breakfast. In fact, I'm not even sure when I last had any water.

Pulling my attention from the food, I look left to the small stage where musicians playing fiddles, flutes, whistles, and a banjo are performing an Irish jig. It's hard not to join in with those who are clapping along to the music. In front of the stage, in an area designated for dancing, a group of guys wearing matching fraternity t-shirts and holding half-empty glasses of Guinness are clumsily attempting to perform their rendition of an Irish dance, much to the amusement of their buddies who are watching and egging them on.

"Hey, Rachel!"

I hear my name over the din. Standing on tiptoe, I scan the crowd and locate Elly. She's seated at a long table near the back of the room, and she's waving her hand high in the air so I can see her. I timidly wave in return and begin weaving a path toward the table, getting jostled to-and-fro by the crowd as I make my way through the fray.

As I draw closer, I discover there are five more ED residents at the table, including Grant.

They're all wearing scrubs, and all of them worked in the department today. Most of the residents have started on a drink, and a few are delving into a shared platter of appetizers. Though they look about as exhausted as I feel, they're still smiling and bantering with one another. They give off a collective vibe of teammates who are really happy and in-sync. It's clear they love what they do, they worked extremely hard, and they're proud of what they accomplished today.

How I would love to be part of their team!

When a couple residents look up and notice that I'm approaching, I sense the color fade from my cheeks. What am I doing here? I'm not part of their team! I'm not even close! These are emergency medicine residents. Emergency medicine residents at Lakewood Medical Center, one of the most prestigious programs in the country. I'm way out of my league. It's like trying to eat lunch with the popular kids at school.

I slow my approach, giving myself time to decide what to do.

I could pretend to get a phone call and slip outside. From there, I could hop a bus and go home. The residents would never know what really happened, and instead of attempting to hang out with a group I don't belong to, I would spend the evening in the quiet seclusion of my apartment . . . miserably alone.

No. I can't do that. Not tonight.

Alternatively, I could stay here and try to make a good impression on the group. If I make a good impression, one of the residents might even encourage the residency admissions committee to grant me an interview. In fact, now that I think of it, impressing these residents may be the best chance I have to salvage an interview. This might be my only hope.

Okay, I'm definitely staying.

As soon as I make my decision, another blast of panic hits me. Exactly how am I supposed to make a good impression on them? This isn't the ED. This is a pub! I don't know them, and I have no idea how to interact with them in this type of venue. Would it be best for me to maintain a professional demeanor? Or would it be a smarter strategy to adopt a more I-hang-out-in-pubs-with-the-cool-kids-all-the-time persona?

I groan at my total lack of preparation. I should have spent my time on the bus studying the residents' bios on the Lakewood website. I could have learned about their interests and, at the very least, drawn up a list of talking points.

But I wasn't thinking clearly on the ride here. I'm still not thinking clearly. And now I'm facing what may very well be my only chance to secure an interview for next year's residency class, and I'm woefully unprepared. I've nearly blown it before I've even started.

"Hey, Rachel. Glad you could make it," Elly greets me in her friendly way. She motions to an empty seat.

"Thanks." I take the seat, which is conspicuously in the middle of the table.

"Welcome to O'Flanagan's." A waiter cruises up to me with a broad smile. "What drink can I get started for you?"

All six residents pause their conversations and look my way. I shift in my seat and glance around. Is this some sort of initiation? A test? Is there a particular drink emergency medicine residents are supposed to order when in a pub? If I order the wrong drink, will the residents shun me from their group?

I definitely need to read up on this later. Perhaps there's an article in the *Annals of Emergency Medicine* about it.

For now, though, all I can do is check what the others are having. Scanning the table, I count three Guinness beers, one wine, one drink that I'm pretty sure is whiskey, and a glass of lemon water. I sigh with relief. Elly is just having lemon water.

"I'll start with water with a lemon, please," I tell the waiter.

"You got it." The waiter hurries off toward the bar.

"Do you not drink?" one of the third-year residents asks me. He's seated at the head of the table, and he's got his shoulder-length blond hair pulled back into a ponytail at the nape of his neck. His tone isn't accusatory or judgmental. He just sounds curious.

I sit up, trying to appear self-collected despite how my stomach has tightened with nerves and my heart is rattling in my chest. I can't help it. I've just been addressed by one of the third-year residents. He's at the top of the residency pyramid. If anyone here might have sway with the application committee, it would be him. Thankfully, he's not quizzing me on how to appropriately fluid resuscitate a septic infant. At least he's asking me a question I've answered lots of time before.

"No, I don't drink. I'm too sensitive to alcohol. I get lightheaded even if I accidentally breathe in a whiff of hand sanitizer," I tell him with a cautious laugh. "So I've found it best for me to steer clear of alcohol, as well as caffeine or anything else that might be mind-altering."

The resident laughs along with me in a friendly way. "Sounds like a wise decision."

"Hey, everybody!"

I turn and see that Zach O'Cain has arrived. He's showing a relaxed grin as he takes the empty chair immediately to my left.

"Hi, Zach." Grant gives him a nod from across the table. "How was Fast Track today?"

Zach leans back, appearing impressively at ease despite the crowd we're with. Then again, Zach isn't trying to get into an emergency medicine residency, so he's not under the same pressure to impress everyone as I am.

"The place kept Doctor Fox and me hopping, that's for sure. I heard Fast Track set a new record for the number of patients seen in one shift." Zach looks my way. "I heard it was even more brutal out front. How was your shift in the main ED?"

I blink, collecting my thoughts. *Well, let's see. I realized I'll never be good enough to get into the residency program of my dreams. My parents are making me feel like a total failure in life. A patient kicked me out of her room because she assumed I'd be too dumb to know anything. And I've figured out that my mortal enemy is extremely attractive, and after three years of trying to ignore him, I'm becoming jealous that he's attracted to someone else.*

I flinch as emotions bubble up inside of me again. Somehow, though, I manage to keep my expression impassive and reply to Zach simply with:

"It was definitely busy."

The waiter returns, places my water in front of me, and takes Zach's drink order. Just then, Hadi and Carrie arrive. Carrie promptly scuttles to the far end of the table plunks herself down by the third-year resident. She lets out a giggle and begins chatting while ogling at him like he's a celebrity. Meanwhile, Hadi greets the group and takes the chair at my right.

As the waiter starts making his way around the table taking food orders, I hear my phone chime with a new text message. Reaching into my jacket pocket, I pull out my phone and read the text from my mom:

I didn't know if you heard, but your brother will be an assistant professor starting next fall.

I don't even have a chance to catch my breath before my phone lights up with another message from her:

*And Julie has already received her invitation to interview
for medical school.*

I stare at my phone. I'm thrilled for my siblings. I truly am. However, the news also reminds me that my parents view me as a failure by comparison. I put my phone away and fix my eyes on the table. When the waiter reaches me, I wave him off. My stomach might be empty, but I don't have an appetite anymore.

After a while, I raise my eyes again and start watching the residents as they chat amongst themselves. They look so happy. So confident. So sure of where they're going in life. And, I realize, I'm nothing like them.

Without warning, the dam breaks and tears flood my eyes. I hastily slide my chair back from the table, stand up, and say to no one in particular:

"I need to make a call. I'll be right back."

Slipping away from the table, I start shoving a path through the crowd to reach the front door. My breathing is growing shallow and my throat is getting thick as I pass the bar and dance floor. Through my watering vision, out of the corner of my eye, I see the frat boys still cheering, laughing, and doing Irish dancing while drinking Guinness and eating cookies. The music is pounding harshly in my ears. I'm starting to feel so claustrophobic in here that I think I'm going to suffocate.

At last, I break free of the crowd, reach the doorway, and burst outside, where I'm met by a much-needed rush of fresh nighttime air.

Sliding to one side, I collapse against the window, trying to settle my rapid breathing.

"Hey, there."

I jump when I hear someone address me. Looking to my left, I see one of the guys wearing the frat t-shirt coming my way. He's smiling and holding a shoebox that's half-filled with chocolate cookies.

"I saw you go by the bar. Looks like you're having a rough time." He holds out the box to me, fixing his bloodshot eyes on mine. "Thought you could use one of these. They're organic."

I stare at him blankly. My thoughts are so jumbled and my emotions are so high that I can barely process what he said. But I think he offered me a cookie. I could actually use a cookie right about now.

I sniff and take one of the biggest cookies from the box. "Thanks. This is really nice of you."

"No worries. Happy to help. Enjoy." The guy cradles the shoebox against his abdomen as he turns around and moves with slightly unsteady steps back into the pub.

Leaning against the building, I resume starting distractedly out at the lamppost-lined street while taking a bite of the cookie. It actually tastes pretty good, and I finish it off fast. After a minute or two passes, I feel the tension in my muscles release. My racing heart slows down, and my mind grows calm. I take in a breath, finally feeling ready to rejoin the others. Pushing off from the wall, I make my way to re-enter the pub.

As I step across the threshold, a wave of lightheadedness and nausea hits me. I stumble into someone who's standing at the bar. Raising my head, I see yet another guy who's wearing the fraternity's t-shirt. He has got one of the chocolate cookies in his hand.

"Sorry," I tell him, my tongue feeling weirdly heavy as I speak, causing my words to come out slurred.

The guy looks me up and down. A grin appears on his face, and he gives me a wink. "Hey, no worries." He raises his glass of beer. "Cheers, and have fun."

I want to roll my eyes at him for being so obnoxiously flirtatious, but my muscles are becoming increasingly loose and I wind up stumbling again. Gathering my footing, I turn away from the guy and clumsily resume maneuvering toward the back of the pub. As I go, my head becomes so light it doesn't even feel like it's attached to my body anymore. I nearly trip again, and I have to place a hand on the wall to steady myself as I go. I think I'm dehydrated. I need water.

Reaching the table, I find Elly and the rest of the group enjoying drinks, dinner, and conversation. I experience another surge of lightheadedness and stagger again, bumping my chair before I'm able to grab hold of it and sit down. My head continues swimming, and more nausea rises up within me. My skin is feeling prickly and warm.

Water. I need water.

I focus on my water glass, which is on the table in front of me. My arm seems to be floating as I reach out, lift the glass, and put it to my lips. I take only a sip, however, because I find that water hitting my stomach only makes my nausea worse. With a grimace, I put the glass back on the table. My grip is now so unsteady that I nearly knock over the glass before I let it go. What's wrong with me? Am I getting sick?

No, I don't think I'm sick. Actually, now I'm starting to feel good. Really good. Really chill. In fact, this is probably the most relaxed I've felt in a long time. I can hardly remember why I was so upset earlier.

Little alarm bells start going off in my head. Me? Relaxed? While I'm at a table with Lakewood's ED residents?

Something is definitely not right.

"Hi, everybody," a familiar voice reaches my ears.

I lift my head. Though my vision is a bit blurry, I can see Tara approaching the group. She's smiling, and it's not hard to figure out why: Austin is strolling alongside her. While everyone else voices a greeting, all I can do is keep staring at them in a daze. I sense I'm growing pale, and my head seems to be filling up with cotton balls. I have no idea what's happening with me, but I think the sight of Austin and Tara together is making my nausea return.

Austin's eyes scan the table, stopping hard when they land on me. I stare vacantly back at him. He watches me for what feels like a long time, and then he strides to the empty chair directly across the table from me and sits down. Tara follows him and takes the chair to his left.

"Hey, Rachel." Hadi has to lean in close so I can hear him over the music. He motions to a huge plate in front of him that's filled with sliders, fries, and pizza bites. "You're welcome to any of this, if you're hungry."

I notice Austin shift his attention to Hadi. I have no idea what Austin is scowling about. This is turning out to be a great evening. I don't care if I feel sick because all the worries of the world seem to have slipped out the door. I'm so relaxed, I'm almost giddy. Swaying slightly, I give Hadi a playful thumbs-up.

"Awesome!" I giggle when I hear my enthusiastic reply carry above the ambient noise. "I'm starving! Thanks so much!"

Hadi slides the plate closer to me. "You're welcome. Eat up."

I'm about to reach for some food when I hear Austin clear his throat. I turn his way and find him studying me with a severe look.

"What's the matter with you?" I ask, my words coming out muddled. I pick up a pizza bite. Half the toppings drop onto the table, but I don't care. I just leave them there. "Why are you so grumpy?"

The muscles in Austin's jaw start twitching as he keeps observing me. "Are you feeling well?"

"I feel great!" I stuff the entire pizza bite into my mouth. "Super hungry, though!"

Austin's posture stiffens. He shoots a steely look toward the front of the bar, where the cookie-eating frat boys are currently trying to build a human pyramid on the dance floor. Austin snaps his gaze back in my direction.

"Rachel, did you, by chance,—"

"I'm super thirsty!" I smack my lips, looking around at nothing in particular while I grab my water glass.

Austin's eyes get big, and he puts out a hand. "Rachel, that's not—"

I don't give him a chance to finish before I take a giant gulp. Then I pause. That wasn't water. That was something that tasted like malt chocolate and coffee. It was kind of sweet.

I check the glass in my hand. It has the Guinness harp on it, and it's half-filled with dark beer. I hiccup and look over at Hadi.

"Is this yours?" I ask sheepishly, feeling my throat tingle from the unusual aftertaste.

Hadi chuckles. "Yup."

"Whoops!" I giggle again and clumsily clap my free hand over my mouth. "I'm so sorry!"

Hadi's friendly grin broadens as he takes the glass from me. "No worries. It's not a problem."

"It is, considering Rachel doesn't drink," Austin interjects, tracking my movements.

Hadi's eyebrows rise. His smile disappears, and he slides his beer out of my reach. "In that case, maybe you shouldn't have any more."

Austin makes a sound and pushes himself back from the table as though he's about to stand up. "Rachel, let's go outside."

"What?" I shake my head. "Why would I do that? I . . ." I trail off when my body flushes with intense warmth. My head swirls again, and I have to grab the edge of the table for support. "Ugh. I think . . . I need some . . ."

"Here."

Austin is holding out my water glass to me. I take it from him with shaking hands while words tumble from my mouth uncontrolled.

"Thanks, Austin. I know how much you hate me, so I really appreciate your help."

Austin becomes very still. He closes his eyes, exhales, and reopens his eyes to resume watching me. I give him a shrug before I tip back my head and take a few sips of water. My movements are becoming increasingly uncoordinated, however, so water dribbles out one corner of my mouth and onto my scrubs top. With a snicker, I unabashedly use my forearm to wipe the water from my chin. Austin's features clench as he keeps staring at me.

Setting the glass on the table, I slide a little lower in my chair and look around. The rest of the people at our table are engaged in conversations and enjoying their food. Meanwhile, Austin just keeps looking at me. He almost seems angry.

"What is the matter?" I demand with a laugh.

Austin tips his head in the direction of the exit. "I think I should help you get—"

The rest of his words are drowned out by techno music, which starts playing from the overhead speakers. I cast another peek toward the front of the pub and note the Irish band is taking a break, hence the change in music. The frat boys begin clapping and whistling, and I soon spot why: a flock of sorority girls is arriving to join the party. Before long, the dance area has turned into a scene from a nightclub. A smile spreads across my face as I watch them moving to the music's heavy beat. They look like they're having a great time.

And I suddenly have the crazy, wild impulse to join them.

I unsteadily spring to my feet. "Dancing!"

Nearly toppling over, I stagger across the pub toward the dance floor. I have no idea what I'm doing, but it doesn't matter. I feel euphoric. Alive. Relaxed. I just want to dance.

The frat boys let out another round of cheers as I join them on the crowded floor. I push into the middle of the throng and start dancing to the music. Everything around me becomes a whirlwind of sound, light, and motion. I'm getting hot. My head is spinning. My eardrums are aching from the pounding music. My nostrils fill with the aromas of beer, food, and marijuana.

I freeze, smacked into a moment of mental clarity.

Marijuana?

Swaying weakly, I turn in a circle, studying the frat boys anew. My gaze shifts to the floor, where the empty shoebox sits discarded in the corner. Lifting my eyes back to the frat boys, a wave of horror washes over me. Did those cookies . . . did I accidentally . . .

"Rachel."

Austin's voice is loud in my ear. Raising my eyes, I find him standing right beside me. He's breathing hard. His jaw is clenched.

"I'm taking you home." Austin puts one hand on my shoulder, and I realize he has my bag and jacket in the other.

The fog moves back in, taking over my mind. I can't make sense of anything. All I know is Austin said something about going home, but I don't want to go home. If I go home, I'll have to deal with all my stressors, hurt, and insecurities. I'm not ready for that. Not yet.

I shake my head, which triggers a bout of vertigo that nearly causes me to topple over. "No. I don't want to go home, Austin."

I move to venture deeper into the throng. Austin grabs my hand, stopping me.

"Rachel, you need to go home."

"No, I don't." I try to get away, but Austin doesn't let go. I feel a rush of indignation and glare up at him. "Don't tell me what to do, Austin. You're always telling me what I'm doing wrong. Just for one night, I don't want to worry about doing things wrong, okay? I don't want to think about my parents being disappointed in me, or how I'll never get into this residency program, or how you . . ." I hiccup and avert my gaze. "I'm not going home," I utter again, though I'm starting to realize there's nothing else I would rather do. I'm miserably queasy, my head is throbbing, I can barely stand up, and I think I might throw up.

Keeping my hand in his, Austin moves so he's standing in front of me once more. "Please, let me take you home."

"No." I attempt again to tug myself free, but between Austin's strength and the fact that my arms are like rubber, I know I'm not going anywhere.

Austin sighs. "Fine. I'm sorry, Rachel, but I'm doing this for your own good."

Austin releases me, but before I can bolt away, he puts both hands underneath my arms and lifts me with ease off the ground. My eyes pop open wide, and I let out a yelp of surprise. The next thing I know, Austin has slung me over his shoulder like I'm nothing more than a sack of potatoes.

"What are you doing?!" I screech, kicking my legs wildly. I feel the blood rushing into my head as I hang halfway down his back with my face against his shirt. All I can see is the dance floor down below, and I can hear the frat boys starting to laugh and cheer Austin on. "You are insane, Austin Cahill! Insane! Put me down! Put me down right now!"

Austin ignores my protests. With his forearm across the backs of my knees to brace my lower half against his chest, Austin begins carrying me off the dance floor. Over the pounding music, I hear more whistling, cheers, and applause from the frat boys, who are clearly enjoying the fiasco. I continue kicking while adding a few fist-pounds against Austin's back for good measure, but he doesn't even seem to notice. He keeps carrying me away from the fray. Before long, I feel a rush of night air and the music fades from my ears as Austin exits the pub. Without breaking stride, he turns right and begins walking up the sidewalk while people we pass laugh and let out amused exclamations.

I finally stop kicking. I'm totally exhausted. "Okay, Austin, you win. You got me out of the pub. You can put me down now." My words drip with frustration.

Austin doesn't reply. He carries me all the way to the street corner before coming to a stop. "Where do you live?"

"Like I would ever tell you that."

"Well, if you don't, since I have your phone, I'll call your parents and explain I need your address because you were drinking beer and doing marijuana tonight."

"No! No, don't do that!" I resume kicking with new fervor. "Austin, I had no idea the cookie was drugged! I swear! I also didn't mean to drink Hadi's beer! I just . . . just . . ." With a weary sigh, I give up. "My apartment building is two blocks straight ahead. The River Ridge complex."

I feel Austin release his hold on my legs and put both hands around my waist. He lifts me off his shoulder and then carefully lowers me to the ground.

"Can you walk?" He hasn't let go of me, and there isn't even a hint of amusement in his expression as he watches me.

"Yes, I can walk. I. . ." I nearly collapse as my legs give out.

Austin catches me. Without another word, he scoops me up in his arms again, this time carrying me against his chest with one arm behind my back and the other under my knees. Fixing his eyes straight ahead, he begins carrying me up the sidewalk. Rocked by the motion of his steady strides, my exhaustion finally gets the better of me. I lean my head against his chest. My eyes close.

"What floor?"

I open my eyes with a start, stunned to realize Austin is already standing in front of the elevator bay on the ground floor of my apartment building. I lift my aching head, doing a double take when I notice two gals standing in front of the next elevator over. Dressed in nightclub attire, the gals are staring at Austin with dropped jaws and wide eyes.

"Um, hello," I say to them, plastering on an awkward smile.

"Hi," one of the gals replies. Her eyes remain huge as they shift from Austin to me. "Where in the world did you find this guy? Handsome, strong, and literally sweeping you off your feet?"

"And wearing scrubs, too," the other gal chimes in, nudging her friend.

The first gal gives Austin another once-over. "Are you a doctor? Please tell me you have brothers. Or cousins. Even cousins will do."

The other gal begins nodding in apparent agreement. "Seriously. Where are the hot guys like you hiding nowadays?" She sighs. "We were just at a pub that was packed with frat boys, and every single one of them was a total dud. They were all stoned out of their minds from some stupid marijuana cookies."

There's a pinging sound as the gals' elevator opens. They step inside, and the first gal spins around to put her attention back on Austin.

"Going up?"

"Thanks, but we'll take the next one." Austin still hasn't cracked even a twinge of a smile. He taps our elevator's call button with the point of his elbow.

The two gals don't hide their disappointment and continue gazing at him until their elevator door slides closed.

In the silence that follows, I clear my throat and look up at Austin once more. He tips down his head to meet my gaze. There's a very intense pause, which causes my heart to flutter.

"What?" I dare to ask.

Austin continues searching my face. "What floor?"

"Huh?" I blink a few times as our elevator pings and the door slides open. "Oh, um, six. I'm in six twenty-four."

Austin says no more as he carries me into the elevator and pushes the button for the sixth floor. The door closes. While the elevator starts to ascend, everything gets really quiet. My stinging eyes slowly shut. My aching head drifts downward until my chin is against my chest. Then everything goes black.

Seven

I let out a groan as I groggily open my eyes. My head is aching terribly. Blinking my vision into focus, I slowly push myself up into a sitting position and peer around. To my total confusion, I discover I've been sleeping on the couch in the front room of my apartment.

I have no idea what time it is, but daylight is streaming in through the partly open window blinds and my stomach is rumbling with hunger. I cast a glance at the clock on the wall, and my jaw drops. It's already ten in the morning. I slept through my entire morning study session.

I spring to my feet, intent on going directly to my office to start reading about the acute management of spontaneous pneumothoraces, but I swiftly realize my hastiness was a mistake. My head gets so light that my vision dims. My legs grow weak. Reaching to the arm of the couch to support myself, I carefully sit back down, lower my head, and stare at the floor, trying to remember how I wound up like this. My mind is weirdly fuzzy, though, making recent memories a blur. In fact, to my alarm, I have no idea what happened last night. All I know is that I feel absolutely awful. Letting out a moan, I list to one side, rest my head on the arm of the couch, and close my eyes.

"Rachel?"

My eyes pop back open when I hear a man's voice. With a cry of alarm, I leap up unsteadily once more and raise my hands in front of me like I'm about to do some sort of martial arts maneuver.

"Get out of here, you psychopath!" I yell, swaying so much I nearly fall over. "I know jujitsu-karate-krav-maga, and I'm not afraid to use it!"

"Rachel," someone repeats, putting his hands on my shoulders. "Rachel, it's me."

I pause. I recognize that voice. Catching my breath, I raise my head.

Austin Cahill is standing in front of me.

Austin is in my apartment.

Why is Austin in my apartment?

Shaking from the sudden adrenaline rush, I take in the sight of him. Austin's hair is disheveled. Facial scruff is on his upper lip and chin. He's wearing scrubs.

Hang on, I'm wearing scrubs, too. Why was I sleeping in my scrubs? Why was I sleeping on my couch?

And why is Austin here?

"Austin, what's going . . ."

My voice peters out as my head starts to pound. I wince and grab the couch to steady myself.

"Lie down."

I don't argue, letting Austin guide me to a seated position. I lower my aching head onto the arm of the couch, and he lifts my legs so I'm lying flat on my back.

"What happened?" I mumble, trying to look at him while holding up a hand to shield my eyes from the sunlight.

Austin doesn't reply. As he peers down at me, I'm pretty certain the corners of his mouth are twitching upward a little bit. At last, he gets down on his haunches beside the couch, still studying me. Yep, there is definitely an amused gleam in his eyes.

"What's so funny?" I demand, the words coming out hoarse. Why is my throat so dry?

Austin starts rubbing his chin with one hand, appearing as though he's deciding what to say. Eventually, he asks, "Do you remember the pub?"

"The what?" I draw my brows together. "What in the world are you . . ."

I fall silent when, in a flash, I remember. I remember everything. Every terrible, humiliating, nauseating, accidentally drugged-and-intoxicated moment of last night.

"Oh no." I put both hands over my eyes, as if trying to hide myself from the world. "Think of all the people from Lakewood who saw me last night, Austin. There were residents, nurses, and other med students there. I've completely destroyed my reputation." I inhale a heavy, strained breath, trying in vain to calm the anxiety that's rapidly rising inside of me. "I'll never get into Lakewood's residency now. I might not get into any residency at all. And then—"

"Rachel. Rachel, look at me."

I slowly uncover my tear-filled eyes to focus on Austin. There's something calming and reassuring in the way he's watching me. I sense my anxiousness fade a little bit.

"It's not that bad. I promise," he says. "In fact, I don't think anyone from Lakewood even noticed. Those who were at our table were preoccupied with their own conversations and meals, and by the time you tried to do a John Travolta on the dance floor, the pub was so crowded that no one at our table could see you."

I flinch. "I wasn't really trying to bring back *Saturday Night Fever* out there, was I?"

"You were." Austin appears to be working increasingly hard to hold back a grin. "Not to mention, you were also adding your own, shall I say, *unique* interpretation to it."

I groan and look away. "I'm so embarrassed."

"Don't be. Like I said, the Lakewood crowd didn't even notice. As for your disco fever, drugged or not, you were still dancing better than the rest of them."

I take a moment before peering at him again. Austin shows another smile. It's a very attractive smile.

He's so ridiculously handsome.

I cough as soon as the thought hits me.

"Are you all right?" Austin reaches out and sits me up.

"Yup. Fine," I wheeze.

"You're not going to throw up?"

I shake my head.

"Good." He slowly lets me go. "Because after how the night went when I got you back here, I would be amazed if you had anything left in you to expel."

I grimace. "You mean, I got sick?"

"Several times."

I drop my head into one hand, embarrassment welling up inside of me yet again. "And let me guess: you had to help me with that, too?"

"It was either that or let you aspirate," Austin replies, "and I wasn't about to let that happen on my watch."

I take a moment before I lift my head to look at him once more. "Thank you, and I'm so sorry."

"You have no reason to apologize. What happened wasn't your fault." He ventures another smile. "However, you've definitely proven it's not a good idea to ingest mind-altering substances when you're small, a novice to chemicals, dehydrated, and running on an empty stomach."

I start shaking my head. "I obviously know all that, too. I'm a medical student, for crying out loud. That's partly why this whole situation is so humiliating. I was so clueless last night. I was so stupid."

"No, you weren't stupid. Like I said, this wasn't your fault." Austin's tone darkens. He gazes off at nothing, and the muscles in his jaw tense slightly. "It took all my restraint not to drag those fraternity idiots outside and have some words with them. They had no idea of the kind of danger they put you in with their antics." He seems to take an extra moment before focusing on me again. The lines in his face relax. "Anyway, I'm glad you're doing better."

Quiet settles over us. It's not the adversarial quiet I would expect to feel around Austin. Instead, it's something very different. Something that causes my pulse to accelerate and my breathing to quicken. Something exciting and powerful deep down inside of me that draws me to him.

"Austin," I begin, feeling the need to fill the charged silence, "thank you again for everything."

His expression is steady as he leans in a little closer. "You're welcome."

There's another beat when neither of us speaks nor moves. The draw I feel to him grows even stronger.

Alert! Alert! This is Austin, and Austin likes Tara. And you have to stay focused because you have an honors grade to achieve and an emergency medicine residency program to get accepted into.

The voice in my mind yanks me back to reality. I force myself to look away. "You must be exhausted. Did you get any rest?"

"A little." Austin tips his head toward the chair in the opposite corner of the room. "Around five in the morning, once your bouts of sickness passed and you finally fell asleep, I was able to doze."

"I bet you're starving. Let me get you something from the fridge."

I move to get up, but Austin puts his hand on mine to stop me. His touch sends an electric sensation zipping up my arm.

"Don't worry about me, Rachel. I'm fine. Seriously. Please stay seated." He shows another grin. "Otherwise, I'm pretty sure I'll have to scoop you off the floor again."

I want to laugh, but I don't. I'm too distracted with studying how his hand is resting over mine.

"You should lie back down," I hear Austin say.

"What?" I whip up my head, almost guiltily.

"Lie down. You're pale."

"Oh. Right." I lower my head back onto the arm of the couch, realizing how woozy I feel.

He lifts his hand from mine. "Can I get you some food?"

"No, thank you. I don't feel up to it yet."

"Do you have a headache?"

"Yeah, as a matter of fact, I do." I start rubbing my temples in an attempt to massage away the relentless aching. "It's awful. How did you know?"

He raises his eyebrows slightly. "I'm not going to incriminate myself."

I snicker. "Oh. Gotcha."

He chuckles—it's a rich, inviting sound that causes me to smile, too—and gets to his feet. "You'll probably benefit from taking something for your headache before it gets any worse. Do you have a medicine cabinet around here?"

"Yeah. It's in the hallway bathroom." I flop my arm back over my eyes to block out the light. "There should be some Tylenol in there."

"Acetaminophen."

I pause, and then I slowly remove the hand from my eyes to fix him with a severe look. "Tylenol."

"Acetaminophen," he repeats.

I stare at him, incredulous. Is Austin seriously going to argue with me? Now? Here? About the correct usage of the generic name of an over-the-counter medication?

Of course he is. Because he's Austin.

I defiantly push myself up on one arm. I might not be at the top of my game at the moment, but I'm not going down without a fight. "Tylenol. People call it *Tylenol* all the time, Austin."

"People are wrong, then, if it's actually generic acetaminophen."

My nostrils flare. Austin is so aggravating. So frustrating. So exasperating. I'm not sure if I want to strangle him or . . . kiss him.

Kiss him?

I nearly gasp aloud. No. That's not right. I do not have a burning desire to kiss Austin Cahill. The thought was just a weird side effect of being drugged last night. I'm still detoxing, which is why anything I think or feel right now can't be used against me.

Austin seems to interpret my wide-eyed silence as defeat. With an infuriatingly victorious look, he strides out of the main room. I still don't move, though my mind is racing . . . racing with thoughts of what it would be like to kiss Austin.

Get a handle on yourself. You're feeling the effect of the tainted cookie. That's all.

Satisfied by the reasoning of the voice in my head, I lower myself onto my back and peer up at the ceiling.

Actually, though, I really do think I want to kiss Austin.

This is a disaster.

"I'll get some water for you, too." Austin reappears from the hall and crosses into the kitchen.

"Okay." I'm suddenly finding it difficult to come up with something coherent to say. "Good. I mean, um, thanks."

I fall quiet again, strangely transfixed by the sounds of Austin moving around my apartment. I hear him open a few cupboards. When he finds the one with the cups and glasses inside, there's a distinct pause. I then hear him turn on the kitchen faucet and shut it off again. A few seconds later, he comes out of the kitchen holding a couple white pills in one hand and what I realize is my One Direction boy band mug, which I got years ago when Julie and I went to one of their concerts. The mug has colorful hearts around the boy band's name on one side and a picture of Liam Payne on the other.

"Nice mug." Austin is clearly fighting off laughter as he holds it out for me to take.

I sit up, snatch the mug from him, and hold it protectively against my chest. "You took this one out of the cupboard on purpose."

He chuckles again and extends his other hand, dropping the pills onto my palm. "It's not my fault it was at the front of the shelf. You must use it a lot . . . but I'm not judging or anything."

"Judge away. I don't care. Liam is a handsome man and a talented singer." I haughtily toss the two tablets into my mouth and wash them down with a gulp of much-needed water. "And he's a gentleman."

"Oh, he is, is he?" Austin is still grinning. "You know him personally?"

I roll my eyes and rest myself back on the couch. "I'm not even going to humor that with a response."

He keeps grinning, though there's now something more probing about the way he's watching me. He takes a seat on the far end of the couch and motions to the mug. "So is that the type of guy you're looking for? A handsome, musically talented gentleman?"

"No," I draw out the word while I set the mug on the floor beside the couch. "I mean, those aren't *unattractive* qualities in a guy, but there are obviously other qualities that are far more important." I peek down at the mug and finally laugh at it myself. "Trust me: a boy band member is not the type of guy I'm looking for."

"Does Hadi sing?" Austin asks unexpectedly.

"Hadi?" I repeat. "Why on earth would I know if . . ." I trail off as realization strikes me. "Hang on, Austin, I'm not romantically interested in Hadi."

He arches an eyebrow with a look of unmasked skepticism. "You're not."

"No, I'm not. We're friends. That's all. Don't get me wrong, Hadi is a good guy, a great nurse, smart, funny, and good-looking. He'd be a great catch." I shrug. "He's just not the right catch for me."

"Uh-huh." Austin scratches his head. "You think Hadi has all those great qualities, and yet you want me to believe you're not romantically interested in him?"

"Yes," I reply immediately, though I find myself getting flustered. Austin always does this to me. He gets in my head. "I mean, no. I mean . . ." I exhale, trying to collect my thoughts. "Like I said, we're just friends."

"So you're just friends who flirt."

I gasp loudly. "We do not flirt! Take that back, Austin Cahill! I do not flirt at work!"

"I suppose I can't argue with that," he mutters, and I'm not entirely sure he meant for me to hear him.

I pick up the mug, about to take another drink, but I can't resist adding, "If you want to talk about flirting at work, then let's talk about you and Tara Hess."

Austin becomes very still. Seconds pass while he stares back at me. His expression is completely unreadable, and he doesn't reply.

"I thought so," I say before taking another drink.

I swallow while keeping a smugly victorious look on my face, even though I'm feeling anything but smug at the moment. The truth is, I'm wishing Austin would contradict me. I wish he would insist he's not interested in Tara Hess. Instead, though, he rubs the back of his neck while diverting the discussion back to me:

"Well, Hadi sure seems to be interested in you."

I nearly spit out my next sip of water. "What are you talking about?"

Austin drops his arm to his side and speaks each word with exaggerated deliberateness. "I'm talking about Hadi being interested in you."

"You're wrong." I shake my head. "We're really just friends."

Before either of us can say more, Austin's phone starts to ring. He clears his throat, gets to his feet, and strides across the room to retrieve his jacket, which is on the floor beside the chair he slept in. As I track his movements, I find myself once again wondering how I went so long without noticing his striking profile and his toned, athletic physique . . . not to mention, his thoughtfulness, humor, and brilliance. Have I been in a coma for the last three years?

You didn't notice because you were scared to notice. You didn't want to get swept up in feelings for Austin. You were so focused on your education, you ignored how you felt about him.

I quickly chug down another swig of water.

Austin retrieves his phone from his jacket pocket and puts it to his ear. "Hello?" There's a pause, and then a hint of a smile appears on his lips. "Hey, Tara."

My stomach crashes to the floor. Tara is calling Austin. On his personal cell phone. I know she's not at the hospital, so this obviously isn't a work-related conversation.

Austin turns to face out the window and leans casually against the wall as the conversation continues. He appears comfortable as he chats with her, speaking in a voice that's just low enough so I can't hear what's being said. From what I observe in his body language, something tells me this isn't the first time he and Tara have talked outside of work. Of course it isn't. Because they're an item.

I lower my head. Austin Cahill is the most aggravating, infuriating, frustrating man on the planet . . . and I'm crazy about him.

But he's falling for someone else.

You never gave him the time of day. You were always too busy studying.

The voice keeps chanting relentlessly in my head, and I know it's true. I never gave Austin a chance. I let him slip through my fingers.

I had to, though. I couldn't get swept up in romance when med school started, and I refuse to get swept up in it now. I'm on the most important rotation of my career, and I will not let these wild, crazy feelings for Austin get in my way. I have to focus. I must earn an honors grade. It's my only chance left to secure an interview for Lakewood's residency class.

Austin ends his call and strides back to the couch. "So how are you feeling after a little hydration?"

"Better," I tell him, keeping my tone impassive. Polite. Unemotional. "Please don't feel as though you have to stay any longer on my account. I'm guessing you have other things you need to be doing with your day."

Austin's gaze flicks to his cell phone before settling back on me. "I don't want to leave you alone, Rachel. Not until I know you're—"

There's a brisk knock on the front door. Austin glances toward the entryway and then back at me with a questioning look.

"Who on earth would be coming over this early on a Sunday morning?" I slowly get to my feet, wobbling as I do so.

"Sit down. Let me get it." Austin puts out an arm, clearly getting ready to catch me if I fall.

I steady my footing. "I think I'm okay. Thanks, though."

Venturing cautiously across the room, I head for the entryway. Austin follows behind me. There's another knock on the front door. Reaching out, I pull it open. And I freeze.

My sister, Julie, is standing outside.

Eight

"Surprise!" Julie lets out an elated laugh and bounds through the doorway with her long, dark blonde ponytail bouncing behind her. She wraps her arms around me, pulling me into one of her enthusiastic hugs. "It's so good to see you, Rach! I . . ."

Julie trails off and becomes very quiet.

Stepping back from her, I see she's frozen in place while staring over my shoulder. Her brown eyes are huge. Her mouth has dropped practically to the floor.

And I remember Austin is a few feet behind me.

I follow Julie's line of sight to Austin, whose eyes are shifting between Julie and me.

Julie makes a choking noise and looks my way again, now viewing me as though she has never seen me before. Her cheeks become an impressive shade of pink. "Oh, gosh, Rach, I'm sorry for barging in. I should have let you know I was . . . I mean, I didn't mean to interrupt . . . I mean, I didn't expect . . ."

My own face ignites when I realize what she's thinking. "No worries at all," I tell her quickly. I motion as nonchalantly as I can from Julie to Austin and back again. "Julie, this is Austin Cahill. He's one of my colleagues. Austin, this is my sister, Julie Nelson, who—"

"Came to stay with my sister for a few days because I'm on vacation and needed to get away after breaking up with Marcus," Julie fills in the rest with a widening smile. She steps toward Austin and confidently extends her hand. "It's nice to meet you, Austin."

"Likewise." Austin shakes her hand in return. He appears about to say more when his focus cuts back to me. "Rachel? Are you okay?"

I've reached out to the wall to steady myself. My head is beginning to get light again, and I think my cheeks have gone from red to pasty. Apparently, I'm not as recovered from last night's adventure as I thought.

Julie also looks my way. Her forehead wrinkles. "What's wrong, Rach?"

"Nothing. I'm fine. I just . . ." I swallow down the nausea.

Austin makes a fast move past Julie, getting to me just as my knees give out. He slings one of my arms behind his neck and scoops me up in his arms. Julie is now unabashedly gawking at Austin, who carries me into my room and lays me down on the bed.

Julie rushes in behind us, looking frantic. "What's happening?"

"It's no big deal. I promise," I tell her. "I wasn't feeling great last night, which is why Austin helped me home, and . . ." I break off as another wave of nausea hits, and I fall back on the pillow.

Julie puts a worried, inquiring gaze on Austin.

He meets her quizzical stare and tips his head toward the door. "Let's go out there and let Rachel rest while I fill you in."

Julie nods, shooting me a last look before she scampers out of the bedroom. Austin starts to follow her. When he reaches the doorway, he pauses to peer at me over his shoulder.

"Are you going to be fine in here by yourself for a couple minutes?"

I nod.

He makes another move to depart, but I call after him:

"Austin?"

He stops and turns back once more.

"Thank you again," I say quietly. "For everything."

He tips his head. "You're welcome, Rachel."

Austin leaves the room and shuts the door behind him. Left alone in the quiet, though I do my best to fight it, weariness takes hold of me. I let my eyelids fall. I don't notice anything more.

***

Sunlight causes me to open my eyes. I'm lying on my still-made bed. One of the blankets I usually keep on the couch in the front room has been draped over me. Through the window, I see the summer sun shining brightly. Pushing myself up and swinging my legs over the side of the bed, I check the clock on the nightstand and nearly choke. It's almost three in the afternoon. I've never slept so late. Ever.

I stand, relieved to find I'm steady on my feet. The nausea is gone, and I'm no longer lightheaded. The pounding behind my temples has resolved. My mind feels clear and sharp. At last, I feel like myself again.

I won't eat a chocolate cookie for the rest of my life.

I cringe as the memories of yesterday start playing again in my head. I cannot believe what happened. What would I have done if Austin hadn't been there?

The question strikes me hard. What *would* I have done without Austin's help? I have no idea. There's no way to truly measure the assistance he rendered. Not only did he get me out of a dangerous situation and bring me home safely, he saved me from humiliating myself in front of several of Lakewood's emergency medicine residents and nurses. Had Austin not been there to get me out of the pub when he did, I have no idea what would have happened, but it wouldn't have been good. I owe him more than I can say.

I gaze out the window and wrap my arms around myself. The image of Austin remains in my mind, and the appreciation I feel for him expands into something more. Something I have been feeling a lot lately when I'm around him. Something that causes a wonderful feeling of warmth to course through me and a smile to touch my lips.

Austin. Austin Cahill. Intelligent, funny, handsome, gentlemanly Austin Cahill. The man I once despised is fast becoming the man I would hold up above all others. The change I feel about him is astonishing. Puzzling. Exhilarating. Why did it take me so long to realize how I really feel about him?

How I really feel about him.

I catch my breath at the thought. I'm falling for Austin Cahill. No, actually, I've already fallen. Completely. I've fallen head-over-heels for him. In the course of a few days, I've gone from despising everything about him to not wanting to stop thinking of him.

No, I take that back. This metamorphosis hasn't happened over just a few days. If I truly study the inner workings of my heart, I think I fell for Austin a long, long time ago, but I was too busy focusing on other things to admit it.

A soft laugh escapes my lips. Can this be real? Austin? My sworn enemy? The most frustrating, provoking man I've ever known is now the man I absolutely adore?

A moment later, my laughter disappears and the warmth inside me ices over. No matter how I feel, my situation hasn't changed. I can't get swept up in Austin Cahill because I'm in the middle of the most important rotation of my life. Besides, even if I could focus on romance, Austin isn't interested in me. He's interested in Tara. There's no question in my mind about that any longer. I could see it while he was talking on the phone with her this morning, and I've seen it when I've watched them interacting in the emergency department. There's no mistaking the meaning in the way Tara smiles at Austin or how he watches her in return. They stand so close. They laugh so readily. They . . .

I growl and yank the drapes across the window to shut out the sunlight. If Austin is attracted to Tara, that's fine. I don't care. I can't care. I've got other things to focus on. I've spent more than three years despising Austin, and I can continue keeping him at arm's length until medical school is over. In less than a year, we'll be graduating and going our separate ways. I'll get over Austin.

Eventually.

I hope.

I spin away from the window, stride to the other side of the room, and head into the bathroom. I turn on the shower. I peel off my scrubs and finish unchanging, and then I step into the much-needed cascade of hot, steamy water. As my head continues to clear, I keep myself distracted with planning how I'll rearrange tomorrow's study schedule to compensate for what I missed due to last night's debacle.

Once my shower is done, I change into jeans and a v-neck, short-sleeved shirt, brush my teeth, and run a comb through my hair. Feeling refreshed, I return to the bedroom and open the door. I find Julie on the other side of the main room, sitting on the couch and reading something on her phone. She has her jacket draped over the arm of the couch and her suitcase open at her feet. Her hair is down and hanging loosely over her shoulders. When I emerge from my bedroom, she whips up her head and gets to her feet. Her gaze is worried.

"Rachel, how are you doing?"

I scan the main room and kitchen, confirming Austin is gone. In spite of myself, I'm unable to ignore the prick of disappointment I feel. What was I expecting, though? I couldn't ask him to hang out here all day, especially since he already stayed last night. Not to mention, once Julie arrived and I had someone else to watch over me, there was no need for Austin to remain. It made sense for him to go. He undoubtedly had stuff to do with the rest of his day off. Perhaps errands. Studying. Laundry. Maybe going out with Tara . . .

I frown.

No, I'm not going to do this. I'm not going to dwell on wondering what Austin is doing. If he's interested in Tara, that's his business. Besides, as I keep telling myself, I've come this far in pursuit of my dreams that I can't get distracted now. I have to remain focused on earning an honors grade and somehow getting an interview with Lakewood's residency application committee.

I set my attention back on Julie, who I'm only starting to process is actually here. I give her a warm smile. "I'm doing a lot better, thanks."

She sets down her phone, comes forward, grabs me by the hands, and pulls me over to the couch. "Austin told me everything that happened at the pub last night."

"Everything?" I repeat, my stomach sinking with dread.

This is bad. If Austin told Julie everything, Julie has surely informed Mom and Dad about what happened. Mom and Dad will be utterly ashamed their daughter was ingesting marijuana, accidentally or not, and making a complete fool of herself in public. In fact, they're probably on a plane out here right now so they can lecture me in person for being so reckless. They'll remind me that my brother and sister never got into this kind of trouble . . . or any trouble at all, for that matter.

Julie sits beside me, her expression one of sympathy. "I'm so sorry you got food poisoning from the pub. Austin said it was a pretty severe bout and lasted most of the night."

"Food poisoning?" I repeat, my mind working fast. Austin told Julie it was food poisoning? With a silent sigh of relief, I hurriedly nod. "I mean, yes. Food poisoning. It was terrible. I'll never eat bangers and mash again."

Julie tips her head to one side. "Austin said it was the shepherd's pie that got you sick."

"Oh, you know, now that you mention it, it might have been shepherd's pie. Everything from last night is so foggy, I can't quite remember the details." I force a laugh. "I was super sick."

"Sounds terrible." Julie shakes her head. She then adopts a scheming smile. "So when were you going to tell me about Austin, anyway?"

My heart sputters. "What do you mean?"

Julie rolls her eyes. "Come on, you don't have to play that game with me. I'm not Mom, you know." She laughs. "There's obviously something going on between you and Austin. I mean, why else would he have brought you home and stayed with you all night?" She slides closer to me, her eyes sparkling with excitement. "So tell me all the details. When did you start dating? What first attracted you to him?" She breaks off and giggles again. "Okay, I can see what must have first attracted you to him. I mean, he's super hot."

I tuck my hair behind my ears, giving myself time to gather my thoughts. "There's nothing going on between Austin and me. Honestly. We've known each other since the first day of med school, and we're friends. That's all."

Friends. A few days ago, I never would have said Austin and I were friends. Now, I'm desperately wishing we could be so much more. But we can't. We can't ever be something more. I've got to focus on my education, and Austin cares for someone else. Someone who wasn't foolish enough to ignore him and brush him off the way I did.

I feel another sting of remorse.

"Wow, you seriously put Austin in the friend zone?" Julie gets to her feet and goes into the kitchen to get herself a glass of water. "I realize I'm stepping into this really late in the game, but forgive me for saying I think you're crazy and should reconsider your decision." She takes a drink of water, sets the glass by the sink, and turns to face me. "From everything I could gather, Austin is a catch. Smart, funny, caring . . . and did I mention hot?" She grins. "He certainly doesn't strike me as the type of guy you would normally pass over." Her lips curve up with amusement. "At least he's not like Lars or any of the other guys Mom and Dad have set us up with."

I manage another strained laugh, but Julie's words are a punch to the gut. It's true: I passed over Austin. All these years, I took his presence for granted. I didn't even consider him romantically. I was too busy with other priorities to notice him in that way. I suppose it never would have worked out, anyway, yet I can't help wondering . . .

Clearing my throat, I focus back on Julie. "Austin will definitely be a catch for someone else, but I'm not looking for romance right now. Besides, I'm pretty sure Austin has something going on with one of the medicine residents."

Julie tips her head to one side. "Is her name Tara?"

My posture stiffens. "Actually, yeah, it is." I hesitate before asking, "How did you know?"

Julie makes her way back to the couch. "While Austin was telling me about what happened last night, his phone rang a couple times. When we were done talking, he called someone back, and he addressed whoever it was as Tara."

I press my lips together and look away, trying to tell myself it doesn't matter. Yet I suddenly find myself immensely irritated by the thought of Tara's sweet smile.

"Well, whoever Tara is, she certainly can't be as gorgeous, intelligent, and awesome as you are." Julie drops back down on the couch beside me. "Frankly, Austin's an idiot for choosing her over you."

"Thanks, Jules, but Tara is actually really nice."

"It doesn't matter. You're nicer," Julie says with authority. "Anyway, their phone call didn't last long, but it certainly sounded like they were making arrangements to meet up for dinner this evening."

I nod. It's all I can do. Though there's no way Austin and I will ever be together, I still feel a horrible ache inside. The thought of him going out with Tara—or with anyone else—feels completely wrong. Tara doesn't know Austin the way I do. She doesn't know that he slightly shakes his head whenever he's annoyed, or that he eats cafeteria oatmeal for breakfast after rounds, or that his eyes always narrow when he's mulling something over . . .

I force myself to change the topic. "So tell me more about what brought you all the way out here?"

"I'm sorry about the surprise." Julie guiltily glances at her jam-packed suitcase. She then gazes out the window, and her expression becomes serious. "After what happened with Marcus, I guess I needed to get away from everything that reminded me of him for a bit. I needed a chance to clear my head so I could start wrapping my mind around the thought of life without him." She sighs. It's a sad, remorseful sigh that makes my heart ache for her. Stoically, she soon adopts another smile and fixes her eyes on mine once more. "Since I had some days off, I decided to come out here to be with you." Her brow furrows. "I'm sorry for imposing. I wasn't exactly in the mood to vacation alone. I couldn't go stay with Mom and Dad, either. They would have been too . . . smothering. They baby me so much, it would have been more than I could take." She makes a sound of exasperation. "You're lucky they actually treat you like an independent adult."

I stare at her in shock. Julie is jealous of the way Mom and Dad treat me? Is she serious?

"You know, Julie, I've always been jealous of how Mom and Dad treat you," I remark quietly.

Julie's eyebrows shoot up. "What? Why? They coddle me way too much. I swear they still think I'm in junior high."

"That's not how I see it. All I ever hear from them is how amazing they think you are, how everything you do is perfect, and how proud they are of you." It's my turn to peer thoughtfully out the window. "I certainly never hear them say those things about me."

"That's because they don't think they need to say those things about you," I hear Julie state. "You've always been independent. You're motivated, driven, and focused. You carved your path and found your niche without relying on our parents. You successfully accomplished all the pre-med requirements on your own. You got into med school on your terms." She begins twirling a strand of her hair around one finger. "Mom and Dad don't interfere with you because they don't think they need to. Their silence speaks volumes of how highly they regard you and how much they trust you."

I stay silent, trying to absorb this. Finally I look at her again. "I've always felt like I'm the middle child they never notice."

"And I've always felt like the baby they never let grow up."

More silence falls between us. It's a pensive, though comfortable, silence. At last, Julie motions to her suitcase and says:

"Again, I really hope you don't mind that I came."

"Are you kidding? Of course I don't mind. I'm actually super excited you're here." I reach out and give her hand a squeeze. "You can stay as long as you need to, assuming you don't mind that I'll be going to work and didactics, studying, and, well, being extremely stressed out about whether or not Lakewood's residency admissions committee is even going to grant me an interview for next year's class."

"Are you kidding me? Of course they'll grant you an interview. Actually, they better not just grant you an interview, they better accept you into their residency program. They will be making a huge mistake if they don't."

"Thanks, but that's not true." I exhale wistfully. "Lakewood has one of the top emergency medicine residency programs in the country. With every day that goes by, I realize more and more that I'm way out of my league."

"I don't believe that. I'm sure you're one of the smartest, most dedicated, and most hard-working med students they've ever had."

"I obviously try to be, yet I still pale in comparison to the current first-year residents. You should see them, Jules, they're amazingly good."

Julie says nothing for a moment, and then her expression brightens. "Hey, maybe I *could* see them. In fact, I was hoping you'd let me shadow you on one of your shifts. Do you think that would be okay?"

"I certainly wouldn't mind. I don't know what the policy on that is, though, so I'll email Dr. Sanders and Lynn to find out." I check the clock. "In the meantime, you're probably getting hungry. Do you want to go out and get something to eat? We can also hit the grocery store, so this place will be stocked with what you like."

Julie nods. "That would be great."

We both get to our feet, and I smile up at my taller-but-younger sister.

"You pick the place for dinner. My treat."

"Really? Thanks!" Julie claps excitedly. "Do you have a favorite place?"

I sheepishly shake my head. "Admittedly, I haven't gone to most of the restaurants around here, though I've heard they're fantastic."

"Well, then I say we stroll around and see what strikes our fancy." Julie loops her arm through mine, and then she pauses and grins more playfully. "I'm guessing, though, you'd prefer to skip the Irish pub."

I blush and begin to laugh. "Yeah. I think it would be a good idea if we skipped that one."

Nine

"Good afternoon, sir. My name is Rachel Nelson. I'm a fourth-year medical student, and I'll be helping take care of you today." I motion behind me. "This is my sister, Julie. She's a pre-med student shadowing me this shift. Would it be all right with you if she observed while I take your history?"

I'm speaking to a thin, dark-haired, fifty-three-year-old man who's wearing a long-sleeved shirt and shorts. He's sitting on the edge of the stretcher, peering at me with a smile. In response to my question, he starts nodding emphatically.

"Absolutely. Of course. Yes. That would be fine. The more, the merrier, in fact. Definitely. It's nice to meet you both. My name is Isaac."

I calmly exchange a glance with Julie before I step closer to the stretcher. Taking my cue, Julie comes up beside me. She has her hair pulled back in a tight bun, and she's wearing a pair of scrubs we borrowed from the hospital locker room. She even has a temporary badge, which she was issued this morning when we checked her in as a hospital visitor. Between her outfit and the extremely serious expression she has on her face, I have to say that she looks pretty official. I smile in the brief moment I observe her, recalling the hours of shadowing doctors in hospitals and clinics I did as a pre-med student. That was when I first fell in love with emergency medicine. That was when I knew I wanted to work as an attending physician in an emergency department one day. That was back when I was sure I could do it.

Those years seem like a lifetime ago.

I refocus on Isaac and continue. "The note obtained when you were triaged over here to Fast Track indicates you have a question about some sort of bite you sustained? Would you please explain more about what's going on?"

"Certainly." Isaac clasps his hands in his lap. "I was using scissors to clip grass in my backyard. I needed to be very meticulous about what I was doing, so I was down on my hands and knees. While working, I felt something poke my leg. I saw a snake in the grass, and I thought the snake had bitten me."

My eyebrows rise. "I'm sorry to hear that. Before you go on, I need to ask if you happen to know what kind of snake it was that bit you. Even if you can describe what it looked like, it would help sort out how to properly care for you."

Isaac doesn't reply. Instead, he spins to his right, leans off the side of the stretcher, and picks up his yellow backpack from the floor. Sitting up again, he unzips the backpack's main pocket.

"It's in here. You can take a look yourself."

I suppress a shudder as I recoil slightly. Out of the corner of my eye, I see Julie scoot about ten steps away. Shifting my attention to the open backpack, I find I can't quite see inside it, but it doesn't matter. I'm already completely grossed out. There's a dead snake in there. This man brought a dead reptile into the emergency department. I make a mental note to tell him a photo will suffice should anything like this ever happen again in the future.

Clearing my throat, I try to act as though the thought of a scaly, cold, dead reptile at the bottom of the backpack doesn't freak me out. "Great. That's very helpful." I slowly start re-advancing toward the stretcher . . . and toward the backpack. "I'll take a quick peek inside to see what type of snake it was, and hopefully we can confirm it wasn't venomous."

Just as I lean forward to peer into the backpack, I hear Isaac say:

"I don't think he's venomous. He's actually pretty friendly. He's a cute little guy."

His words register in my mind, and I freeze with my head hovering over the open backpack. A split-second later, I realize I'm staring down at a live snake. A long, thin, dark brown snake with a cream-colored stripe running down the length of its back.

The snake puts its beady eyes on me and sticks out its tongue, which starts wiggling in the air.

"Arg!" I leap back, arms flailing.

Julie shrieks and stumbles into the curtain that leads out of the room.

Isaac watches us, his bland expression not changing in the slightest. He gently pulls the backpack closer to his chest, gazes down at the snake, and murmurs something to it under his breath. He then raises his eyes to me once more. "I think you startled him, but he's okay."

I put a hand to my chest, gathering my footing while I catch my breath. "I'm . . . sorry for scaring the snake." I straighten my white coat as my heart continues thumping from the unexpected blast of adrenaline. "I suppose we're not accustomed to having reptiles in the emergency department. Especially live ones."

"Really? I wouldn't have guessed that." Isaac shrugs. "Anyway, I really should be going now. I need to get home and let my little friend go back to playing in my yard."

Julie's eyes are still wide as she flicks a puzzled glance my way. I discreetly smile back at her. This might be the first snake I've handled in the emergency department, but it certainly isn't the first case I've had that makes absolutely no sense.

"Hey, is everything okay in here?" The curtain for the room is pulled aside a few inches, and Zach O'Cain pokes his head inside. "I heard yelling, and I wanted to make sure everyone is . . ." he trails off when his eyes come to a stop on Julie.

"Hello, Zach." I face him, maintaining my professional demeanor in front of the patient. "Yes. We're all okay. Thanks for checking."

"Oh . . . good." Zach's attention stays on Julie a moment longer before he seems to collect himself and look my way. "Sorry for interrupting. I'll see you later."

Zach's eyes dart Julie's direction once more before he slips out of the room and shuts the curtain behind him. In the beat of silence that follows, I peek at my sister. Her cheeks have taken on a faint shade of pink, and her glossed-over gaze is still lingering on the place where Zach just stood.

Hmm. This might be even more unexpected and interesting than a man bringing a snake to the emergency department.

I focus back on the patient. "Sir, are you sure you want to leave? I thought you were worried about having sustained a snake bite. We certainly want to help you with that."

He shakes his head. "No, I said I *thought* I had been bit. I realized, though, it was only a piece of bark that had poked my leg." He pats the backpack lightly. "My little buddy didn't do anything wrong."

"I see." I shift my stance. "So may I ask what prompted you to come to the emergency department? Do you have a wound from the bark we could assist you with?"

"Of course not. I didn't get any wound, and I don't need any medical care. I simply thought the people in the emergency department would want to see this lovely snake. I thought you would *appreciate* the opportunity to view it." Isaac actually sounds a little offended now. He haughtily zips his backpack closed and gets to his feet. "As you appear to have no interest, however, I would like to leave." He carefully pats the backpack again and speaks at it. "Don't worry, buddy. You'll be in the yard again in less than ten minutes."

Isaac tips up his chin, strides past me, draws aside the curtain, and heads toward the exit, carefully cradling the backpack as he departs. I watch him go, slowly feeling my calmness and confidence give way to dismay. There goes my chance to start off this Fast Track shift impressing Dr. Sanders. Now I don't have anything medical to report to her. I don't even have a patient.

"Rachel, was that your patient who just left?"

I flinch when Dr. Sanders steps into the exam room. I was hoping to have a few minutes to decide how I was going to explain to her what happened, but now I'm going to have to wing it. Blinking fast, I keep my tone businesslike as I reply:

"It was, yes. Isaac was a fifty-three-year-old male who was working in his yard today. He thought he got bitten by a snake but realized he had actually been poked by a piece of bark. He had no concerns and didn't want medical care. He came in only because he thought the emergency department staff would appreciate viewing the snake he found in his yard." I pause before making sure to add, "It was a non-venomous garter snake."

Dr. Sanders stares at me for a drawn-out second. "He brought a dead snake into the emergency department."

"Oh, no, it wasn't dead." I actually feel myself on the verge of smiling. "It was most definitely alive."

Dr. Sanders lifts up her glasses and rubs her eyes. "Okay, that's extremely creepy."

I nearly laugh, but I stop myself. I must show Dr. Sanders that I take every case seriously, including ones involving innocent reptiles. I need to—

A snort from Julie causes me to look her way. A grin has spread across her face, and her eyes dance with humor as she starts laughing.

"I cannot believe that guy brought in a snake! A live snake!" Julie claps a hand over her mouth as she keeps giggling. "I thought I was going to die. I have no idea how you kept your cool that whole time, Rachel. It was really impressive how you handled it."

Dr. Sanders starts chuckling, too. "I've certainly heard lots of good stories from med students over the years, but this is the first time anyone's story has involved a live snake at the bedside." She shakes her head and focuses on me once more. "Since your first patient made an early exit, there is another low-acuity patient who was brought back a couple minutes ago, if you're interested. Or, if you'd like to wait to take on something more medically interesting, I hear they're going to bring over from the main department a woman with longstanding abdominal pain." She glances out past the curtain. "The main department is already so overcrowded this morning, they asked if Fast Track could take some of the overflow."

I take about a millisecond to consider my options. "I would be happy to take both patients, Doctor Sanders," I tell her. There's no way I'm passing up the opportunity to show my attending that I can multi-task in the emergency department. After all, managing several patients at once is a vital skill in emergency medicine.

Dr. Sanders gives me a nod. "Sounds good. When you're done meeting your patients, let me know what your plans of care will be. In the meantime, I'm going to start checking on the admitted patients who are boarding down here. We've got several this morning."

"Will do," I reply before turning to Julie. "Ready to go?"

"Yup," Julie replies, still giggling.

Together, Julie and I exit the room. I lead the way to the circular nursing station in the middle of Fast Track and peer up at the patient tracking board to find where they put the first of my two new patients. This patient is a forty-one-year-old man named Oscar Watts. I'm about to motion for Julie to follow me to his room when I hear her phone start to buzz.

"Whoops. Sorry. I forgot to put it on silent." Julie hurriedly pulls her phone from her back pocket. She moves to tap the phone's screen but pauses. Her breathing hitches.

"What's wrong?" I ask quietly.

Julie slowly raises her eyes to mine. "Marcus is calling. I . . . I should probably answer this."

"Of course, Jules. I totally understand." I point behind her. "That way takes you to an exit into a staff-only courtyard. It's pretty secluded out there. You can use your badge to get back in when you're done."

Julie nods appreciatively. Her hands are trembling as she answers the call and puts her phone to her ear. Spinning around, she starts speaking softly into the phone as she hurries away.

I watch her until she turns a corner and disappears from view. Poor Julie. I hope everything is—

"So, Rachel, who's the cute pre-med student shadowing you today?"

I pause, and then I turn toward Zach, who's coming toward me with a self-assured smile on his face and a distinct swagger in his walk. He purposefully shifts his eyes in the direction Julie went before focusing on me once more.

I arch an eyebrow, and then I let a grin show. "Before you say anything else incriminating, I should probably inform you that that cute pre-med student happens to be my little sister."

Zach halts. His eyes get big, and his smile disappears. He coughs. "So this is awkward."

I snicker. "It's okay. My sister, Julie, is visiting from out of town, and she's staying with me for a few days. And yes, she is pre-med. She's applying for early acceptance into med school right now."

Zach adopts another grin. "Well, if your sister decides to come out here for med school, I might be asking you for her phone number one day . . . that is, if she's single."

My grin fades, and my eyes flick in the direction of the courtyard. "Good question. She just broke up with her boyfriend—actually, he broke up with her—but he's apparently calling her right now."

Zach's brows pull into a scowl. "Her boyfriend broke up with her? He sounds like an idiot."

"Thanks. I'll tell Julie you said so."

"You do that." Zach nods, his smile returning yet again. "Yeah, you do that."

Saying no more, Zach walks off in the direction of the main department. I snicker again as I watch him depart, and then I go the other direction toward the room of my next patient. When I reach the curtain, I halt outside.

"Mr. Watts? Is it okay if I come in?"

"Um, are you alone?" a nervous-sounding man replies from the other side.

I stand up straighter in surprise. "Yes, I'm alone."

"Okay. You can come in."

I maneuver around the curtain and immediately put my eyes on the patient. He's of average build, and he has tanned skin and blond hair. He's dressed in a bright red t-shirt and jeans. Sitting on the edge of the stretcher, he's fidgeting restlessly. His eyes are anxious, and he's sweating a little. I peer at him more closely.

"Sir, my name is Rachel Nelson. I'm a fourth-year medical student. What's going on?"

The man flinches. "I think I'm in serious trouble."

"Oh?" I step closer and lower my voice. "Mr. Watts, I want to help you in any possible way I can. Could you please explain why you think you're in trouble?"

He takes in several breaths, and then he leans toward me and drops his voice to nearly a whisper. "I drank the punch."

I peer back at him for a moment or two. Apparently, this is just going to be one of these kinds of days here in Fast Track. Resigned to my fate and determined to make the best of it, I sit down on the stool beside the stretcher.

"I see." I make sure to keep my tone calm. This man seems so panicked, I'm afraid any sudden movement or loud noise might spook him.

Oscar's arm is shaking as he runs a hand through his hair. "I did. I drank the punch, and now I'm gonna pay for it."

I'm starting to wonder if I should be calling security. I mean, is this man in real danger? Did Oscar join some sort of cult, and now he's regretting it and trying to hide? Has he been followed here by—

"It was grape. The punch was grape. My favorite flavor." Oscar groans. "I couldn't help myself. Now my brother is going to be so mad."

I do a double take. "Sir, just so I can be clear: do you mean you literally drank punch?"

Oscar stops shaking his head and looks at me as though I'm a complete moron. "Of course. What else would I be talking about?"

"Fair point." I relax and tip my head in acknowledgement. "Why don't you tell me more about what has you so worried about drinking grape punch."

Oscar's nervous demeanor returns as he begins wringing his hands. "Well, you see, I live with my brother. Last week, he bought himself groceries, which included some punch. I really love punch. The next day, while my brother was at work, I drank all the punch without asking permission."

"I see." I maintain my professional expression and even make a few notes on my paper so Oscar will see I'm giving his issue my full attention.

Oscar sighs dramatically and goes on, "Anyway, my brother got home from work and asked where all the punch went. I didn't want to tell him what I had done, so I told him I accidentally spilled it on the floor and had to throw it away." He draws his brows together. "I lied, but I thought it was for the best. I thought I would learn from the experience and never do something like it again. I thought I could move on." He heaves yet another tremulous sigh. "Today, though, my brother came home from the grocery store, and I saw he had bought more punch. The punch was grape this time. I tried to be strong, but when he left the house I . . . I couldn't resist."

I stop scribbling on my paper. "So you drank his punch for a second time."

"Yes." He hangs his head. "All of it."

"And you think your brother will be upset when he comes home and finds out."

"What if he yells at me? I don't know if I could take that."

I study him. "Is there anything else that made you decide to come to the emergency department today?"

"Isn't this enough?" Oscar demands, his voice rising.

"Of course. I simply want to make sure we're addressing all your needs."

"There's nothing else I need. I only need to hide here while someone calls my brother and tells him not to yell at me when he figures out the punch is gone."

I fix a harder gaze on him. "Sir, has your brother yelled at you before? Does he yell at you often?"

Oscar actually scoffs. "Of course not. My brother is the kindest man I know. He's a preacher. That's why he buys punch. He gives it to the children in his congregation." He waves a hand dismissively. "My brother lets me live with him for free, and he tells me I can eat his food whenever I want."

"I understand," I say, even though it's a lie. I don't understand at all. It's like I entered the *Twilight Zone* of Fast Track this morning. However, I stay composed as I get to my feet.

"Mr. Watts, here's what I propose: I'd like to examine you, as I do all my patients. I'll also ask our social worker, Dwayne, to contact your brother and explain what happened. If your brother is as kind and understanding as you say, I'm sure he'll forgive you for drinking his punch."

"Oh, I know he will." Oscar scoots back on the stretcher and adjusts himself into a lounging position, now appearing completely calm and comfortable. "I just wanted someone else to tell him what I did, so I didn't have to fess up myself."

"Of course."

I wash my hands at the sink and proceed to perform a basic examination on Oscar. Not surprisingly, it's unremarkable. I then politely excuse myself from the room. As the curtain shuts behind me, I scan the department. Julie is still gone. I feel another ache of sympathy for her. I hope her conversation with Marcus is going okay.

As I continue surveying the place, I also don't see Dr. Sanders, which means she's still busy caring for all the admitted patients who are boarding down here. With the place this full, the most helpful thing I can do is get a patient moving toward appropriate discharge, so I scurry down the hall to the social worker's office to inform him about Mr. Watts. I find Dwayne on the phone, attempting to arrange a room at a voluntary detox facility for a patient. I wait in the corner, and once Dwayne's call is over, I explain to him that my patient is requesting someone to call his brother about grape punch. Dwayne asks me to repeat the story. He then states that he'll head to Oscar's room to get the brother's phone number.

Leaving Dwayne's office, I hurry back to Fast Track, which is becoming increasingly crowded by the minute. I halt and do another check of the area. I still don't see Julie. Pricked with concern, I dash over to the doorway that leads out to the courtyard. I see her sitting on a bench, bent at the waist while holding her phone to one ear and resting her forehead in her other hand. Seeming to sense me watching, she raises her eyes and spots me. I give her a questioning look. She mouths that she's all right.

Leaving Julie to her call, I head back to the nursing station and read the patient tracking board. The second of my two new patients, a seventy-two-year-old woman with abdominal pain, has been brought over from the main department and triaged to a room. I charge that direction. I reach the curtain and tap lightly on the wall beside it.

"Hello, may I come in?"

"Yes," a woman says in reply.

Sliding around the curtain, I find a healthy-looking woman sitting on the stretcher. She has already changed into a hospital gown, and there's a blanket across her lap. Her hair is styled, and the rims of her large glasses are a fun shade of pink. As soon as I step into the room, she smiles warmly at me.

"Hello, dear. My name is Vicki Fitzgerald."

"Good day." I smile in return, appreciative of a friendly greeting. "My name is Rachel Nelson. I'm a fourth-year medical student who will be helping you today."

Vicki motions to her hospital gown with a sheepish expression. "I'm sorry to be using your time, Rachel. I feel so self-conscious about all this. The only reason I'm here is because I decided I should get seen for my stomach pains, but my regular doctor couldn't see me for weeks and so she directed me to come here instead." She adjusts her glasses. "I realize this isn't an emergency, and I apologize for being here at all."

"You have nothing to apologize for. We're always happy to help." I take the stool beside the stretcher. "Please tell me more about your stomach pains, and we'll figure out how to best assist you today."

"Well, for the past several weeks I've had constant stomach pain . . . no, not pain, actually. Rather, it's more of a bloated sensation in my lower abdomen." She shrugs. "That's really all. I know it's not a big deal, but since it has been going on for so long and it's getting worse, I thought I should get it checked out."

I keep my expression impassive despite the unease rising inside me. Something about her story has me worried. I get to my feet, wash my hands, and commence performing an exam.

"Are you having any other symptoms?"

"None," Vicki tells me. "That's why I feel so silly for being here."

I continue with my exam, pausing as I palpate the lower right quadrant of her abdomen. I'm almost convinced I feel something there. I push on the area again, and though Vicki doesn't seem to be in any discomfort or even notice what I'm doing, there's definitely a mass. The question is: what kind of a mass is it?

I finish my exam, and then I take in a breath and step back from the stretcher. I obviously don't have any idea if what I palpated in her abdomen is serious or completely benign, yet I only have about one second to decide what to say to Vicki about it. No one ever wants to worry a patient unnecessarily—that can be traumatizing for someone. However, it can be equally traumatizing for a patient if he or she is caught completely by surprise with horrible news. In situations like this, there's no easy answer on how to proceed.

"Ms. Fitzgerald, I—

"Please call me Vicki, dear," she tells me, still smiling pleasantly.

I nod and take another moment to choose my words. "Vicki, when I examined you, I thought I felt something like a mass in your lower abdomen. I don't know what it is, so to be thorough, I think we should get some pictures to take a look."

Vicki's smile falters only a moment. "Of course, dear. Please do whatever you think you should."

I motion toward the curtain. "If you'll excuse me, I'm going to step out and place orders for lab work and imaging. We'll get some IV fluid going as well, so please don't eat or drink anything until I have a chance to see your results."

"I understand. I appreciate your help."

"You're more than welcome." I rest a hand on her shoulder for a moment, and then I turn and exit the room.

I move fast across the department to the computer beside the attendings' desk. Sitting down, I log in and begin placing orders for Vicki's workup. Once I'm done, I raise my head and look around. I see Dwayne going into Oscar's room, presumably to get his brother's phone number so Punchgate can be resolved. Meanwhile, one of the nurses, Kathy, is heading into Vicki's room to place the IV and draw the blood I ordered.

I do another check of the patient tracking board. Fast Track is full now, as are all the exam rooms and hallway spaces in the main emergency department. Once again, we're so busy that we're essentially on lockdown, with what little space that's remaining being saved for the sickest and most emergent patients. It's always unnerving when it's like this, knowing the waiting room is bursting at the seams. There's always the chance that somewhere in the crowd is a person who looks well and whose vitals are normal but who's actually extremely ill—like someone with early sepsis or a person with abdominal discomfort that's really cardiac in etiology. As always, it is a race against time to get each person back for assessment and treatment before someone takes a turn for the worse.

I return to my feet, about to go check on Julie again, when I see the curtain of a nearby exam room get drawn aside. Dr. Sanders steps out. My insides twist when I realize she's accompanied by Austin and Tara. They must be discussing one of the admitted patients who's boarding down here. As I observe them, I note Tara is looking even more dolled-up than the previous time I saw her. Meanwhile, dressed in scrubs with his stethoscope draped casually around his neck, Austin looks as staggeringly handsome as ever. His eyes are focused on Tara as she talks, and there's something subtle in the way he's watching her that leaves no doubt they're more than work associates. I wonder how their date went the other night. Or maybe I don't want to know.

I turn away.

"Rachel, how are your patients doing?"

I snap to attention when I hear Dr. Sanders address me. Spinning back around to face her, I see Tara also begin to watch me with her doe-eyed expression. Austin, too, peers at me with an expression that's impossible to read.

I concentrate on Dr. Sanders, acting unruffled though my anxiety is escalating. I can't help it. I'm not only speaking to my attending, I'm being stared at by the man I simultaneously adore and despise. It's like Austin is just waiting to swoop in and say something to outdo me in front of the attending.

Austin is like a vulture, I decide. A drop-dead gorgeous vulture.

"Things are going well," I answer Dr. Sanders, keeping my voice even. "My first patient is a man who wants someone to call his brother and explain he consumed all his grape punch, and—"

Something between a snort and a chuckle escapes Austin's lips. I break off from what I'm saying and look his way. He clears his throat while watching me with eyes that are now sparkling with amusement. We exchange a glance that sends my heart into a frenzy of delight, and I nearly smile back at him before I remind myself that I'm in the middle of presenting to my attending. I hastily refocus on Dr. Sanders and continue:

"My other patient is a seventy-two-year-old woman with several weeks of abdominal bloating. She has a palpable mass in her right lower quadrant. I've already put in labs, as well as orders for CT and ultrasound imaging."

Dr. Sanders was smiling about the grape punch, but as soon as she hears about Vicki, her smile fades. "Sounds good. Thanks, Rachel."

Dr. Sanders turns to resume talking with Austin and Tara. I watch her as disappointment crashes down around me. *Sounds good. Thanks, Rachel.* That was it. That was all the feedback my attending gave me. In other words, I'm not impressing Dr. Sanders in the slightest. I shouldn't be surprised, though. I haven't done anything to stand out. There's nothing I've done to set myself apart from the countless other med students who are also applying to Lakewood's emergency medicine residency program. The competition is fierce, and with every passing day, I'm obviously fading more and more into the background.

I lower my eyes. This Fast Track shift could have been an opportunity to work efficiently and independently, see lots of patients, and demonstrate that I can capably manage the care of several chief complaints. Instead, I've got almost nothing to show for my time here today. I've blown it. Again.

"I really appreciate you guys coming down," I hear Dr. Sanders saying to Tara and Austin. "If you have a couple more minutes, there's one other boarding patient I want to update you about."

I raise my eyes.

"Of course." Tara's perfectly curled hair is dancing on her shoulders as she nods. She looks up at Austin, and there's a meaningful pause before she goes on. "Why don't you put in orders for the patient we just met, and I'll go with Doctor Sanders to see the other one?"

"Sure," Austin says, his eyes squarely on Tara now.

Tara's gaze lingers on his before she turns and departs with Dr. Sanders.

Suddenly, it's just Austin and me.

I clear my throat and peer up at him. Austin swings his focus back my way. I'm about to open my mouth to say something to diffuse the silence, but my eyes shift past him to where

Dwayne is stepping out of Oscar's room. Dwayne leaves the curtain open behind him, which gives me a view of inside. I can see Oscar sitting on the corner of the stretcher. He's fidgeting restlessly again.

"I'll go make that phone call," Dwayne informs me.

"Thanks," I reply, giving Dwayne a wave as he heads off in the direction of the social worker's office.

"So you're managing the acute care of punch ingestions now?" I hear Austin quip.

I spear him with a glare, though I'm actually trying to decide if Austin's teasing jab infuriates or charms me. "As a matter of fact, I am. And don't you dare make any snarky comments about it, Austin, because I'm not in the . . ."

Motion far behind Austin causes me to trail off from what I'm saying and look past him once more. Oscar is now pacing in front of his stretcher while gripping his hands in his hair. He comes to a halt, peeks out of his room, and casts a panicked glance around the department. Grabbing the curtain, he whips it closed, concealing his room from view.

"Excuse me for a moment," I tell Austin.

Slipping by him, I stride to Oscar's room and pause outside, listening through the curtain. I hear rustling noises, followed by the sound of something scraping, and then it gets quiet.

"Mr. Watts?" I call through the curtain. "May I please come in?"

Only silence replies. With a rush of alarm, I slide by the curtain to enter the room. I come to an abrupt halt, letting the curtain swing shut behind me.

Oscar is gone.

I stare at the unoccupied stretcher. Apparently, Oscar is the Houdini of the emergency department because he has vanished. The only thing amiss is the white sheet on the stretcher, which is now wrinkled and has a man's shoe prints on it. In fact, it's like someone was standing on the stretcher and . . .

I shift my gaze upward, and my eyes widen even more. The ceiling panel directly over Oscar's stretcher has been dislodged and pushed aside to expose the dark, cavernous space above.

My mouth slowly falls open as the realization strikes me. Oscar escaped. My patient escaped through the ceiling.

An instant later, my shock wears off and I start grinding my teeth. No, Oscar. Not today. You're not going to go all Alcatraz on me. I have an honors grade on this rotation to obtain. I have a residency program to get into. So I am not about to lose a patient on my watch. No, sir.

Rushing forward, I climb onto the stretcher, get to my feet, and stand up as tall as I can. Cranking back my head, I peer into the void. I can't see anything but blackness above me.

"Mr. Watts?" I whisper sternly. "Mr. Watts, come back down here right now." I pause, giving him a chance to answer. When there's no response, I go on in the same chastising tone. "There are pipes up there. And wires. And dust that might trigger allergies. Perhaps mold. And maybe rats, spiders, and other creatures carrying infectious diseases. Trust me, you do *not* want to have to start a rabies vaccination series."

I jump when I hear someone come around the curtain and step into the room. Cringing, I pull my attention from the ceiling and look to see who it is. It's Austin. Of course it is. Why do things like this always happen whenever he's around?

As I've said before, Austin Cahill is a curse.

He comes to a stop at the foot of the stretcher. Standing completely still, his lips part slightly while his eyes shift between me and the opening in the ceiling.

"Rachel," he finally says with exaggerated deliberateness, "What are you doing?"

"Shh!" I wave my hands, motioning for him to lower his voice. I point to the opening in the ceiling and bark in a whisper. "I've lost a patient, and I need to get him back!"

Austin blinks. And blinks again.

Deciding I don't have time to banter, I look upward once more and stretch my arms as high as I can. I'm still far too short to reach the opening. In desperation, I peer down at Austin once more. "Well, don't just stand there! Come up here and help me!"

"Help you do what, exactly?" Austin hasn't moved.

I start jumping on the stretcher in an attempt to grab hold of the edge of the opening above. "Help . . . boost . . . me . . . up!"

Austin comes closer to the stretcher, holding up his arms as if to catch me if I fall. He starts shaking his head. "Rachel, I am not going to help you climb into the hospital's attic space. That's dangerous and totally unnecessary. Let's go get security and notify them that—"

"No." I stop jumping. I'm panting as I fix a slightly crazed, pleading look on him. "Austin, my entire future is on the line with this rotation. I need an honors grade so when Lakewood rejects me I can still get an interview with another residency program." I point emphatically toward the curtain that leads out of the room. "So I cannot go tell my attending that my patient escaped into the ceiling. It would be a fiasco I'd never live down."

Austin watches me for another long moment. He then sighs and climbs up onto the stretcher beside me. He's so tall, his head is nearly touching the ceiling. Bending at the waist a little, he clasps his hands together down low and out in front of him, interlocking his fingers.

"Here you go." He now seems to be fighting a grin. "Operation Ceiling Rat underway."

Moving fast, I put my hands on Austin's shoulders and lift my right leg to place my foot on his overlapped palms. In one swift movement, Austin stands up straight to boost me upward. My head and shoulders poke through the opening above. I wobble as I grab the edge of the hole in the ceiling to brace myself.

"Mr. Watts?" I whisper harshly again. "Where are you?"

There's a pause, and then I hear his disgruntled reply:

"I'm over here."

As my eyes adjust to the darkness, I see Oscar on his hands and knees a few feet away. He stops crawling to look over his shoulder at me.

"Mr. Watts, this is completely unacceptable behavior. Where on earth did you think you were going to go?"

"I . . . I don't know." He sits back on his haunches. "When the social worker said he was going to call my brother, I panicked, I guess."

I feel Austin adjust his grip on my foot. Keeping my attention on the runaway, I continue, "Mr. Watts, you said you had nothing to worry about from your brother."

"I don't. My brother is the nicest guy in the world." Oscar does another one of his exaggerated sighs. "I just didn't want him to know I stole his punch."

Dust is filling my nose, nearly making me sneeze. "Your brother is going to find out, whether you like it or not. That is, after all, why you came to see us in the first place. So I suggest you come out of the ceiling now. Right now."

He sighs yet again. "Fine."

I look down through the opening at Austin, who's watching me with that ridiculously attractive grin. I give him a nod, and he slowly lowers me to the stretcher beside him. Letting me go, he steps off the stretcher, and then he extends up his arm. I place my hand in his steady grip, the touch causing a tingle to rush up my arm as he helps me to the floor. There's a beat before Austin releases my hand and backs up.

I make myself busy brushing the dust off my shoulders. "Thanks."

"You're welcome." Austin's eyes track back up to the ceiling. "Good news: it looks like your escapee is going to be just fine."

I spin around, watching as Oscar rolls himself onto his stomach, dangles his legs down through the hole, and then holds onto the lip of the opening to lower himself onto the stretcher. He at least has the courtesy to slide the ceiling panel back into place before he hops down to the floor and takes a seat on the edge of the stretcher once more.

"I'm impressed you managed to get up there," Oscar tells me. "It was a stretch, even for me."

I cross my arms over my chest. "You're lucky I didn't call security and instead recruited the assistance of . . ." I trail off as I motion behind me.

Austin has already slipped out of the room.

I pause before facing Oscar once more. "Mr. Watts, now that you're no longer in the hospital's ceiling, is there anything else we can help you with today?"

He shakes his head. "Nope. I'm all good. I'd like to leave now, actually. I'm gonna text my brother and ask him to pick me up right now, in fact."

"Your brother?" I echo, sensing my patience waning. "The same brother you wanted us to call for you?"

"Uh-huh." Oscar seems completely nonplussed as he removes a phone from the pocket of his jeans and starts typing a text. "He should be here any minute."

I close and reopen my eyes, telling myself to remain calm. "Very well, Mr. Watts. I'll go write up your discharge instructions."

"Thanks," he says, not looking at me while he continues composing his text.

Spinning on my heels, I pull open the curtain and step out. After straightening my white coat, I start making my way to the computer. There's a twinge of nerves inside me when I see Dr. Sanders sitting at the attendings' desk. She raises her head, putting her eyes on me as I approach.

"How's it going with your patient, Mr. Watts?"

I take my seat, making sure to have an I-wasn't-just-climbing-in-the-ceiling-to-retrieve-an-escaped-patient expression on my face. "Things are going well. Dwayne placed a call to the patient's brother, and the patient is requesting to leave now." I motion to my computer. "I was going to type up his discharge paperwork."

Dr. Sanders tips her head. "Great. I'll leave you to it."

Saying no more, Dr. Sanders gets up from her desk and walks to another exam room. For once in my life, I'm actually glad my attending isn't paying me any attention. I doubt having to explain that one of my patients felt compelled to flee through the ducting system would lead to high marks on my evaluation for the shift. Thank goodness Austin helped me sort out that mess.

I sigh. Austin. The guy I never appreciated until it was too late.

Forcing my emotions aside, I begin typing Oscar's discharge instructions. As I do, my mind drifts to thoughts of Julie, and I begin wondering how her—

"Here you go, back where you started from," I hear Zach say in a friendly, humorous way.

I lift my eyes, which widen in surprise. Zach and Julie are walking together into Fast Track. I observe Julie closely. She's gripping her phone in her hand, and I can't read her expression . . . subdued, perhaps? Distracted? It's hard to tell. Meanwhile, Zach is staying alongside her with an attentive smile on his face. When Julie sees me, she heads over to the desk.

"Hey, Rach. Sorry my call took so long."

As she gets closer, I note Julie has been crying. To her credit, she adopts a smile and goes on:

"My visitor badge wouldn't let me back in through the security door. I tried texting but realized you probably didn't have your phone on you." She motions to Zach, who has stopped a few feet behind her. "Thankfully, Zach was going down the hall. He saw me stranded outside and let me in." She faces him. "Thanks again for your help. It was nice to meet you."

"Likewise." Zach's smile brightens.

With the swagger back in his step, Zach turns and starts strutting toward the main department. I bite the insides of my cheeks so I don't break into a giggle. I have to hand it to him, Zach definitely goes after what he wants. He's clearly interested in Julie, and he doesn't mind . . .

How, though, does Zach expect to have time for love? I still don't understand how anyone in our situation can think they have time for romance. What's the point of trying?

With a shake of my head, I shift my attention to Julie, who's taking the empty chair beside me. "So how did the call go?"

"About as I would have predicted." Julie's shoulders slump. "Marcus and I care about each other. We miss each other. We wish we didn't have to be apart. Yet Marcus is looking at my trajectory for the next several years and still feels it isn't right for him." She inhales as tears well up in her eyes. "Love sucks sometimes, Rach."

I nod. "I know, Jules. I really know."

Julie puts her phone into her pocket. "Frankly, it's a miracle love ever works out. Think of all the elements that have to line up perfectly on both sides for a relationship to be successful:

feelings, jobs, finances, family . . . I'm surprised it ever happens."

"I couldn't agree more," I say softly. I quickly turn back to my computer and use the mouse to click the *print* button for Oscar's discharge instructions.

Julie slides closer. "So what are you going to do?"

I glance Julie's way again. "About what?"

"About Austin? About your own love life?"

I face her squarely. "I still have no idea what you're talking about."

Julie rolls her eyes and doesn't keep her voice down as much as I would like. "You know exactly what I'm talking about. Have you given the situation with Austin any more thought? Would you, perhaps, consider taking him out of the friend zone?" She nudges me and ventures a smile. "After all, he did care enough to bring you all the way to your apartment from the pub, Rach."

I clear my throat and focus on the computer once more. "Like you said, for romance to work, all the elements have to fall into place at the same time. With Austin, the elements are most definitely not in place. They're not even close, and they never will be."

Julie leans back in her chair with a disappointed sigh. "That's too bad. I think you and Austin would be good together."

Saying no more, I keep my focus on the computer and open Vicki's chart. I begin scanning her results, which are starting to post. Her labs reveal her sodium level to be a little low and that she's mildly anemic, otherwise they're within normal limits. I next open up the CT of her abdomen and pelvis, which was completed only a few minutes ago. Once the images finish loading on the screen, I begin scrolling through them. I soon stop scrolling and stare at an image more closely. A sickening sensation develops within me.

Vicki has cancer.

"What are you looking at?" Julie slides her chair closer, her tone brightening with interest.

I keep staring at the mass on Vicki's right ovary. "One of my patients, a lovely, kind woman, came in for weeks of abdominal bloating." I wet my lips. "Based on this, it looks like she has ovarian cancer."

"Oh." Julie sits back again, her expression falling fast. "That's awful. I'm so sorry."

I open the radiologist's official report. In the impression, as I dreaded, the radiologist states the mass on the right ovary is indeed suspicious for a primary malignancy.

I sit still in my chair, taking a few seconds to collect my thoughts. Every new cancer diagnosis is devastating. From the moment the diagnosis is made, the lives of the patients—the people—are drastically changed forever, and so are the lives of their loved ones. In an instant, they are forced to grapple with cancer every minute of every day. Their schedules suddenly have to revolve around extremely expensive medications with horrible side effects, doctor appointments, surgeries, pain, imaging, biopsies,

IVs . . . and all the while, there's the fear lurking in the background that the cancer is stealthily spreading nonetheless. I hate cancer.

Though it's nothing compared to what patients endure, it's also horrible to have tell a patient in the middle of a noisy, crowded emergency department that they have cancer. Most people don't come to an ED expecting to hear their back pain, recurrent headaches, bruising, abdominal discomfort, or cough are due to a malignancy, and the totally unexpected nature of the diagnosis makes the utter devastation and disbelief upon hearing the news even worse. Unfortunately, however, it happens often. Emergency medicine providers—essentially strangers to their patients—frequently must be the ones to deliver this type of shocking, awful, life-altering news. The emergency medicine provider must put everything else on pause and try to find a good way, in the middle of a busy, loud department, to explain to a patient a new diagnosis that will alter their lives forever. And most of the time, they must explain this when there are no definitive answers yet to give.

Thankfully, in the case of malignancies, there are some cancers that are easier to talk about than others. Localized testicular cancer, for example, has a fairly straight-forward treatment and good prognosis. Other cancers, however, are the opposite. They hide in deep spaces within the body, growing and spreading unnoticed for a long time before they even start causing symptoms. Ovarian cancer is one such occult cancer. By the time someone becomes symptomatic and is diagnosed, the cancer is often so advanced that the prognosis is poor.

I close my eyes and breathe out slowly. I stepped into Vicki's path only an hour or so ago, and now I must give her what is undoubtedly the most terrible news she has ever received.

Julie bites her lip while her gaze shifts between the computer monitor and me. "Are you okay?"

"No, but I can't complain." I look at my sister. "I'm not the one whose life is about to be torn apart."

Almost reluctantly, I pick up the phone receiver and ask the operator to page the on-call resident for OBGYN. Before I talk with Vicki, I at least want to have a gynecologist's expert opinion about the diagnosis and anticipated plan for care. It's the only thing I can offer to Vicki amidst the frightening unknown.

The phone soon rings, and I answer.

"Hello, this is Rachel Nelson in Fast Track."

"Oh, hi, Rachel!" A familiar voice reaches my ear. "It's Danielle Gillespie. How are you doing?"

I smile, grateful to have a friendly person on the other end of the line. Danielle is another fourth-year med student, and she was also on the emergency medicine rotation here at Lakewood last month. She's really nice, fun, and bubbly, and she's roommates with Savannah Drake. (She also somehow miraculously finds time for romance—she has been in an exclusive relationship with her boyfriend, Joel, for quite a while now.) Anyway, Danielle is going into OBGYN, so I'm guessing she must be working with the on-call team today.

"Hi, Danielle. I'm doing pretty well," I reply. "Unfortunately, I have a patient who presented with weeks of lower abdominal bloating."

I hear Danielle suck in a breath, and I know she already knows where this conversation is going.

"I just got the results of her CT," I continue, "and the radiologist is concerned it looks like a primary, right-sided ovarian malignancy. Her ultrasound is still pending."

"I'm so sorry," Danielle utters softly. "I'll let the resident covering for Gyn-Onc know, and we'll be down to Fast Track shortly. What's the patient's name?"

"Vicki Fitzgerald." I peer at the CT images for a long second or two, and then I look away again. "Hey, Danielle, just out of curiosity: I thought you were rotating at University Hospital this month. Are you also covering patients here at Lakewood?"

"Yup," Danielle replies. "Some days, they have me working here so I can have a broader experience during the rotation. It's awesome." She sounds as though she's starting to smile again. "I'm impressed you remember my schedule, Rachel. Then again, you have an amazing memory. You probably remember my schedule for the entire year better than I do!"

I laugh quietly. "Well, I guess keeping track of a lot of details comes with the emergency medicine territory, right?"

"For sure." She pauses, and the levity in her voice fades once more. "I'll go speak with the Gyn-Onc resident, and I'll see you down there soon."

"Thanks, Danielle." I hang up the phone.

Julie is watching me closely. "Now what?"

"Now I have to go tell Vicki." I get to my feet, filled with dread. "This is going to be hard."

"Can I help somehow?"

I shake my head. "Thanks, but no. Normally, I would take you in there to observe, but with something like this, I think it's better to only have people she has already met. I'll have her nurse come with me."

Julie is nodding. "I'll wait here. Do you want me to tell Doctor Sanders about it, if I see her?"

"That'd be great." My eyes sweep the department. "She has been so busy managing all the boarding inpatients, I haven't had a chance to update her yet."

Julie gives me a thumbs-up. "I'll wait here, and if I see her, I'll let her know where you are."

"Thanks."

Leaving my desk, I head to the nursing station. I quietly tell her nurse, Kathy, what's going on and ask her to come with me. It's always better to have a support team for the patient, especially for something as awful as this.

Kathy comes to my side, and I lead the way to Vicki's room. When we reach the curtain, I say:

"It's Rachel and Kathy. Is it okay for us to come in?"

"Of course," Vicki replies in her friendly way.

Sharing a glance with Kathy, I push aside the curtain, and we enter the room together.

"How are you feeling?" I inquire to break the ice.

Vicki smiles. "I'm doing great. Everyone here has been so kind and attentive, and I've been happily passing the time reading on my phone."

My own smile is reserved as I take a seat on the stool. Out of the corner of my eye, I see Kathy go to the other side of the stretcher. Keeping my focus on Vicki, I go on. "Vicki, I have some of your results back, and I'm afraid I don't have good news."

There's a stark pause as Vicki stares at me, and I don't rush things. Long ago, a mentor told me to always fire a warning shot before delivering bad news, and I've found it to be invaluable advice. It gives someone a few seconds to recalibrate before the conversation proceeds, just as I can see from the way her brow is furrowing that Vicki is doing now.

"Is it . . . cancer?" she finally asks in almost a whisper.

Vicki isn't the first person who has asked this seemingly out-of-the-blue. In fact, it's often the patients who appear the most relaxed and unbothered about their symptoms who are actually harboring the horrible hunch.

I nod. "Right now, the radiologist who reviewed your CT suspects right-sided ovarian cancer." I make sure to speak clearly and slowly, giving my words a chance to sink in. As another mentor taught, once someone hears they may have cancer, they don't hear much else.

"I knew it." Vicki stares straight ahead. "I don't know why, but I knew it. That's the reason I waited so long to be seen. I didn't want to know."

Reaching out, I place a hand on hers. "I took the liberty of asking the gynecology team to come down here and meet with you. They'll review your CT and ultrasound images, and then they'll talk with you. They'll be a great resource for answering questions you may have."

Vicki turns to me again. I see the recognizable mixture of shock, resignation, and denial warring in her expression. It's a look I've unfortunately seen many times already in my short career.

"Thank you for your help." Vicki gives me another gracious smile despite the fear I can see behind her eyes. "I really appreciate it."

I nod again. I realize she's not only generously thanking me, she is kindly asking for a few minutes to be alone. I give her hand a squeeze and get to my feet. I feel so worthless. So guilty. She's thanking me, but I've done nothing to help her. All I've done is tell her devastating news.

"Is there anything I can get for you or anyone we can call on your behalf?" I inquire.

"No. I think I'll just take a few minutes to process the news, and then I'll call my husband and have him come join me here." Vicki looks between Kathy and me. "Thank you again for everything."

I want to stay. I want to comfort her. I want to try to fix this for her. I know I can't, though, and I know she wants to be alone. Taking a step back from the stretcher, I share a look with the nurse. Saying no more, we exit the room and quietly close the curtain behind us.

Kathy makes her way back to the nursing station. I slide over to the wall, my emotions churning as I start peering around. It's a strange thing to watch everyone continuing to go about their tasks unaware that the life of one woman in here has been so drastically altered. Behind me, on one side of a curtain, there's a patient with an ankle sprain. On the other side, there's a woman who has learned she has cancer.

I inhale, my breathing getting shallow, and continue looking around. Julie is still at the desk; she has her head down and appears to be reading something on her phone. A glance at the patient tracking board shows we're still packed beyond capacity and there are no new patients waiting to be seen. Dr. Sanders is bustling from one room to the next as she manages all the boarding patients, leaving me with no chance to interact with her and redeem my reputation in her eyes. Standing outside another patient's room are Tara and Austin, who are smiling meaningfully at each other as they talk. Farther down the hall, I catch a glimpse of Elly Vincent— a clear example of the amazing emergency medicine residents who get accepted into the program here at Lakewood—racing to the room of another critically ill patient in the main department. Behind me, I hear Vicki on the phone explaining to her husband that she has some really bad news.

As I continue taking in the scene, my emotions finally spill over. I duck my head, flee down the hall, and escape out the back exit of the emergency department. I race into the nearest bathroom, slam the door behind me, and turn the lock. In the quiet, I drop back against the door and let tears fall.

Ten

I swipe my badge against the outdoor card reader, causing the hospital's main doors to unlock and slowly slide open. Stepping inside the building, I glance at the fancy clock on the wall, which shows it's a little after ten at night. I pull my eyes from the clock and scan the dimly lit lobby. The information desk is empty, and there's not a soul in sight. Other than the hum from vending machines in the corner, the place is silent. It's a striking contrast to the crowded, busy atmosphere around here during the daytime. Hospitals always feel so differently—so dark and quiet—during overnight hours.

Except for the emergency department, that is. It's never quiet in the emergency department. Especially not at night.

I'm beginning a run of overnight shifts in the main department, which means I'll be working from eleven pm to seven am for the next few days. I've arrived an hour early, like always, intending to squeeze in some review of the syllabus beforehand. However, now that I'm standing in the middle of the empty lobby and listening to the silence, I find I'm not in the mood for studying. Tonight, I want to use the time just to think.

My footsteps echo as I make my way over to a chair and take the seat. Dropping my bag at my feet, I breathe out slowly, absorbing the stillness that immerses me. This is the first time I've been by myself in days; having Julie in town meant I really didn't have any time alone. Not that having Julie here was a bad thing. To the contrary, it was wonderful to have her company, and she expressed the same sentiment about having the chance to spend time with me. Each for our own reasons, I think we both needed and appreciated one another's support.

Unfortunately, Julie's vacation ended yesterday, and she caught a flight back to school last evening. Though I wished she could have stayed longer, we at least managed to pack in a lot before she left. In addition to shadowing me during my Fast Track shift, Julie came to last Wednesday's didactic session (clearly to Zach's pleasant surprise) and shadowed me when I worked in the main department on Friday afternoon. Fortunately, I happened to have this past weekend off, so Julie and I got to spend the time exploring the area where I live. After three years, I finally visited several of the great restaurants, shops, parks, and museums around my neighborhood. We stayed up late each night to talk, eat junk food, and watch movies. I didn't study once . . . and, to my surprise, that didn't bother me too much. This past weekend was a welcome diversion for both Julie and me. I sensed we both relished the opportunity to talk, laugh, and break out of our usual routines.

Another good thing about this past week was that Julie seemed to begin working through her sadness about Marcus. With each passing day, I could see her acute pain waning a little bit more. As impossible as I knew she thought it seemed when Marcus initially ended their relationship, by the end of the week, it was clear to me that Julie will be able to heal and move on, continue pursuing her dreams without regret, and, hopefully, find love again one day.

Meanwhile, I think my own heart also went through a change. Regarding Austin, I count myself lucky that I haven't seen him since the Fast Track ceiling debacle; time has allowed me to distance myself from the sadness and regret I feel over him. Knowing he has found love elsewhere has also helped reinforce my resolve not to pursue romance at this stage of my life. A relationship right now would never work out and would only lead to heartache. There's no point in getting swept up in love and losing focus when I'm so close to accomplishing the goals I've dreamed of, sacrificed for, and worked toward for so long.

I've also grown to accept that I'm not going to get into Lakewood's emergency medicine residency program. I doubt I'll even get an interview. It's devastating and humiliating, and I dread my parents' disappointment when I tell them, yet I can't complain. I simply don't deserve to get accepted into the program. There's nothing I've done to stand out from the crowd. I haven't done anything to impress the attendings or current residents. My attending barely pays me any attention during our shifts. I just blend in with all the other med students who have cycled through Lakewood's ED over the years. In other words, I've missed my chance with Lakewood, so all I can do now is double my efforts to earn an honors grade on this rotation and hopefully land an interview with an emergency medicine residency program elsewhere in the country.

I take another look at the clock and realize it's almost time for my shift to start. Springing to my feet, I pick up my bag and sling it onto my shoulder, and then I begin jogging through the maze of empty corridors that takes me through the ground level of the hospital to the emergency department. As I round the final corner, my heart starts pumping with anticipation. It's undoubtedly going to be a wild, crazy night shift in the emergency department, and . . .

I come to a stop as I step through the department's back entrance, and my eyebrows rise in surprise. The emergency department is quiet. Really quiet. By far, it's the least busy I've ever seen it here.

Stunned, I peer up at the huge tracking board mounted on the wall. It shows all the regular exam rooms are occupied by patients, but only a few hallway stretchers are in use. Additionally, there's just one patient in a trauma bay. Fast Track actually has a couple of open rooms at the moment. Even the waiting room is oddly empty; there are only a few patients awaiting triage and room assignments.

I peel my eyes from the tracking board and resume peering around, still dumbstruck by the sight. Though it's noisy in here, the ambient commotion is nothing compared to the usual volume of screaming patients, phones ringing, pagers going off, EMS providers giving report, overhead announcements blaring from speakers, and conversations between doctors, nurses, and patients being spoken above the ruckus. Looking around, I see staff members busily working, but they aren't running from one room to the next like they usually need to do. Granted, this would still be considered immensely busy compared to most emergency departments around the country—both in terms of patient number and patient acuity—but for Lakewood, this has got to be some sort of low-census record.

Taking a few steps farther into the department, I spot Dr. Sanders. She's at the other end of the department chatting casually with the charge nurse, Laura, and Dr. Kent. Soon, Dr. Godfrey saunters out of the trauma bay and joins them. As I watch, I'm again not entirely sure I can believe my eyes. I have never seen the emergency medicine attendings with time for conversation before. This is bizarre.

Eerily bizarre.

Another look up at the board shows that Dr. Kent is officially working in Fast Track tonight. He's got the first-year resident, Grant Reed, and one of the other med students with him. Hadi is the nurse assigned to work with them. Out here in the main department, it looks like Dr. Sanders and Dr. Godfrey are the two attendings on for the shift. I'm the only med student. Elly Vincent is the first-year resident, the second-year resident is one of the guys who was with us at the pub, and the third-year resident on tonight is the guy with the ponytail who was also at the pub. It looks like Kathy, Pete, and Carrie are some of the nurses covering the main department for the overnight shift.

Recovering from my shock at the relative quiet, I tip up my chin, adopt a professional air, and make my way toward what will be my workstation for the shift. Just because it's not insanely busy doesn't mean I'm going to act less businesslike. If anything, I need to be even more at the top of my game tonight. Since they're not overloaded with patients to care for themselves, the attendings are going to be able to watch me even more closely than usual. Plus, it just so happens that both of the attendings I particularly need to impress in order to obtain a good grade on this rotation—Dr. Sanders and Dr. Kent—are on tonight. It's crucial I do everything I can to impress them.

I silently begin cursing the fact that I didn't use the time before this shift to come in here and study. I had forty-five minutes to demonstrate to my attendings how dedicated I am to learning, and I blew it. Again.

With a despondent shake of my head, I reach my selected work station and set out my belongings. I quickly don my white coat, log into the computer, and review the tracking board again. There's only one patient waiting to be seen: a fifty-nine-year-old man named Bob Wang. He has just been triaged and put into Room One. His chief complaint is listed as "*Palpitations.*"

After making sure my light blue scrubs are wrinkle-free, I turn from the computer, about to go notify Dr. Sanders that I'm willing to pick up the new patient, when I see she's already coming my way. My stomach promptly seizes into a giant knot of nerves.

"Good evening, Rachel." Dr. Sanders is as composed as always. "I was talking with Laura, who's acting as charge tonight. Sounds like this place has been fairly mellow for the past few hours. We have a few admitted patients still boarding down here, but it's anticipated their inpatient beds should become available before too long."

I nod. "I also note a patient with palpitations was just brought back from the waiting room. Would you like me to go begin the workup?"

"Sure." Dr. Sanders smiles. "In fact, I was coming to let you know about him. I figured you'd be interested in picking him up."

"Absolutely." I adjust my stethoscope around my neck. "I'll go right now."

Darting around Dr. Sanders, I cruise across the department toward Room One. It's funny it's referred to by a room number, because Room One isn't actually a single exam room at all. Room One is a large, enclosed area that's more like its own mini emergency department. It has a big workstation with four computers, its own supply closets, and three patient treatment areas, which are separated by privacy curtains. Apparently, years ago, when overcrowding began to be an issue in the department, the space was converted from offices to provide additional patient treatment areas.

Since it's an add-on to the department, Room One can only be accessed via a narrow doorway near the ambulance bay. Needless to say, the fact that it only has one way in or out is less-than-optimal, and the space definitely isn't fancy (if the peeling paint and cracks in the walls are any indication, it should probably be knocked down entirely), but at least it provides more places to care for patients. Because it's tucked away in its own alcove, making it quieter than the rest of the main emergency department, Room One is often where boarding patients are kept until their beds become available. Truth be told, as old, crumbling, and out-of-the-way as Room One is, I actually like caring for patients in here.

Stepping through the doorway, I take a moment to glance around. Lining the long wall at my left are the three patient treatment areas. The treatment area farthest to the left has the curtain drawn closed across it; it looks like that's where Mr. Wang has been put. The curtain for the middle treatment area is drawn open, revealing an unoccupied stretcher. The curtain around the treatment area on the right is partly ajar, and I can see an older man inside who is currently receiving supplemental oxygen via a high-flow nasal cannula; I'm guessing he's a patient with a CHF exacerbation who has been admitted and is waiting for his inpatient bed.

Directly across from where I'm standing, against the back wall, are supply closets and other equipment, including an ECG machine, intubation kits, the machine where medications are stored, bags of IV fluid, a linens cart, orthopedic items such as crutches and walking boots, the laceration repair cart, I&D tools, the ENT cart, and two defibrillators on code carts.

To the right of where I'm standing is the big workstation. Pete is currently seated in front of one of the computers, inputting something into a patient's chart. He raises his head when I enter Room One and greets me. I give him a polite, professional wave in response. I finish scanning the area; it doesn't look like there's anyone else in here tonight.

Once I've gotten my bearings, I make my way to the curtain that leads into the treatment area for my patient.

"Hello, Mr. Wang? May I come in?"

"Yes," comes the reply.

Stepping around the curtain, I find a healthy-appearing man who looks his stated age. He has already changed into a hospital gown, and he's resting back on the stretcher. He has been hooked up to the cardiac monitor, which shows his most recent blood pressure check was mildly elevated, otherwise his vitals were within normal limits. As I take a second to watch the tracing of his cardiac activity rolling across the monitor's screen, I note he's in a normal heart rhythm except for occasional premature ventricular contractions, or "PVCs."

I focus on the patient and give him my most official, doctor-ish smile. "Good evening. My name is Rachel Nelson. I'm the fourth-year medical student who will be helping take care of you tonight."

"Hi, Rachel," Mr. Wang replies politely.

I reach over to the counter next to the sink and pick up an ECG that's sitting there. It was performed on Mr. Wang when he arrived to the emergency department a few minutes ago. Glancing it over, I find it appears normal but for a couple PVCs, consistent with what I saw on the monitor. Raising my eyes back to the patient, I continue:

"I read the triage note, which said you're having palpitations. Please tell me more about what's going on."

Mr. Wang nods. "It's nothing major, but for the past couple of days, I've been feeling what I think are palpitations."

"Have you ever experienced anything like this before?"

"Occasionally, I've felt a few over the years, but it has never been anything that has really caught my attention. However, the past week or so, they've been happening a lot more often, and they seem to be getting stronger."

I take a seat on the stool beside the stretcher. "Have you noticed any pattern to the palpitations you're experiencing? For example, is there anything that seems to trigger the sensation or cause the palpitations to stop?"

Mr. Wang takes a moment to think this over. "They're the worst during or after a workout at the gym."

"When they're occurring, do you have any other symptoms?"

"Sometimes when the palpitations get really bad, I also feel short of breath."

I peek back up at the monitor. "Are you experiencing a feeling of palpitations right now?"

"Yeah, though it's not bad at the moment. Earlier this evening, however, after I got home from the gym, they were becoming pretty intense. That's why I decided to come get checked out."

I get back to my feet, my sense of worry increasing as I hear more of his story. "Do you have any significant medical history, or do you have any immediate family members with significant medical issues?"

"I have high blood pressure, but it's controlled with the medication my regular doctor prescribes," Mr. Wang explains. "My father had something wrong with his heart, which wasn't diagnosed until he was in his seventies. I'm not sure what the problem was, but I remember him saying something about the electricity going through his heart in an abnormal way."

I step to the sink and start washing my hands. "Mr. Wang, what I'd like to do is examine you and then order some labs and imaging, which will help us determine if your heart and lungs are all right."

"Sounds good." He shrugs. "Whatever you think is best."

Removing my stethoscope from around my neck, I commence performing an exam. When I place the stethoscope upon his chest to listen to his heart, I can hear its strong, steady rhythm getting disrupted intermittently by an extra beat.

The rest of his exam is unremarkable, and once I'm done, I place the stethoscope into the pocket of my white coat and step back from the stretcher.

"Are you okay for the moment? If so, I'll step out to place some orders."

He gives me a thumbs-up. "Yes, I'm fine. Like I said, I'm doing much better than earlier."

"Great. I'll be back soon. In the meantime, please don't hesitate to let us know if you need anything."

I give him another smile, and then I make my way out of the treatment area. As soon as the curtain closes behind me, I pick up my pace and beeline over to the nearest computer to start placing orders: IV access, lab work, continue the cardiac monitoring, and chest imaging. I also make a note that we're going to perform a repeat ECG and a recheck of his cardiac enzyme levels in a few hours.

"Looks like you've put in everything for Mr. Wang?" Pete asks me, getting up from his computer.

"Yes. Since his story is a bit concerning, I'm going to go let Doctor Sanders know about him shortly."

"Sounds good." Pete starts making his way over to the supply area to gather what he needs to place an IV. "I'll get started on those orders, and then I'll go check on the boarding patient."

"Thanks, Pete."

While Pete gathers the necessary supplies and then goes into the Mr. Wang's room to place the IV and draw labs, I settle in to review my patient's chart. It's not difficult to commit his information to memory, since there's not much information at all. As Mr. Wang said, he has been a pretty healthy guy, and he only checks in periodically with his primary care doctor to make sure his blood pressure remains well-controlled on medication.

Once I'm done reviewing the chart, I exit out of the computer. Before starting on Mr. Wang's chart note, I want to notify Dr. Sanders about him. So I leave the workstation and make my way toward the narrow doorway that leads out of Room One and into the rest of the main emergency department.

"Hey, Rachel?" I hear Pete call from behind me.

I stop and turn around. Pete is approaching.

"Would you mind taking a peek on the CHF patient who's boarding in here? I just finished a reassessment, and he looks like he's having a harder time breathing than before."

"Of course."

Reversing direction, I pass Pete and head over to the treatment area of the patient in question. Pete follows. Reaching the bedside, I find the older gentlemen sitting up, leaning forward slightly, and gripping the railings of the stretcher. His hospital gown has slipped off one shoulder, which lets me see that he's retracting as he breathes. From a glance at the information on his wrist band, I learn he's a seventy-eight-year-old named Richard Ames.

"Sir, I'm Rachel Nelson. I'm one of the med students here in the emergency department. Are you feeling worse compared to when you came in?"

He nods. He's too winded to reply.

I quickly use my stethoscope to listen to his lungs. Sure enough, I can hear a recognizable crackling sound, which indicates fluid is building up. I rapidly finish an exam and then move to the foot of the stretcher.

"I'm going to have respiratory therapy come in here to start you on BiPAP, and we'll have the radiology tech bring the portable chest x-ray machine to get a new image of your lungs." I motion to the work station. "While that's happening, I'll call the admitting team to notify them that you're feeling worse. I expect they'll want to give you some medication and come down to re-evaluate you."

Mr. Ames nods again in reply.

"I'll call respiratory for you," Pete offers, jogging over to one of the phones at the workstation.

While Pete gets on the phone, I go to the closest computer and place the order for the STAT, portable chest x-ray. Once the order is in, I use one of the phones to ask the operator to page the admitting medicine team to my number.

While I'm waiting for the medicine team to call back, I start reviewing Richard's chart to get caught up on his medical history. In contrast to Mr. Wang's chart, Mr. Ames's medical history is quite lengthy and complex, and my lips begin moving slightly as I read and mentally file away his information.

A noise causes me to look up from the computer. A radiology tech has arrived with the portable x-ray machine, which she can barely squeeze through the narrow doorway that leads into Room One. Once she gets the machine inside, she pushes it over to Mr. Ames's treatment area and begins setting up. A few moments later, another radiology tech enters, goes to Bob Wang's treatment area, and wheels him away on his stretcher so he can get imaging done in the radiology suites. As soon as the doorway is clear, the nurse, Carrie, comes prancing in with a friendly smile on her face.

"Can I help you guys in here?" She uses her manicured hands to gesture around Room One. "Looks like it's getting a little busy, and there's not much going on elsewhere right now."

Pete nods. "That'd be great, Carrie. Thanks."

I also give Carrie a smile. "Yes, thanks. Why don't you help with the care of Mr. Ames until his inpatient bed becomes available? He's here for a CHF exacerbation. We're getting a repeat chest x-ray now, and RT is coming to start him on BiPAP. I've paged the admitting medicine team, and someone should be calling me back shortly."

"You got it!"

Carrie waits until the radiology tech is done taking the x-ray, and then she practically skips over to Richard's treatment area and begins introducing herself to him. Meanwhile, I go to the radiology tech's side and check the x-ray image on the machine's little digital monitor. Not surprisingly, I can see evidence of pulmonary edema—an indicator of fluid in Richard's lungs. After I'm done reviewing the x-ray, I thank the radiology tech, who then wheels the clunky machine across Room One and carefully manages to maneuver it out the door.

No sooner has the radiology tech left than Brenna from respiratory therapy slides into Room One with the BiPAP machine. She heads to Richard Ames's treatment area and gets him started on BiPAP. It doesn't take long for Richard to start appearing more comfortable as his breathing becomes less strained. I continue to observe from nearby while Carrie obtains a new set of vitals. Though Mr. Ames remains hypertensive, his numbers are improved compared to before.

"I'll be back in about thirty minutes to see how it's going with the BiPAP," Brenna tells me, speaking over the noise of the machine. "I'll be in another room helping with an intubation, so feel free to let me know if something comes up in the meantime."

"You got it," I reply. "Thanks."

Brenna heads for the exit. She has to dart aside to allow the radiology tech who's bringing Mr. Wang back from the radiology suites to get through the doorway, and then she departs Room One. As the radiology tech guides Mr. Wang's stretcher into his treatment area, Pete goes to the bedside to reconnect Mr. Wang to the cardiac monitor and obtain a fresh set of vitals. I'm about to join Pete to reassess the patient when one of the phones at the workstation begins to ring. Since both nurses are busy, I dash over to the workstation and answer the phone myself.

"Good evening. This is Room One in the emergency department."

"Rachel?"

There's a rush of heat inside my chest when I hear Austin's voice, and my heart begins racing. Apparently, I'm not as over him as I thought. I'm not over him at all, in fact. Just hearing him say my name has been enough to put a smile on my lips and make my cheeks flush.

"Hi, Austin."

"Are you working down there tonight?"

I make sure my tone sounds as unaffected as his. "Yes, I'm starting a run of overnights this week."

"That's cool. Tara and I are on-call. We got a page from Room One. Do you know anything about it?" Austin waits a beat before adding, "Please tell me you don't have a patient lost under the flooring this time."

I snicker. "No. But I was the one who sent the page. I wanted to update you about one of the admitted patients who's boarding down here." I check behind me, looking into Richard's treatment area to see how he's doing. "Mr. Ames, the gentleman with the CHF exacerbation, is becoming increasingly symptomatic. You should probably come down and reassess him. I got him started on BiPAP, which appears to be helping, and I ordered a repeat chest x-ray. I can also get some Lasix ordered, if you'd like."

"Furosemide," he corrects me without hesitation.

I exhale to convey annoyance, but to be honest, I'm not annoyed at all. In fact, I'm starting to love these little spats of ours. It's something just between Austin and me. Something only we share.

A moment later, however, I mentally slap myself to my senses. I'm once again getting distracted by my feelings for Austin, but I can't do that. I'm here to work hard, learn, take excellent care of patients, and get an honors grade. I am not here for romance. Besides, Austin isn't even interested in me like that.

"Yes, if you could get another dose of furosemide ordered, that would be great," Austin goes on, filling the silence. "Thanks for helping out with him. Tara and I will come right down."

Austin hangs up. With the alluring sound of his voice lingering in my ear, I put down the phone receiver and enter the medication order. I also place an order for a repeat ECG, as well as a repeat blood draw to recheck his BNP and troponin levels. Once I'm done, I open the chart for my first patient, Bob Wang, and start looking at his results. His chest imaging is unremarkable. His labs also look normal. So far, we're on track for a repeat ECG and a recheck of his cardiac enzymes in a couple more hours, and if those are normal a second time, I'll consult cardiology to determine what his disposition and follow-up plan should be.

Out of the corner of my eye, I see Carrie heading over to the medication machine to pull out a dose for Mr. Ames. I turn the other way, deciding to check on Mr. Wang before I go update Dr. Sanders on what I've been doing in here—no doubt, she's starting to wonder what's taking me so long. Then, after I report to Dr. Sanders, I'll begin typing a full chart note for Bob Wang, and I'll also do a brief note in Richard Ames's chart to explain the interventions I made while he was boarding down here.

I reach the curtain that leads into Mr. Wang's treatment area. The curtain is slightly ajar. I see Pete at the bedside, chatting with the patient, and Mr. Wang smiling in response. He continues appearing comfortable and well, and after a glance at the monitor, I confirm his vitals remain normal. I note, however, that there are still PVCs running across the tracing on the screen.

"Is it okay if I come in and join you?" I ask.

Mr. Wang looks my way. "Of course."

I step around the curtain. "I wanted to check how you're feeling."

"Still doing well," Mr. Wang replies pleasantly. "Occasionally, I'm having palpitations, but they're nothing serious."

I glance again at the cardiac monitor. "So far, your chest imaging and labs are unremarkable. You're on-schedule for repeat cardiac testing in about two more hours. If the repeat tests also look good, I'll be consulting cardiology and coming up with the best treatment and follow-up plans for you."

"Excellent." Mr. Wang reaches over to the little table beside his stretcher and picks up his phone. "I'll call my wife and let her know she can go to sleep. I'm sure she has been worrying about me."

I smile at him and then turn to Pete. "I'm heading out to update Doctor Sanders. I'll be back in a few minutes."

Pete gives me a friendly salute. "Sounds good."

I slide back around the curtain, leaving Mr. Wang's treatment area. Walking fast, I head for the doorway that leads to the rest of the main department, intent on finding Dr. Sanders so I can tell her about Mr. Wang and what I've done for Mr. Ames. When I reach the doorway, I nearly crash into someone who's coming from the other direction and trying to enter Room One. I stop and raise my head. I gulp. It's Austin.

For a second or two, we just stand face-to-face in the doorway observing each other. Austin is wearing navy blue scrubs, and he's once again going without his short white coat. His pager is clipped to his waistband. A pen and a folded piece of paper are in the breast pocket of his top. His stethoscope is around his neck.

In only the moment I use to take in the sight of him, all my feelings for Austin are reignited. My heart pounds harder. My cheeks get warmer. My skin begins to tingle.

"Hi." Austin is studying me with that mesmerizing gaze of his.

"Hi," I say quietly.

Austin motions past me into Room One. "I'm here to see Mr. Ames. Tara had to go take care of a new admission in Room Nineteen."

Tara. Hearing her name is like a splash of cold water to the face, and I'm glad. It's exactly what I need to snap out of my trance.

"Wonderful." My professional demeanor returns. "The nurse has given him the medication, and she's getting a repeat ECG and labs on him right now. RT should be back to check on him shortly, and I believe the radiologist's report of the new chest x-ray should be available."

Austin's mouth turns up into a smile. It's a genuine, appreciative, very handsome smile . . . and it nearly takes my breath away.

"Awesome. Thanks, Rachel."

Just the way he says the words sends another thrill through me.

I need to get away from this man.

"You're welcome." I briskly gesture past him in the direction of the rest of the main department. "Now, if you'll please excuse me, I'm going to update Doctor Sanders about my patient. Please let me know if there's anything else I can do to help with Mr. Ames."

"Will do. Thanks again for . . ." Austin trails off. Looking past me, his eyes narrow slightly as they start darting around the room. "Do you hear that?"

"Huh?" I peer up at him in confusion. "What are you . . ."

But I, too, fall quiet when I begin hearing a faint, high-pitched sound. It's a humming sound, and it seems to be coming from inside Room One. I spin around to face the room and, like Austin, start shifting my gaze around to figure out where the noise is coming from. The sound rapidly gets louder, and its pitch begins to rise. The noise now seems to be radiating out of the floor itself . . . and the walls . . . and the ceiling . . .

Over the humming, I hear something start to rattle. My eyes localize the sound to a coffee mug that Pete left sitting by his workstation. I stare as the mug rattles faster and faster on the countertop, the vibration soon growing strong enough to cause the mug to slide to the edge of the counter and topple off. The mug hits the floor and shatters with a startling crash.

"What was that?" Carrie steps out from behind the curtain of Mr. Ames's treatment area, her eyes wide.

At the same time, Pete whips open the curtain of Mr. Wang's treatment area. "Everything all right out there?"

Austin's jaw muscles are working as he continues surveying the room. He slowly reaches over to me and wraps a hand securely around my upper arm. "I think this is the start of an—"

There's a deafening bang as the floor suddenly shifts underneath us. I let out a cry as the jarring motion throws me from my feet. Austin tightens his hold on my arm, stopping me from falling, and grips the doorframe with his other hand. There's a split-second when everything is hauntingly still. Then the earth begins to shake.

A terrible, deep rumbling noise fills the air as the ground starts churning violently below our feet. I hear Carrie scream. Pete shouts something. The ground shakes harder, and I stagger again, nearly tossed to my knees by the sickening motion. Austin pulls me in against him, bracing me as the force of the shuddering earth intensifies even more. Now clinging to one another in the doorway, Austin and I struggle to stay upright as the relentless, terrifying shaking continues. An ear-piercing alarm starts going off. Strobe lights begin to flash. Something crashes on the far side of the room. I hear shouts and screams from the rest of the main emergency department far behind us.

Holding onto Austin, I grit my teeth, mustering all my strength to remain on my feet against the power of the quake. I squint through the thick, dusty haze that's collecting in the air, doing a frantic scan of Room One. In horror, I watch chairs topple over, supplies tumble out of the cabinets, and the empty stretcher start slamming against the wall. There's a blinding flash followed by a shower of sparks as one of the overhead lights pops and goes dark. Carrie lets out another scream as she trips and lands at the foot of Mr. Ames's stretcher. Pete is grunting with exertion as he tries to stabilize himself with his back against the wall while holding onto Mr. Wang's stretcher.

The merciless shaking continues. Computers slide off the workstation and smash upon the ground. More supply carts tip over, spilling their contents. Empty IV poles roll across the room and clatter to the floor. A ceiling panel shakes loose and drops to the floor with a heart-stopping crash. Another light goes out. More panicked screams burn in my ears.

Seconds seem to take hours as the ground continues unleashing its fury. Austin tightens his hold around me while we hover helplessly in the doorway. Choking from the dust, I cough and duck my head against his chest, hanging onto him as tightly as I can.

I suddenly start hearing a strange, loud crumbling noise. Raising my head, I flick my gaze around until I trace the sound to its source: a huge crack that's appearing in the floor not far from where we're standing. The crack swiftly expands, shoots up the wall, and spreads over the doorframe. Plaster and paint-covered pieces of drywall start crumbling down on top of Austin and me. I then hear the sound of splintering wood directly overhead, and I look straight up. I only have time to register that the crossbeam of the doorframe itself has split before I hear Austin shout:

"Rachel!"

He shoves me forward and out from underneath the doorway. I stumble to the floor, catching myself on my outstretched hands. I hear the blood-chilling sound of an avalanche behind me. Thick, dark clouds of dust and debris spill into the air. There are more screams. Another light fixture shatters and goes out.

Then the earth becomes quiet.

For one long, terrible second, nothing stirs. Sprawled on the ground and breathing fast, I cough out a wheeze and lift my head. I stare through the thick haze, sensing myself go pale when I see the extent of the earthquake's destruction spread out before me. It's a surreal, apocalyptic sight.

I begin hearing the sounds of movement. To my relief, I spot Carrie pulling herself to her feet and going to attend to Mr. Ames, who thankfully appears unharmed. Farther to my left, Pete is ignoring a bleeding wound on his arm as he begins to assess Mr. Wang, who looks stunned but also uninjured. Exhaling hard, I slowly rock back on my haunches and check over my shoulder.

I let out a horrified scream.

Eleven

My entire body is trembling as I push myself to my feet and turn to face where the doorway used to be. The air seems to get sucked from my lungs. My head gets light, and my vision dims. I stagger weakly as a rushing sound fills my ears.

No. Not Austin. Please, not Austin.

Austin is on the ground, lying on his right side amidst a giant pile of rubble from the collapsed doorway. His eyes are closed. He isn't moving. A thin stream of blood is trickling down the left side of his scalp, the red hue making a sickening contrast to the chalky white dust and debris that covers the rest of him.

My heart slams in my chest, and I'm yanked from my shock when a surge of adrenaline unlike anything I've felt before comes over me. I sprint forward, drop to my knees next to Austin, and grab his wrist to feel for his pulse. Tears of relief begin rolling down my cheeks. He's alive.

"Austin?" I lean down over his ear. "Austin, can you hear me?"

He doesn't reply. He doesn't move. Growing frantic, I snatch my stethoscope from the pocket of my white coat and put in the earpieces. Bending lower, I place the diaphragm of the stethoscope against Austin's chest and then reach over him to listen to his back. I hear his slow, steady heartbeat and air moving through both of his lungs.

"Oh my gosh!" Covered in dust, Carrie emerges from Richard Ames's treatment area and beelines toward me. "Is he okay? What can I do?"

"Go get help from the main department," I say while I continue trying to assess Austin for injuries without moving him. I don't want to reposition him without assistance. He could have a spinal injury, and we have to keep him as stable as possible.

Pete jogs out of Bob Wang's treatment area and crouches down beside me. "I'm afraid we aren't going to be able to get help for a while, Rachel."

"What?" I sit up fast, pulling the stethoscope from my ears.

Still not seeming to notice the bleeding wound on his arm, Pete motions in the direction of the doorway. "I think we're trapped until the debris gets cleared out from the other side. For now, we're on our own."

It takes one awful second for Pete's words to sink in, and then I shift to look at the doorway again. Only now do I really see the true extent of the damage sustained in the earthquake. The entire doorway came down, leaving a massive pile of wood and stone piled up in its place.

My body goes cold as the devastating reality hits me. There are three patients in here now, and there are only two nurses and me to take care of them. We're cut off from the rest of the department, and there's no telling how long it will be before anyone can come to our aid. We have no way of knowing how much damage was inflicted to the rest of the facility, or how many people have been injured . . . or worse. We could be trapped in here for hours. For days.

My breathing is becoming more and more strained as panic begins coursing through me. I can't take care of these patients. I don't know what I'm doing. I'm just a med student. I need help from an attending. I . . .

My gaze drops back to Austin. His face is so pale. He's so still. So quiet.

The sight causes something to stir deep inside me. It's an intense, powerful feeling, which rises up from my core and fills my whole body, driving my panic away. I can do this. No, I *have* to do this. I have to help Austin, for his life may depend on it. I have to help Mr. Ames and Mr. Wang, for their lives may also hang in the balance.

I cannot—I will not—let my insecurities get the better of me now.

Pulling my eyes from the huge pile of rubble, I take in a fortifying breath and face the nurses. "We need to get to work. Carrie, bring the empty stretcher over here. Pete, go grab a cervical collar and a backboard."

Carrie nods and rushes off to the empty treatment area to retrieve the stretcher. Pete leaps to his feet and charges to the back of the room, where he starts digging through the mess of overturned carts and spilled supplies in a hurried effort to find what we need. Focusing again on Austin, I start throwing the debris off his body while looking for other injuries. More relief fills me when I see he landed in front of the collapse rather than getting trapped directly underneath the rubble.

A faint moan escapes Austin's lips. I hunch back down to get a better look at his face.

"Austin?" I force my words to remain steady. "Austin, it's Rachel. I need you to listen to me. You must hold still. Don't move at all. We're going to get you in a collar and on a backboard."

Pete returns at a sprint, carrying a dust-covered cervical collar with one hand and dragging a backboard with the other. I reposition myself by Austin's head, place my hands on his shoulders, and brace his head and neck between my forearms. Pete lays the backboard behind Austin and then works around my arms to secure the collar on Austin's neck. Carrie pushes the vacant stretcher to my side before she dives down to assist Pete. Once the nurses are in position, I continue stabilizing Austin's cervical spine while the three of us carefully logroll him onto his back so he's lying on the board. Letting go of Austin, I slide to the opposite side of the board from the others and motion for Carrie to come help me. Once she's at my side, I grip the board's handles and look between Carrie and Pete.

"Ready?"

"Ready," Pete replies, gripping the handholds on his side.

Carrie nods while also grabbing the board. "Ready."

"On my count." I get into a crouching position, channeling my strength into my legs. "One, two, three, lift."

Clenching my teeth, I help Carrie and Pete lift the board off the ground. Austin lets out another incoherent moan as the three of us carry him on the backboard over to the stretcher and set the board down upon it.

I immediately dart to the top of the stretcher, lean forward so I'm hovering over Austin's head, and open his right eye and then his left. Thankfully, his pupils are equal and reacting normally to the light in the room.

"I'll wheel Austin into the empty treatment area and get him connected to the monitor," I say to the others. "Carrie, go check on Mr. Ames. Pete, go see how Mr. Wang is doing. Once we've assessed everyone, we—"

The rest of my words are drowned out by the distant sound of an explosion, like a transformer just blew. The remaining lights in Room One go out, and the windowless space falls into complete darkness.

"Oh my gosh." Carrie's tremulous whisper carries through the blackness. "Now what are we going to—"

A few overhead lights flicker back on, filling the space with an eerily dim hue while casting strange shadows into the corners of the room.

"The hospital is running on auxiliary power from the generator," Pete remarks in a low voice. "I'm guessing it's all we're going to have for a while."

I wet my lips and unlock the brakes on Austin's stretcher. "We'll make it work. Let's go."

Pete and Carrie charge off in opposite directions to check on the other patients while I push Austin's stretcher into the empty treatment area. Moving as fast as I can, I wrap the blood pressure cuff around his upper left arm and clip the oxygen saturation monitor to one of his fingers. I yank up his shirt to the base of his cervical collar and stick ECG leads to his chest. Once I've gotten Austin connected to the machine, I pull down his shirt, stand on tiptoe to reach the monitor, and hit the button that turns it on, praying the device is wired to get auxiliary power. There's an agonizingly long pause before the screen lights up and a tracing of Austin's cardiac activity starts scrolling across the screen. As the machine finishes obtaining his vitals, I note his oxygen saturation, pulse rate, and blood pressure are within normal limits.

Exhaling the breath I was holding, I spin around and face Austin once more, ready to resume doing an exam. But as my eyes land on him, another flood of crippling emotion washes over me. I grip the stretcher railing while working to hold back a sob. Seeing Austin this way—seeing him so hurt and vulnerable—is almost more than I can bear.

Austin can't leave me. He can't.

It takes everything I have to suppress my feelings and focus on doing the rest of the exam. First, using the otoscope, I check in and around his ears. There's no sign of blood pooling behind either eardrum, and there isn't any bruising around the backs of his ears to suggest a skull fracture. Next, I check Austin's scalp wound. The bleeding has nearly stopped, the wound itself is fairly shallow, and the underlying scalp feels normal when I palpate it. After inspecting his head, I finish the rest of his exam. I don't find any other obvious signs of trauma.

Nonetheless, a terrible sense of fear is gnawing at me. Without Austin being able to communicate, and without having imaging of his head, neck, and anything else that might be hurting him, there's no way of knowing for sure that Austin doesn't have an occult, life-threatening injury. He could have a slowly expanding bleed in his head, which won't clinically manifest until it's too late. He may have sustained a laceration to his liver or spleen. He could have an injury to his spinal cord. As the devastating possibilities run through my mind, I cling harder to the stretcher railing to steady myself. Distraught and feeling utterly helpless, I shift my worried gaze to the collapsed doorway, wondering how long it will be before help reaches us.

"Rachel!" Pete shouts from the adjacent treatment area. "Come in here!"

Pulling myself away from Austin's bedside, I run to Mr. Wang's treatment area. I pass around the curtain and halt in alarm when I discover that he's sitting up stiffly, breathing fast, and clutching a hand to his chest. His lips are pale. His eyes are wide with that haunting look I've seen in patients before they die.

"This started a couple seconds ago." Pete speaks rapidly as he begins cycling another set of vitals. "He was doing fine until just now."

"Mr. Wang, what's going on?" I use my stethoscope to begin listening to his heart.

He shifts his glazed-over stare to me. "I . . . don't know. I think . . . I was startled by the earthquake . . . palpitations . . . getting . . . worse."

I keep a hand on Mr. Wang's arm while my eyes flick to the monitor. Consistent with what I heard when I examined him, Mr. Wang's heart rate is dangerously fast, and more and more PVCs are filling the screen. Before my eyes, the extra beats begin taking on a new morphology—one that causes my stomach to drop with dread. He's developing ventricular tachycardia, or "v-tach." The large chambers of his heart are beating so fast and so inappropriately that his heart won't be able to properly refill between beats and circulate blood around his body for much longer.

The monitor finishes obtaining a new round of vital signs, which light up the screen. As

I feared, Mr. Wang's blood pressure is also dropping.

"Pete, place another IV," I say. Leaning out past the curtain, I call across the room, "Carrie, bring the intubation and code carts in here."

A whirlwind of motion and noise begins swirling around me while I lower the head of Mr. Wang's stretcher so he's lying flat. Pete runs out of the treatment area to go search for IV supplies in the mess at the back of the room. Carrie bursts in pulling two carts behind her: one that contains intubation equipment and the other that has the defibrillator on top of it. While Carrie scrambles to get the equipment ready and connect Mr. Wang to the defibrillator, Pete returns with supplies in his hands. He swiftly places a second IV and gets fluid running through it, pushing it in fast with the help of a pressure bag.

I keep my attention on my patient, pressing my fingers into his wrist to monitor his pulse, which is growing ominously fainter by the moment. "Mr. Wang, your heart is now beating in a dangerous rhythm. I recommend we cardiovert your heart—meaning we hit it with a brief pulse of electricity—immediately. Otherwise, you might . . ."

I don't even get a chance to finish before Mr. Wang's eyes roll back in his head, and he becomes unresponsive. The pulse in his wrist disappears. Mr. Wang has gone into cardiac arrest.

"Pete, start chest compressions. Carrie, start bagging him." Releasing the brake on the stretcher, I push it farther away from the wall to give us more room to work. I dart to the code cart. "We'll shock him once and then plan to intubate."

In another rush of coordinated chaos, Pete begins pushing on Mr. Wang's chest while Carrie rushes to the head of the stretcher and starts administering supplemental oxygen to him. I hit the button on the defibrillator to charge it up. The machine's alternating, two-toned alarm soon goes off, indicating it has reached the necessary charge.

"Everybody clear?" I ask in a loud voice.

Pete stops compressions and steps back, holding up his hands. "Clear."

"Clear." Carrie slides away from the stretcher.

I press the button on the defibrillator. A shock is administered to Mr. Wang's heart via the patches Carrie applied to his chest. Mr. Wang's body arches slightly as the electricity hits and then becomes still once more.

Pete immediately resumes chest compressions, and sweat soon forms across his brow. Carrie continues bagging Mr. Wang to provide oxygen. Facing the code cart, I yank open the drawers in a hunt for epinephrine as well as intubation supplies. Over the chaos, I hear Mr. Wang let out a groan. I whip around. He has opened his eyes, and he's pushing Pete's hands away from his chest.

I shoot another look at the monitor. Mr. Wang's heart is back in a normal rhythm.

"We have return of spontaneous circulation," I announce, almost breathless from the latest surge of adrenaline that's coursing through me. "Carrie, put the patient on supplemental oxygen via nasal cannula with the goal of keeping him at or above ninety-four percent." I push the button on the cardiac monitor to get a new set of vitals. "Pete, keep Mr. Wang in a supine position with fluid going. As long as his vitals stay within normal limits, we'll continue relying on IV fluid for hemodynamic support." I lean back, peering past the open curtain to view the mess of supplies at the back of the room. "Do we have a cooling machine in here?"

"Nope, I'm afraid not," Pete replies with a shake of his head. "They're both kept in the trauma bays."

I sigh before putting my attention back on Mr. Wang. I watch as his stunned gaze shifts from the nurses to the defibrillator and finally to me. He takes in a few more breaths. At last, he seems to find his voice.

"Did you shock me with that thing?" he asks weakly.

I venture a slight smile. "Yes. Welcome back, Mr. Wang. You certainly gave us some extra excitement to go along with the earthquake. How are you feeling?"

"Not too badly." He winces as he slowly motions to his chest. "My ribs ache, but it's nothing I can't handle."

"I'm glad you're doing as well as you are, all things considered," I tell him sincerely. "We're obviously going to continue keeping a very close eye on you, and there are some tests you'll need once we get out of here." I pause, my words nearly catching as I anxiously wonder yet again how long it might be before we're rescued. Clearing my throat, I force myself to continue. "In the meantime, Pete will perform another ECG and you'll remain on cardiac monitoring. You must tell us if you start to experience any new or returned symptoms, okay?"

"Okay." Mr. Wang glances at his cell phone. His voice remains hoarse, but I can hear it gaining strength. "I wish I could call my wife."

Carrie pulls her own phone from the back pocket of her scrubs. She frowns. "Unfortunately, cell reception is still down."

"Don't worry, Bob. I'm sure your wife is well," Pete says before he starts stepping away to get the ECG machine. "Anyone who was in a building with even remotely better infrastructure than this place made out better than we did, I can guarantee that."

Mr. Wang is still pale as he nods and rests back his head. I stay at the bedside to observe him a while longer, confirm his repeat vitals are within normal limits, and do another exam. Once Pete returns to the treatment area, I finally step back from the stretcher and say to the nurses:

"While you get the post-resuscitation care going in here, I'll go check on the other patients."

Pete begins setting up to get the ECG. "Sounds good. Thanks, Rachel."

I make a move to exit but pause and look back. "By the way, Pete, do we need to put any stitches in that wound on your arm?"

Pete stops what he's doing and glances down at his arm. His eyebrows rise in an expression of surprise, like he's noticing his injury for the first time. "Nope. Appears to be a hefty abrasion but nothing that needs stitches." He looks at me again. "I'll get a dressing on it as soon as I'm done."

With a hasty nod, I exit and dart back toward Austin's treatment area. My heart is pounding with both hope and apprehension as I maneuver around the curtain. I set my eyes on Austin and come to a stop. A whimper escapes my lips. Austin is still frighteningly pale, his eyes remain shut, and he hasn't moved.

"Austin?" My voice wavers almost pleadingly as I advance closer to the stretcher. "Austin, can you hear me?"

His eyelids flutter. His lips barely part. Nothing more.

It's a losing battle to keep my silent tears at bay as I proceed to perform a repeat exam and recheck Austin's vital signs. There's nothing more I can do for him until we get out of here, and the realization is torturous.

Once I'm done reassessing him, it takes everything I have to make myself step back from his stretcher and walk out of the treatment area. Wiping the tears from my eyes, I do my best to collect myself before I go into Mr. Ames's room.

I'm relieved to find Mr. Ames seems to be doing fairly well. He's still sitting up on the stretcher, and the BiPAP machine—one of the most helpful treatments he can receive—continues running. When I recheck his vitals, I find his blood pressure and heart rate are up a little, though this isn't surprising considering what we've been through.

"I apologize it took me a while to get back in here." I face him and rest a hand on his shoulder. "We've had a rather exciting night. How are you doing?"

Mr. Ames gives me a thumbs-up and speaks through his BiPAP mask. "Can't complain."

I use my stethoscope to listen to his lungs. There's less fluid in them now, which suggests the medication and the BiPAP are helping. The rest of his exam is stable except for a new, large contusion on his left leg. I'm guessing he hit his leg against the stretcher railing during the earthquake.

"Since you're improving so much with treatment, I'd like to give you another dose of that medication, if we can get it out of the machine, to help continue removing the excess fluid from your system." I put the stethoscope around my neck. "Is there anything else I can get for you right now?"

"How about hamburger?" Mr. Ames grins.

I actually manage a laugh in appreciation of some much-needed levity. "I think we'd all like—"

The rest of my words are drowned out by what sounds like a loud roll of thunder. The ground lurches, tossing me against Mr. Ames's stretcher, and then starts shaking violently once again. I stumble and fall, reflexively sticking out my right arm to catch myself. I wince when I feel a sharp pain in my wrist as I hit the heaving floor.

The earth continues to rock. Sprawled on the ground, I see the lights surge and dim. Water begins spraying out from a broken pipe in the ceiling. I hear Carrie let out a panicked yell. Another computer slides off the work station and hits the ground with an ear-splitting crash.

I begin feeling something falling on my head, and I look up. Through the thick shower of plaster and dust that's falling from the ceiling, I see one of the panels directly over Mr. Ames's stretcher rattling loose. Clenching my teeth, I wrap my good hand around the stretcher railing and fight against the merciless motion of the aftershock to pull myself to my feet. I release the brake on the stretcher and tighten my grip on the railing while grabbing the BiPAP machine with my injured hand. Staggering against the shifting ground, I tug Mr. Ames on his stretcher and the BiPAP machine out past the curtain. Just as we clear the treatment area, the dislodged ceiling panel drops and smashes to the ground where Mr. Ames's stretcher was situated only moments before.

The earth stops rocking. All is still.

Breathing fast, I let go of the stretcher and the BiPAP machine. My pulse is thumping so hard I can feel it up in my throat and ears as I spin around to make sure Mr. Ames is okay. He's wide-eyed but doing fine. I cough a few times to clear the dust and debris from my airway, and then I call out:

"How is everyone?"

"We're all good in here," Pete replies, though his tone is tense.

Carrie comes out of Mr. Wang's treatment area, does a double take when she sees me, and scurries my way. "What happened, Rachel? I . . ." She freezes, her eyes nearly popping out of her head when she gets a view of the mess on the floor of what used to be Mr. Ames's treatment area. She claps a hand over her mouth. "Rachel, if you hadn't been in there. . ."

I blow a strand of hair from my eyes. "Carrie, if you feel like Mr. Wang is stable enough for Pete to manage him on his own, would you take over tending to Mr. Ames? He needs another dose of the diuretic, if you're able to get it. In the meantime, I'll go make sure Austin is okay."

Carrie nods fervently. "Of course."

I leave Carrie and Mr. Ames, hurry next door to Austin's treatment area, and slide around the curtain. His stretcher was knocked slightly askew by the aftershock, yet Austin still hasn't stirred. He hasn't even opened his eyes.

My throat gets thick as anguish overcomes me. Austin could be dying right here in front of me, and I have no way to save him. I'm training to become an emergency medicine physician, but I can't save the life of the man I care so much about.

I hang my head in agony. It's hopeless. There's nothing I can do.

Except talk to him.

And maybe, just maybe, he'll be able to hear my voice.

Everything feels solemnly quiet as I settle myself on the stool beside Austin's stretcher. Inhaling a stuttering breath, I reach out and take his limp hand in mine.

"Austin, it's me. I know you don't like it when I tell you what to do, but I'm going to do so anyway. I need to tell you that you have to get better." Lowering my quivering voice to a whisper, I go on. "Austin, we've spent the last three years doing this crazy thing called med school together, so you can't leave me now. Not when we're so close to finishing. You have to stay with me, Austin. I don't want to finish this journey without you. I . . . I can't finish it without you."

Austin remains completely still. All I hear is the slow, repeating beep from the monitor. I'm crying so hard now that I'm barely able to speak, but force myself to continue.

"Austin, I know it seems like all we've ever done is fight, but that's not what it really was, was it? We were pushing each other. Challenging each other. Making one another strive to be the very best we could be. So I want to thank you for that. Thank you for all the times you pushed me to be better. I'll be a better doctor and take better care of patients because of you."

My voice finally fails me, and I start sobbing, silently and uncontrolled. Dropping my head, I watch as my tears land on the cracked, dirt-covered floor at my feet. Over these past few weeks, I thought I had figured out how much I truly cared about Austin. However, now faced with the possibility of losing him—really losing him—my eyes have been opened completely. The truth is, Austin means everything to me. He has been my closest and most stalwart companion since the first day of med school. He has pushed me, and he has challenged me. He was the one person I knew would always be at my side. I fought, teased, and bantered with him not because I hated him but because I cared about him.

Because I loved him.

I love him.

And now I might lose him forever, and he'll never know how I really feel.

"Austin?" I swallow past the lump in my throat. "There's something else I want to say to you. I want you to know that—"

"Room One! Room One, does anyone copy?"

A man's shout causes me to sit up with a gasp. Giving Austin's hand a last squeeze, I leap to my feet and sprint out past the curtain. At the same time, Carrie and Pete emerge from the other patients' rooms, and we all come to a simultaneous halt, exchanging wide-eyed looks while we wait in tense, anxious silence.

"Room One!" the man shouts again. "Does anyone copy?"

I clasp my hands to my chest. I recognize the voice. It's Dr. Kent. He's calling to us from the other side of the collapsed doorway.

"Yes, Doctor Kent! We copy!" Moving as fast as I can over the debris, I get closer to the huge pile of rubble. "This is Rachel, and we copy you!"

I hear several people break into applause and cheers on the other side of the wall. I smile as new tears, this time of relief, begin rolling down my cheeks.

"Rachel, we have two fire crews here now, and they're making fast work of stabilizing the area while digging a path through the mess to reach you." Dr. Kent's voice stays steady and firm. "What's the status of everyone in there?"

I glance over my shoulder at the nurses, who have come up behind me. "I'm fine. Carrie is fine. Pete sustained a large abrasion to his arm, but he's otherwise fine." I face forward again and continue speaking fast. "Patient number one, Mr. Wang, needs critical care. He went into v-tach arrest, but we got return of spontaneous circulation after a first shock. Patient number two, Mr. Ames, will require ongoing care on the medicine service for his CHF exacerbation. His symptoms have been improving with the use of medication and BiPAP." I pause briefly to make sure I can keep my voice from catching. "And we have a third patient, Austin Cahill. He was hurt when the doorway collapsed. He's hemodynamically stable and maintaining his airway, but he remains minimally responsive. He needs STAT imaging of his head and neck, at least."

There's a long silence.

"Rachel, I copy," Dr. Kent tells me before he lowers his voice and starts speaking to those who are with him. Sound is so obstructed by the rubble that I can't hear what he's saying. Dr. Kent then raises his voice again and resumes addressing me. "Rachel, we copy that you have one patient requiring critical care after v-tach arrest, one patient requiring care for a CHF exacerbation, and one trauma patient requiring STAT workup and imaging."

I'm about to respond when there's a loud bang on the other side of the wall. I jump back with a cry, pulling the nurses with me, fearing the pile of debris is about to topple down.

"Don't worry, Rachel! The crews have almost reached you!" I hear Dr. Sanders yell above the din. "Hang in there, everyone! They'll be through soon, and we'll be coming in with medical support!"

Deafening noises continue, making it sound like a construction zone in here. As more dust fills the air, the nurses and I hurriedly retreat farther from the mess while watching the rocks and wood in the huge pile start to shift, revealing peeks of light and movement on the other side.

"Let's get back to our patients while the fire crews finish making their way through," I say to the others.

Pete nods and jogs back to continue monitoring Mr. Wang. Carrie, who's starting to cry herself, gives me a relieved hug before she scampers off to Mr. Ames's treatment area. With the commotion from the collapsed doorway getting even louder, I spin away and run into Austin's room.

"Austin, help is coming." I grab his hand. "Hang in there. Help is coming."

The noise from the firefighters' work continues to crescendo. I lean past the curtain to check what's happening, and I see more light through the rubble and glimpses of a crowd of people waiting on the other side of the fallen doorway. Quickly focusing again on Austin, I resume speaking to him:

"The firefighters have almost finished clearing away the mess, which means we'll be out of here in no time. We'll get some imaging of your head and neck to make sure everything is okay." I bend down closer to him, as if it will help him hear me, though I fear he isn't hearing anything anymore. Nonetheless, I keep talking. "Best case scenario is that you've only sustained a concussion, which isn't anything some rest and a little Tylenol can't help fix, right?" My words catch in my throat. I close my eyes in despair and hold his hand even more tightly.

His hand moves.

Inhaling sharply, I reopen my eyes. Austin's lips part, and I hear him make a sound, as if he's trying to speak.

"Austin? Austin, say that again. I couldn't quite understand you." I give his hand a gentle shake. "Tell me again. What did you say?"

There's a pause that seems to last forever, and then I hear Austin faintly utter:

"Acetaminophen."

I stare until I'm convinced I'm not hallucinating. Then my heart erupts with joy. The Austin I know and love is back.

He's back.

"It's acetaminophen," Austin mumbles again. His eyes slowly open. He stares vacantly at the ceiling before his vision seems to come into focus. His attention slowly tracks down to our hands, which remain clasped together. At last, he puts his eyes on mine.

"It's acetaminophen," he says again, and he breaks into the faintest hint of a smile.

I laugh elatedly and shake my head. "You can call it whatever you want. I won't argue with you. This time."

He opens his mouth to say more when a startling, deep rumbling noise suddenly fills the air. I gasp in fear of another aftershock, but a moment later, a crew of firefighters wearing full bunker gear bursts into Room One.

I get to my feet, watching as Dr. Kent, Dr. Sanders, Dr. Godfrey, Elly, a group of nurses, and several other members of the ED staff run into the room behind the firefighters. The entire group comes to a stop. Expressions of shock appear on everyone's faces as they take in the scene.

"We're glad you're here," I say, breaking the stunned quiet while pushing open the curtain that leads into Austin's treatment area.

A blink later, everyone burst back into action. Shouts fill the air. The firefighters continue their work. Dr. Godfrey leads two nurses and a tech into Mr. Wang's treatment area, and before long, his team is wheeling the patient out of Room One. Elly charges over to Mr. Ames with a team of her own, and he, too, is hastily wheeled off toward the rest of the main department. Meanwhile, I have to hop out of the way as Dr. Kent, Hadi, and the rest of the ED staff surround Austin's stretcher and take over his care.

"Austin! Are you okay?"

The panicked call came from Tara, who has just run into Room One. She joins the throng around Austin and keeps talking at him, but her voice blends into the ambient noise so I can't hear what she's saying. In fact, there are so many people gathered around his stretcher now that I can't even see Austin anymore. A few moments later, Dr. Kent is guiding the way as Austin's stretcher is pushed out of the treatment area.

Suddenly, I find myself alone. Everything in Room One is still and quiet. I slowly turn in a circle to let my eyes wander over the scene. The damage in here is even more extensive than I realized.

"Rachel."

I look to my left and see Dr. Sanders carefully navigating over the rubble to come my way. She gives me a smile, though her brow is furrowed. She points to my wrist. "In addition to getting you to somewhere to rest and hydrate, we should probably obtain an x-ray to make sure that's not broken, huh?"

I lower my eyes to my wrist, which I realize has become swollen and taken on a dark purple hue. I had actually forgotten about my injury, and only now do I realize how much it's aching. I raise my head and nod. "That would probably be a good idea."

Dr. Sanders reaches my side, puts a hand around my upper arm, and starts guiding me through the apocalyptic mess. Together, we navigate the trail that was carved out by the firefighters and exit Room One. When we emerge into the rest of the main department, I halt, stunned by the sight that meets my eyes.

Out here, things are also running on limited auxiliary power. In the dim light, I can see ED staff members hurrying past as they rush to take care of patients. There are cracks in the floor and running up the walls. Water is spraying out from a broken pipe in the ceiling. Stretchers that rolled loose during the quake are lodged at weird angles along the walkways. Chairs and supply carts are tipped over. People's belongings are scattered across the ground. Phones and computer monitors are hanging off desks by their cords. The damage is immense, but at least the extent of the structural damage doesn't appear as severe as it is in Room One.

"We've got one x-ray machine up-and-running," Dr. Sanders tells me. Concern remains etched in the lines of her face, and she motions for us to continue onward. "Let's head over there so we can make sure your wrist isn't fractured. Then we're going to let you get some rest."

I can only nod in reply while I continue gaping at the altered state of the emergency department. It's more staggering proof of how, in only a matter of seconds, everything can drastically change. As I continue peering around, trying to process what I'm seeing, flashbacks of the earthquake start swirling in my mind. I sense the color drain from my face, and I begin feeling faint. I stagger slightly.

Dr. Sanders puts her hand back on my arm, and she assists me as we resume heading toward the radiology suites. Before we round the corner to leave the main department, I glance over my shoulder one last time. Through the open door of the trauma bay, I can see Dr. Kent examining Austin and getting him ready to go for imaging. I smile, overcome with joy and gratitude. Austin is going to be all right.

Twelve

I take in deep breaths while chanting meditation phrases in my head, focusing my energy on settling my nerves. Slowly but steadily, my anxiety fades, replaced by a sense of calmness.

I can do this.

Reaching out, I open the door that leads into the Discovery Conference Room. As I step across the threshold to enter the vacant room, I see that the long table where we normally sit during the Wednesday didactic sessions has been pushed aside, and in its place are twelve desks and chairs. While the door closes behind me, I glance around again, confirming there's no one else in here yet. I'm not surprised, considering the written exam doesn't start for another forty-five minutes.

I came early this morning with the intention of doing some last-minute studying before the test. After all, the grade I get on this final exam matters even more than the score I received on last month's final. Since I achieved a perfect score on the final last month, as well as an honors grade on that rotation, the pressure

I'm under to excel this time around is especially high. I have to prove my grade last month wasn't a fluke. If I don't pull off another exceptional score on this exam and get an honors grade on this month's rotation, many emergency medicine residency programs won't even bother to offer me an interview.

Basically, this is the most important day of my medical education thus far.

So why am I not a nervous wreck?

Surprisingly, despite the immensely high stakes, I'm not the fidgety, panicked mess I anticipated I would be by this time of the morning. In fact, rather than anxious, I feel quietly confident. I know how hard I've studied the syllabus. I know I've spent countless additional hours doing independent reading and research. I know I tried to learn everything I possibly could from each attending, resident, didactic session, and, most importantly, each patient. I've truly done everything within my power to prepare for today's exam.

And, I realize, that's enough.

When this is over, no matter the outcome, I can walk away with my head held high. Regardless of what others may think, or what my exam score or grade on this rotation turns out to be, I will know how hard I worked. I will know how much I sacrificed. I will know the dedicated effort I put into my training. Most importantly, I will know that I gave it my all, and I gave it my best.

I smile at this thought. It's a pretty monumental paradigm shift. For years, I've been focusing so much on impressing others that I stopped paying attention to my opinion of myself. Relying solely on others for validation, I got lost in always worrying about my shortcomings without acknowledging what I was accomplishing.

Thankfully, the earthquake helped me begin to see things differently. That night, faced with the stark reminder that life can change in an instant, I started rethinking what was most important and what really mattered. This new understanding has been getting clearer and clearer in my mind ever since.

Still smiling to myself, I venture across the room and take a seat behind one of the desks. I place my bag at my feet, reach inside it, and pull out my phone. As I put the phone on silent mode, I notice I received a text from Julie:

> *Good luck on your test today! Then again, you don't need luck, Rach. You're going to do awesome because you are smart, brave, and amazing!*

I smile again. It has been just over a week since the earthquake, and in that time I've been communicating with my family a lot more than before. When news first broke about the earthquake, my parents and siblings were thrown into a panic. The torturous uncertainty they experienced was made exponentially worse by the fact that cell phone communications were down and they couldn't find out whether or not I was okay. When my family and I were finally able to connect over the phone, several tearful conversations followed. I think the experience caused all of us to be reminded of how much we love and appreciate each other. We each have our faults, quirks, and differences, but we're family. And I wouldn't have it any other way.

My family members weren't the only ones who were thrust into a worried frenzy when they heard about the earthquake. In the days afterward, I also fielded calls from my high school and college friends. Though a massive earthquake isn't exactly the reason one wants to be catching up with friends, it was nonetheless wonderful to hear from each of them, to laugh and cry, to reminisce, and to be reminded of how much they care. In fact, we're so excited about seeing each other over the holidays that we've already made plans for our annual get-together in a few months.

Anyway, those calls with my family and friends compromised the bulk of the first round of post-earthquake phone conversations. The second round of phone calls ensued very soon afterward, starting the same night my news interviews aired on television.

Yes. News interviews.

I don't know who was responsible, but someone leaked to the media what happened in Room One during the earthquake. Of course, the local news stations couldn't resist pursuing the story of "the young medical student who kept critically sick patients alive in the rubble." A few days after the earthquake, when I returned to work for the first time, I was basically ambushed outside the hospital by a herd of news reporters and camera crews. Thankfully, Dr. Kent and Dr. Sanders had been tipped off about the media's arrival, and they came out of the hospital to protect me from the onslaught. They handled the bulk of the interviewers' questions themselves, keeping their responses professionally brief. I mostly just stood next to them, staring into the camera with an awkward smile plastered on my face. Let's just say, I realized I'm not cut out for television.

Of course, once the story about my role in the ED after the earthquake was broadcast all over the news, my phone resumed ringing with new fervor. Julie couldn't stop saying how awestruck she was by me. Jacob repeated several times that he was extremely impressed and proud of what I had done in Room One. As for my parents, to say they were stunned would be a drastic understatement. At least, I assumed they were stunned, since they listened in almost complete silence while I relayed to them the full account of what occurred. Come to think of it, they said so little that I suppose I don't really have any idea how they feel about it.

Breaking from my thoughts, I text a reply to Julie thanking her for the message, and then I put my phone away in my bag. I resume inhaling and exhaling, deciding that instead of cramming last-minute information from the syllabus, I'm going to relax and let my mind clear before the test.

I lean back in my seat while my eyes start wandering around the room. I notice a crack in the far corner of one wall, undoubtedly a casualty from the quake. It's hard to believe over a week has already passed since that night. Officially rated as a six-point-eight, the earthquake was deemed the worst this region has had in decades. Thankfully, because my apartment building and most structures around the region are fairly new construction, they were built to withstand a tremor of that size. The damage to most buildings was minimal. Even better news was hearing there were no fatalities in the event, and that those who did sustain injuries were able to obtain timely treatment at various medical facilities in the area.

As for Lakewood Medical Center itself, since most of it has been well-maintained, updated, and renovated over the years, the hospital also made it through the earthquake fairly unscathed. Except for the emergency department, that is. As the oldest and least-maintained part of the hospital, the emergency department sustained the most damage by far. Room One was hit worst of all; the wreckage was so bad, in fact, that the area was condemned and shut down permanently.

The rest of the emergency department is now running at about half-capacity, using the rooms that were the least damaged in the quake. Meanwhile, work is happening around-the-clock to clean, repair, and salvage more of the ED, in the hopes that additional space can get put back into use over the next few weeks. Dr. Kent is also advocating for the hospital administration to allocate additional funding toward accelerating construction of the new emergency department, but there's a long way to go, courtesy of the layers of bureaucratic approval that must be obtained before any change to the construction's funding or timeline can happen.

In addition to the significant impact the earthquake had on the emergency department itself, it also forced a change to the schedule for those of us who are rotating there. Since the ED currently has fewer functional exam rooms and, therefore, fewer patients being treated at any given time, the twelve med students were put on modified, shortened shifts for our final week of the month. This allowed all of us to still work enough shifts to get credit for completing the rotation.

My final shifts with Dr. Sanders took place over the past three days; I was given off the first four days after the earthquake. Actually, I wasn't given the days off, I was commanded by Dr. Sanders to stay home. She insisted I needed to rest and recover after what I had gone through. As I tried pointing out each day when she called to check how I was doing, I felt four days was more than enough time off for a sprained wrist, but Dr. Sanders wouldn't even entertain the idea of letting me return to work sooner. In fact, I think she would have made me stay home longer, if it weren't for the fact that I had to accrue enough shifts to meet the requirements of the rotation.

"Rachel? What are you doing here so early?"

I sit up in my chair and spin around. Lynn Prentis is coming through the doorway with a stack of exam booklets in her hand. As she informed all of us via email a couple days ago, because the earthquake knocked out a lot of the hospital's Internet servers, doing an online exam this month wasn't feasible. So we're once again doing the final exam on paper, and Dr. Kent will have to wait until next month to try out the new online testing format he finally got approved to set up.

I give Lynn a smile. "I just wanted to clear my head before the exam."

Lynn sets the stack of booklets on a table near the front of the room. "Well, it's actually great you came early. Doctor Sanders was hoping you could stop by her office."

My smile disappears. "Doctor Sanders wants to see me?"

"Mmm-hmm." Lynn nods as she starts organizing the booklets. "She's in her office now, if you want to head over there. This would be a perfect time."

"Oh. Okay. Um, sure." I swallow while I get to my feet and pick up my bag. "I'll go right now."

Turning around, I slowly exit the conference room. My mind is whirring. Dr. Sanders wants to see me? Now? Why? What have I done?

I make my way to the end of the hallway, cross the large foyer with the elevator bay, and proceed down the window-lined hall that leads to the attendings' offices. In the quiet, I continue racking my brain for a reason why Dr. Sanders would possibly want to speak with me today.

Suddenly, the realization strikes me, and a pit forms in my stomach. I know what this is about: Dr. Sanders wants to inform me that the residency committee has officially decided not to grant me an interview. If the committee had decided to extend an invite to interview, I would be receiving an email about it. But I'm not being invited to interview, and Dr. Sanders is trying to do me the courtesy of privately letting me know.

I rub my fingers against the palms of my hands as I continue down the hallway, focusing on keeping my negative self-talk at bay. I'm not going to let this news mess with my head. Devastating as it is, and embarrassing as it will be to have someone tell it to my face, it's not a surprise. I determined long ago that I wasn't going to make it into Lakewood's emergency medicine residency program. I'm not of the same caliber as those who do residency training here, and that's why I've already shifted my focus toward trying to get into residency elsewhere.

I break from my thoughts when I realize I've reached the office. The door is slightly ajar. I reach out and knock on the doorframe.

"Yes?" I hear Dr. Sanders call from inside.

I clear my throat. "Doctor Sanders, it's Rachel Nelson. Lynn said you wanted to see me?"

"Yep. Come on in."

I push open the door and start walking into her brightly lit office. I halt abruptly when I see not only Dr. Sanders, who's seated behind her desk, but also Dr. Kent. He's leaning casually against the window frame. I stare for a moment, but my confusion soon passes. Of course Dr. Kent would be here. He's in charge of the med student rotation in the ED, so it's only fitting he would be part of this conversation, too.

"Please, have a seat." Dr. Sanders motions to the chair in front of her desk.

I shut the door behind me and do as I'm told. Poising myself on the edge of the seat and clasping my hands in my lap, I look between the two attendings, staying silent in the hopes that they'll break the news to me fast. There's no reason to beat around the bush. The sooner they get this over with, the better.

"Rachel, how are you feeling?" Dr. Sanders has genuine concern in her tone.

"I'm doing well. Thanks for asking." I motion to my wrist. "I removed the splint this morning, and it only ached a little. So I think I'm pretty close to recovered."

"That's great," Dr. Sanders replies. She pauses and exchanges a glance with Dr. Kent before concentrating on me again. "So I wanted to ask: are you planning on taking the written exam today?"

My eyebrows rise. This definitely wasn't the question I was expecting. "Yes. Of course."

Dr. Sanders breaks into a relaxed smile. "Why?"

I peer back at her, trying to figure out if this is yet another one of her attending-level mind tricks. "Well, um, because it's the written final for the rotation."

"True." Dr. Sanders is still smiling. "And remind me: what was your score on the written final last month?"

I squirm in my chair. Does everyone get interrogated like this before they're told they've been rejected by Lakewood's emergency medicine residency program?

"I, um, scored one hundred percent," I say.

Out of the corner of my eye, I can see Dr. Kent also starting to smile. More mind tricks, apparently. Great. They're ganging up on me.

"That's what I thought," Dr. Sanders remarks with a nod. "In that case, you definitely don't need to take the written exam again. I'm sorry I didn't think to let you know sooner. It has been pretty hectic these past several days, and it slipped my mind. I'm sorry."

I draw my brows together, not hiding my confusion. "But isn't passing the exam necessary to complete this rotation?" Yikes, are they not even going to let me pass the rotation this month? Has my performance really been that subpar? Did Dr. Sanders learn about Oscar escaping into the ceiling during our Fast Track shift? Is that what this is about? Are they going to fail me because I make patients feel the need to flee into the hospital's ducting system?

"Yes, passing the written final is required to complete the rotation," Dr. Kent chimes in.

He's speaking evenly, though the corners of his mouth remain incriminatingly curved upward in apparent amusement. "And something tells me you would not only pass the test again but score one hundred percent . . . or higher, if there were extra-credit questions."

My brow furrows even more. "So why wouldn't you want to let me—"

"You're welcome to take the test again, if you really want to, Rachel," Dr. Sanders assures me. "We're just letting you know that you don't have to take the exam, since it's exactly the same test you aced last month. From our perspectives, there's no reason to make you take it again."

"It's the same test?" I hadn't considered this possibility before. "Exactly the same test?"

"It's exactly the same test." Dr. Kent chuckles. "Hence the reason I'm pushing to get the online testing format up-and-running so we can have a larger bank of test questions and mix things up from one month to the next." He crosses his arms in a relaxed manner over his chest. "Most students who are going into emergency medicine do one rotation here in Lakewood's ED and one rotation in University Hospital's ED, where the written exam is different. But in the occasional instance when a student is assigned to work in the same ED for both rotations, as long as they passed the test the first time, the requirement to take it again is waved. That is, unless the student wants to try and improve his or her score." He pauses, his dark eyes sparkling with humor. "Like I said, though, we don't have extra credit, so I doubt your score could improve by much."

"Oh." I finally dare to smile a little. "Thanks."

Dr. Sanders continues observing me, and her expression grows pensive. "Don't thank us, Rachel. You earned the right to be in this position. You studied extensively, worked hard, and continually dedicated yourself to becoming the best student you could be. That's something you should be extremely proud of." She pauses a moment before going on. "Even more importantly, you passed a very different kind of test—a test no medical student has ever been asked to undertake before."

I peer back at her. "What do you mean?"

"I mean what you did last week—the patient care you provided and the leadership you demonstrated after the earthquake—was far more important than any score on a written exam, any evaluation from an attending, or any grade on a rotation." Dr. Sanders continues observing me. "You helped save three lives, Rachel, and you did it under incredibly difficult circumstances. Far more than any exam ever could, what you did last week reveals the kind of medical student you are and the outstanding physician you're on the road to becoming."

I blink hard as a rush of emotion fills my chest. "Th-thank you."

"Like I said, don't thank us. We're the ones who thank you for your hard work. Your dedication is the reason you were prepared to take such good care of those patients that night."

Dr. Sanders leans back in her chair and breaks into another smile. "Now enough of this seriousness and formality, eh? Feel free to go home and enjoy the rest of your day."

I'm smiling, too, as I reach down and pick up my bag. "All right. I will."

"Oh, by the way, you earned an honors grade on this rotation," Dr. Sanders adds, as if this is no big deal whatsoever. "You earned it starting the first day we worked together, and you continued to show you deserved it all the way through the last. So congratulations."

My eyes pop open wide. "What? Really? Are you serious?"

"You sound surprised," Dr. Sanders notes, appearing a little surprised herself.

I nod. "I am surprised. I honestly thought I wasn't impressing you at all, Doctor Sanders." I bite my tongue to stop myself from saying more. What am I doing? Trying to talk her out of giving me the honors grade? Am I insane?

Dr. Sanders looks even more stunned. "Rachel, why in the world did you think you weren't impressing me with your work in the ED?"

I wet my lips, choosing my words carefully. "Well, because we barely spoke during our shifts together. I figured it was because you had decided there was no hope for me."

Dr. Sanders actually laughs and begins shaking her head. "Oh, Rachel, I can't tell you how sorry I am that you felt that way because nothing could have been further from the truth."

She stops laughing to fix her attention on me, and her expression becomes serious once more. "The reason I allowed you to work so independently was because I trusted you. I knew you would do an excellent job caring for patients. I knew that about you from the very first day of the rotation, long before you saved those lives after the earthquake." She points at me. "You're that good, Rachel, and you have showed us how good you are over and over again. Because of your hard work, dedication, and determination, you excelled in the emergency department, earning both my trust and my respect."

My lips part, but no sound escapes them, so I just gawk at Dr. Sanders as her words sink in. Then an incredible mixture of disbelief and joy begins coursing through me. Dr. Sanders trusts me? She respects me? While it matters most how I feel about myself, knowing an attending believes in me and sees my potential is worth far more than any honors grade.

Dr. Sanders keeps studying me, and I get the sense she's somehow able to read the thoughts that are flying through my mind. "Rachel, you're an extremely skilled medical student, and you are going to make a phenomenal doctor. So you have to promise me that you're never going to let anyone make you feel otherwise."

I nod earnestly. "I won't. I promise. I've learned a lot on this rotation, but I think the most important thing I've learned is the need to believe in myself."

"Good. You should believe in yourself. Because you're that good," Dr. Sanders emphasizes again.

Dr. Kent nods. "I couldn't agree more."

I get to my feet and hike my bag onto my shoulder. "Thank you."

Dr. Sanders smiles once more. "Go enjoy your day. You've earned it."

I'm on the verge of bursting into a puddle of happy tears as I turn around and scurry for the door.

"Oh, Rachel?"

I halt and look over my shoulder. "Yes?"

Dr. Sanders is now grinning in a humorous way. She lowers her voice to almost a whisper. "I probably shouldn't tell you this, but let's just say a little birdie informed me you'll soon be receiving an invitation to interview for Lakewood's emergency medicine residency program." She gives me a thumbs-up. "The interviews are being held the first week of December. Mark your calendar."

I slowly face her squarely once again. And I stare. For a very long time.

"Are you serious?" I finally eke out.

Dr. Kent laughs. "I think Doctor Sanders is serious."

I clasp my hands to my chest, looking between them. "Thank you! I'll go make a note of it on my calendar right now!"

It's like I've been hit with a bolt of adrenaline. Whipping around, I scurry out of the office and practically fly down the hall to the elevator bay. I press the elevator call button but wait only a micro-second before deciding to take the stairs. Dashing to the other side of the foyer, I push open the door that leads into the stairwell. My heart is thumping. My mind is racing. Everything is a blur as I take two stairs at a time down to the ground floor. Bursting out from the stairwell, I emerge into the lobby. I don't slow my pace as I zoom through the crowds, pass by the information desk, and head out the hospital's main doors.

Hit by the late-morning sunshine, I scamper over to a wall where there's some shade and finally come to a halt. I'm breathing fast and my hands are trembling as I pull my phone from my bag and call my mom.

"Hi, hon," Mom answers quickly with a hint of worry in her voice. "Are you all right?"

"I'm all right," I reassure her, as I've had to do every time I've called since the earthquake. "In fact, I'm more than all right. I'm doing great."

I can almost hear Mom's sigh of relief. "Wonderful. Tell me what has you doing so great today. No, wait. Let me put you on speaker phone so your father can hear what you have to say, too."

There are muffled noises on Mom's end as she walks around the house until she finds Dad, says something to him, and switches over to speaker phone. She then says to me:

"Okay, go ahead, hon. We can both hear you now."

There's an expectant pause.

I clear my throat. "Well, I've got two pieces of really good news. First, I earned an honors grade on this month's emergency medicine rotation. Secondly, I was informed Lakewood is going to invite me to interview for a position in their residency class." Another flutter of joy dances inside me. "Obviously, an interview is no guarantee I'll get accepted into the program, but at least they're interested enough to interview me, and with a program as competitive as Lakewood, just getting an interview is really cool."

There's another pause.

"Oh. That's great, sweetheart," Dad eventually says, not sounding particularly impressed in the slightest.

"Yes, that's quite nice. Congratulations," Mom adds politely, also not even remotely enthused.

With a silent, crestfallen sigh, I lean back against the building and lower my eyes to the ground. No matter what I do, I can't make my parents proud of me. I'll never understand why.

But, I remind myself, I can't let my feelings be dictated by others' opinions of me. What matters is how I feel about myself. Like Dr. Sanders said, I shouldn't let anyone make me feel less than I am.

I break the quiet, "Well, I'll let you two get back to whatever you were doing. I just wanted to let you know."

"Thanks for calling, hon. Great to hear your voice. I do have to say, though, I have no idea what took Lakewood so long to invite you to interview." Mom makes a tsking sound. "You're such an outstanding candidate, it's almost laughable they waited until now."

My eyebrows rise. Was that Mom's version of . . . a compliment?

Dad huffs. "I totally agree. Clearly Rachel should have been offered an interview after her excellent performance in the emergency department last month. I suppose, though, the residency selection committee had to wait until it was officially time to extend interview invites to applicants."

My mouth falls open. What is happening right now? Dad is praising me, too? Is this for real?

"Hon?" Mom seems to pull the phone nearer to her mouth. "Are you still there?"

"Y-yes," I stutter, trying to wrap my mind around what I'm hearing. "Sorry . . . I . . . I guess I'm sort of taken aback by your praise."

Cue another pause.

"What do you mean?" Dad asks, and he sounds completely serious now.

I rub my nose with my free hand, working to collect my thoughts into something I can articulate. "I don't know, exactly. Actually, I've never known why you guys are always disappointed in me." I pause when my words catch in my throat. Despite my rising emotion, however, I also find myself growing more comfortable discussing how I feel with them. The earthquake proved life can change in an instant, and I know now how important it is to express the way we feel to those we care about. "I've always tried to make you proud, so I've never understood why you don't praise me the way you praise Jacob or Julie."

Another pause. This time, it's a really, really long pause.

"Rachel, I . . . I'm sorry." To my shock, Mom sounds as though she's getting more choked up than I am. "As much as I would like to deny it, looking back, I can see you're right. I don't think we've done a good job conveying to you how proud you've always made us." She sighs. "I suppose it was easy to assume you understood how we felt, but I realize we should have expressed our feelings more openly. I'm sorry."

"Please don't apologize," I say. "I'm truly not fishing for attention or compliments. I simply wanted to let you know how I wish— rather, how I *used* to wish—I made you as proud as Jacob and Julie do. Recently, though, I've come to accept it's okay if I don't."

"Rachel, no one could be more proud of you than we are, and we're not just proud of your accomplishments but of who you've become as a person." My father's usually unflappable tone is becoming emotional, too. "You always made parenting easy. We never had to worry about you. You did well in school, didn't get into trouble, and pursued your goals with dedication. By trying not to interfere or micromanage your life, I suppose we thought you understood how greatly we admired and respected you. But, as your mother said, we should have told you, too." He takes a moment before going on. "I think it can be easy to forget that even those who are successful need support. I'm very sorry. We love you."

"I love you guys, too."

There's more silence, but this time it's silence of a different kind. It's a warm and wonderful silence, which somehow allows us to convey emotions too powerful to put into words.

A gentle breeze brushes my face as I eventually break the quiet by saying again, "I love you guys."

"We love you, too," Mom tells me softly.

"And congratulations," Dad adds. "We'll talk to you soon."

The call concludes. I lower my phone to my side, cherishing how it feels to have reconnected with my parents. After today—after this past week or so—I think they understand me a little better, and I understand them better, too.

With a sigh of contentment, I slip my phone into my bag, push off from the wall, and hoist my bag higher on my shoulder. Tucking my hair behind my ears, I start walking toward the bus stop. I quickly halt, though, as a realization strikes me: I'm done with my emergency medicine rotations. With the exception of when I might go to the ED to admit patients while I'm rotating on other services, I won't work in an emergency department again until next July, when residency starts, wherever that may be.

I look behind me at the hospital. I'm done with emergency medicine as a med student. I've accomplished my goal of earning an honors grade on both rotations. I earned an interview with Lakewood's residency selection committee. Most importantly, I've learned a lot about myself and what really matters. It may have taken an earthquake to literally shake some sense into me, but at least I've finally started to understand.

I'm still gazing up at the hospital when another thought strikes me: for the first time in weeks, I don't feel compelled to rush home and study. My next rotation doesn't start until Monday, which means I have the next several days entirely to myself. I can do anything I want to do. I can function on my own schedule, or I can have no schedule at all. I'll be able to sleep in. Exercise. Get caught up on errands. Watch movies. Go out to eat at any restaurant I desire. Shop for fun. I could even take a road trip somewhere. The possibilities seem almost endless.

The first thing I think I'll try is that adorable French eatery a block or so from my apartment. It was one of the places Julie and I didn't have time to visit while she was in town, and I've always wanted to check it out.

Today I will.

I resume walking toward the bus stop but soon pause once more. There's no need for me to ride the bus. After all, I'm in no rush. I have the entire day to relax. The weather is beautiful.

So I'm going to walk.

Spinning the other direction, I begin retracing my steps toward the sidewalk that leads from the hospital and down the giant hill that Lakewood Medical Center is perched upon. As another brush of wind tousles my hair, a carefree smile appears on my face. Today has been almost perfect.

Almost.

My smile fades, and an all-too-familiar ache fills my heart as my thoughts shift to Austin. He has been on my mind constantly. I haven't seen him since the earthquake; I haven't even called him or sent him a text. With every passing day, the void in my heart caused by his absence has grown deeper, and though I've been desperate to see him or at least hear his voice, I have left him alone. I know this is how Austin wants it. If he had any interest in being in touch, he would have reached out to me. But he hasn't. Because Austin doesn't care about me the way I care about him. He undoubtedly has beautiful, intelligent, sweet Tara Hess doting on him, and it would only be awkward, presumptuous, and embarrassing for me to insert myself into the situation. So although it flies in the face of everything I've recently come to believe about telling the people you care for how you feel, I've forced myself to stay silent. Not saying anything to Austin has been the hardest thing I've ever done, yet it's for the best.

Thankfully, at least I know Austin is doing well. On that surreal night of the earthquake, while I was in the emergency department getting my wrist attended to and then resting under the care of Dr. Sanders, I was relieved to overhear Austin's workup was unremarkable and he was getting admitted to the hospital for monitoring of his post-concussive syndrome. I also noted Tara stayed in the ED the entire time Austin was there and that she was the one who led the team that admitted him.

A couple days later, when I was home, during one of the calls Dr. Sanders made to check in on me, she let me know Austin had been discharged from the hospital in satisfactory condition. She didn't disclose anything else, but I have no doubt Austin was given credit for finishing his internal medicine rotation and instructed to remain at home with minimal activity for several more days, if not weeks, so he could continue recovering from his concussion. I was elated to hear the news, obviously, but it was brutally hard knowing Tara would surely be going to Austin's apartment to visit and care for him.

I should be the one visiting and caring for Austin. I'm the one who knows him best.

I'm the one who loves him.

I tip back my head to the cloudless, blue sky as regret hits me more strongly than ever. Austin was my perfect match, but I was too distracted and stubborn to admit it. I was so focused on my studies, I didn't realize what was most important. I was too blind to see what was right in front of me . . . until it was too late.

It was the night of the earthquake, while I rested on a stretcher in a remote corner of the ED, when I finally came to understand that life is too short and unpredictable to delay love. If you care about someone, you shouldn't pass up the chance to be with them. Love is hard. Love might not always work out. Yet you shouldn't wait for a better time for romance. The time is now.

Except I came to this realization too late. I ignored Austin, and Austin found love elsewhere.

I'm yanked from my thoughts when, out of the corner of my eye, I see the main doors of the hospital slide open. Tara Hess herself steps outside. I duck my head, about to dart away before she notices me, but then I realize Austin is walking out of the hospital with her. Instantly, my heart explodes and my stomach leaps into my throat. From where I'm standing, I can see that Austin's expression is relaxed. He's dressed casually in a t-shirt and jeans, which sit well on his fit, strong frame. He has grown a goatee during his week at home. He appears healthy and well.

Tara blinks in the sunlight and tosses her hair. The sound of her adorable giggle reaches my ears as she faces Austin and says something to him. Austin smiles at her. She giggles again and hooks her arm around his as she keeps talking.

My breathing stutters. I need to get away from here. I need to get away from *him*. If I'm lucky, my schedule will be such that I won't cross paths with Austin again until medical school graduation in June. Then, at last, we'll go our separate ways and this misery will be over.

Austin suddenly turns his head and does a double take when his eyes land on mine. My breathing hitches harder as I stare back at him.

Tara stops talking and follows Austin's gaze. When she spots me, Tara gives me a wave.

It takes everything I have to muster a smile and wave back. I then quickly spin on my heels and flee down the sidewalk, getting lost amidst the crowd, leaving Austin and Tara behind.

Thirteen

I finish putting away my fourth load of clean laundry for the day and close the dresser drawers. After returning the empty laundry basket to the bathroom, I step from my bedroom into the main area of the apartment. I come to a halt, letting my eyes drift around the space. My apartment feels particularly quiet tonight. Poignantly quiet.

Turning to look out the large windows at my left, I see the sun is starting to drift lower in the sky, casting its golden light across the buildings and parks below, seeming to make everything glow.

Lost in thought, I make my way to the couch and sit down. I don't know how much time passes before I'm brought to attention by my growling stomach, which reminds me I haven't had anything to eat today. I never went to that French eatery. After seeing Austin and Tara outside the hospital this morning, my appetite vanished. So instead, I came directly home.

Over the course of the day, I kept myself busy: laundry, vacuuming, washing windows, going through boxes of savings to throw away what I no longer wanted, catching up on emails, and even a much-needed run to the grocery store. While I may not have spent the day relaxing as I had originally hoped, it was cathartic to pass the hours channeling my energy into the process of getting things back in order. It was like wiping the slate clean. It feels as though I've set the stage for a fresh start and taken the first steps toward going forward in life with my new perspective.

Now, though, as the afternoon is waning, I'm growing a little bit hungry and a whole lot restless. With my chores done, my thoughts are already drifting back to Austin. I can't stop thinking about those few moments when I saw him outside the hospital this morning. Just that brief memory triggers an ache of longing in my heart. No matter how I try, I can't deny the strength of my feelings for him. He is deeply imprinted on my heart and mind, and I can only hope time will gradually ease the pain and allow me to move on one day.

I turn away from the window. My eyes land on the television, which is dark and silent, like it usually is. I suppose I could watch TV to distract myself . . .

No, I don't feel like watching a show tonight.

My gaze continues moving over to the kitchen, and I actually pull a face. Even though I did a full stock-up run at the grocery store today, nothing I have sounds even remotely appetizing.

With another despondent sigh, I resume staring out the window. In my mind's eye, however, I'm still seeing Austin striding out of the hospital this morning. I'm guessing he was there to take the final exam for his rotation, and he and Tara probably went out to lunch after he was done.

I squirm and start drumming my fingers on the arm of the couch. I wonder how long Tara and Austin have been officially dating? I wonder if they're telling their friends and family about the relationship yet? I wonder if . . .

I sit up, shaking my head as if doing so will somehow clear Austin from my mind. I can't keep on like this. I can't keep thinking about Austin and what might have been. The regret is too acute. The emotions are too raw.

I need to get out of here. I need to find something to occupy my mind.

I impulsively leap to my feet and dart back into my bedroom. Moving fast, I change out of my sweats and into the first items I grab from my closet: a pink top and a Bohemian-style skirt. Charging into the bathroom, I run a brush through my hair, and then I apply lip gloss and mascara. Once I'm done, I pause to study my reflection in the mirror. This is the first time in weeks I've worn nice clothes and makeup, and I nod to myself with satisfaction. I may feel like an emotional wreck, but that doesn't mean I'm going to look like it. At least, not tonight.

Whipping around, I head out of the bedroom. Going toward the foyer, I grab one of my favorite purses and sling it by its cross-body strap over my chest. I continue moving to the basket by the front door where I keep my shoes. I dig out a cute pare of sandals and slip them on. Finally, I pause and look around my apartment to make sure I haven't forgotten anything. Once I'm sure everything is in order, I pull open my apartment door, step out into the corridor, and lock the door behind me. Shoving my keys into my purse, I start walking down the hallway toward the elevator bay. I'm still not sure where I plan to go tonight, but it doesn't matter. Doing anything is better than staying in my apartment pining over Austin.

I reach the elevator and tap the call button. The elevator soon makes a chiming sound, and its door slides open. I step inside and push the button for the lobby. The door slides shut once more, and the elevator begins its descent. Moments later, the elevator chimes again.

I step out of the elevator and stride across the lobby to the glass doors that lead outside. Emerging into the pleasant warmth of the summer evening, I begin meandering down the tree-lined path toward the street, letting my feet lead the way and not particularly paying attention to where I'm headed.

Before long, I find myself in the center of the area's bustling nightlife scene. I continue strolling absentmindedly, passing shops and restaurants while weaving around the people on the sidewalk. The lampposts are coming on, and the string lights hanging over the road are beginning to glow against the darkening sky. Music from each restaurant crescendos and fades in my ears as I pass by, and I can smell delicious aromas of foods mixing in the air. My stomach growls again. Still, though, I keep walking.

It's not until I begin hearing another type of music—traditional Irish music—that I come to attention. I realize I'm approaching O'Flanagan's pub, which looks and sounds as busy as always. Memories of the last time I was here swiftly fill my mind, and I feel another squeeze around my heart as I recall how Austin intervened and got me home safely that night.

Austin.

I suddenly halt in the middle of the sidewalk. For some strange, crazy reason, the pub is where I want to eat tonight. I don't know why, but I want to go in one last time before I bury the memories of this place—and the memories of the help Austin rendered me here—forever.

Running my hand along the strap of my purse, I resume heading up the sidewalk, now with determination in my steps. With the music inside the pub getting louder, I navigate a path through the throngs of people gathered outside the establishment. I reach the pub's entrance just as someone tries to exit.

"Rachel?"

I freeze when I hear his voice.

It can't be him. It can't.

Yet I'm barely able to breathe as I raise my eyes to the man who's trying to leave the pub.

It's Austin.

For one long moment, we stare at each other while the crowds swirl around us, Austin from just inside the pub and me from the sidewalk right outside. Since I saw him last, Austin has changed into a button-up shirt and a dark pair of jeans. His hair is combed. The golden evening light is hitting his face at an angle, highlighting his strong, handsome features. I gulp as a sensation like lightning zips down my spine.

"Um, hi," I barely manage to say.

Austin's eyes do a rapid scan of the area. He then focuses on me again and steps out the door. "I take it you're coming in for dinner?"

I nod as my heart continues thundering in my chest.

He glances around again. "Are you . . . with anyone?"

"No." My face threatens to ignite, but I set a more pointed look on him and divert the discussion. "What about you? Are you here with Tara?"

"Yes," he tells me.

I look away and don't reply.

"That is, I *was* on a date with Tara," I hear Austin add. "She has gone home."

I pause, and then I face him again, my brows drawn together with genuine concern. "Is everything okay?"

Austin doesn't reply. Instead, he just peers at me, the corners of his eyes wrinkling with concentration as he does so. I stare back at him, waiting and trying—but failing—not to get lost in his hypnotizing gaze.

Austin finally motions behind him to the pub. "It's a little loud around here for conversation. Would you mind taking a walk somewhere quieter where we could talk?"

My eyes get bigger in unmasked surprise. Austin wants to take a walk? He wants to talk?

A split-second later, it dawns on me what Austin wants to talk about: Tara. Austin is looking for advice regarding Tara. He might be trying to get ideas for a great date to take her on, or perhaps he's seeking help deciding on a gift to buy her. Whatever the reason, he wants a female's opinion, and since I happen to be standing here with nothing better to do with my night, he figures he might as well ask me.

A heavy ache radiates through my chest, but I don't show it. Instead, I adopt a smile that matches my impassive tone. "Sure. I'd be happy to talk, Austin."

He takes a step but stops again. His forehead creases. "Wait. You were here to get dinner not to hang out with me. I'm sorry." He shakes his head, actually appearing sheepish. "Forget about taking a walk. I'll leave you to enjoy your evening."

"No, it's okay. I'm actually not very hungry." I study him more closely. He looks uncharacteristically uncertain. Uneasy. It's not like him at all. Though it will hurt terribly to help him with Tara, doing so will be far better than seeing him this troubled. "I was really just looking to get out of my apartment for a bit. I'm happy to take a walk, if you'd like."

Austin analyzes my face while the muscles of his jaw work. At last, he steps forward to join me. Turning around to walk alongside him, I do my best to keep pace with his long strides as we start venturing down the sidewalk. People we pass give us knowing smiles, clearly assuming Austin and I are a couple, which makes the painful reality of the situation even worse. Nonetheless, I'm going to stick this out. If Austin needs help, I want to be here for him.

We go a couple blocks without saying anything. I glance up at him a time or two, but I find that his attention remains fixed straight ahead and his expression is impossible to decipher. With a silent sigh, I refocus on the sidewalk and try to figure out how I got myself into this strange mess. Instead of spending the night distracting myself from thoughts of Austin, I'm walking next to him. Rather than confessing how much I love him, I've agreed to help him secure the love of someone else. If I wasn't so close to crying about the situation, I would probably laugh.

Austin takes an unexpected turn off the main sidewalk and starts guiding the way down a side path between two buildings. His movements are certain, making it clear he knows where he's going. Evidently, he's far more familiar with the area than I am. I can't help wondering how many dates he has gone on while I've been holed up in my apartment staying buried in my studies.

Another surge of regret courses through me, and I can't handle the silence any longer.

"You shouldn't have been in a noisy pub, by the way," I remark, making sure to keep my tone all-business. "You're still recovering from a significant concussion."

He looks my way and nods. "I agree. Two hours of boisterous Irish music, among other things, was a bit much."

He resumes looking straight ahead and says no more, so I do the same.

We eventually emerge out from behind the buildings, and to my surprise, I actually recognize where we are. Austin is leading us toward an open gate that marks the entrance of the same park Julie and I briefly explored while she was in town. The park is gorgeous, sprawling out for acres with its lush lawns, charming fountains, flower beds, ponds, groves of trees, and lamppost-illuminated pathways lined by cute benches. This place is nothing short of idyllic.

Tonight, in contrast to when Julie and I came here, the park is quiet and nearly empty, so it feels as though it's just Austin and me. Without talking, we make our way deeper into the park and finally reach a large pond, which is shining beautifully in the reflection of the lamplight. Still without a word, we begin crossing a bridge that spans over the water, but when we reach the middle of the bridge, Austin comes to an unexpected stop. I halt beside him, waiting. Shifting to face the water, Austin places both hands on the railing of the bridge and stares out at the pond.

"My date with Tara ended early," Austin eventually tells me. "I called it off. I called off everything between us."

I need a moment to process what he just said. So Austin wants my help figuring out how to mend his broken relationship with Tara? This is going to be even more gut-wrenching than I expected.

But for Austin I'll do it.

I come up right beside him. "I admit I haven't known exactly what your status was with Tara. So the two of you were exclusive?"

His eyes remain fixed on the water. "We were getting to that point, I think. She made her interest clear a long time ago, but I wanted to wait until my rotation was over before we pursued anything official."

I press my lips together and, like him, gaze out across the pond. "That makes sense." I let some silence go by before glancing sideways at him. "So tonight you guys were having a discussion about the future of your relationship?"

His returns my glance. He continues to grip the railing. "Yes."

"And instead of moving forward with the relationship, you called it off?" I prompt, trying to get him to open up more so I can help him better.

He keeps his eyes on mine for a protracted moment before he resumes looking straight ahead. "Yes," he repeats.

I manage to keep a slightly exasperated sigh to myself. For a guy who wants my help, Austin sure isn't being very forthcoming. Then again, maybe he's not ready for a real discussion. After all, the breakup with Tara is new. Perhaps he simply needs to talk. To vent.

"I'm sorry about what happened," I tell him, and I mean it. Regardless of my feelings for him, I don't want Austin to suffer.

"Don't be," Austin surprises me with his unaffected response. His words remain even, and his expression is steady. "It was the right thing to do. I knew it wasn't fair to Tara to pursue anything with her." He breaks off to look at me again. "Not when I really wanted to be with someone else."

There's a wild rush inside my chest. Is it possible . . . ?

I swallow and hold onto the railing a little tighter.

"Oh," is all I say in reply.

Austin opens his mouth as if he's about to say more, but he doesn't. Silence falls between us yet again as we watch the water. I don't know how much time passes before Austin suddenly releases his hold on the railing and faces me squarely.

"Rachel Nelson, I'm in love with you," he declares.

I snap my head in his direction.

Austin's eyes get big. He takes a step back, flinching as he runs a hand through his hair. "Sorry, I shouldn't have . . . I mean, it wasn't fair of me to. . . I . . . I just wanted you to know." Jaw clenched, he looks away.

I don't move. I don't even know if I'm breathing anymore. Still clinging to the railing, I'm too afraid to stir, scared I might wake myself and find this is only a dream. Is Austin truly in love with me? Is it possible?

Finally, slowly and tremblingly, I let go of the railing and turn toward him while trying to gather my racing thoughts. My heart is pounding. How can I possibly tell Austin how I feel? How can I ever convey how much I truly care?

Austin breaks the quiet with a sigh. He looks down and rubs the back of his neck. "I'm sorry," he says again. "I don't know what I was thinking. I realize you don't want to hear this. I understand how you feel about me, and—"

"No you don't," I interrupt almost breathlessly. "Austin, I realize I've given you every reason in the world to believe I don't like you . . . to think I hate you." I cringe at the memories of my foolishness. I was so stubborn. So blind. "But I don't hate you."

Austin actually laughs a little. Dropping his arm to his side, he puts on a platonic smile. "That's nice of you to say, but you don't have to sugarcoat things. I understand how you feel. I—"

"No, you don't understand how I feel," I insist. "Because I only came to understand how I truly feel about you a few weeks ago."

Austin becomes very still.

My mind and heart are racing even faster now. I take a step closer to him. "Austin, the truth is that I love you, too. I've loved you for over three years, but until recently, I refused to admit it." My words are shaking so much that I have to stop to inhale another slow breath before I can go on. "I was focused on my studies and afraid to get swept up in romance, so I convinced myself I didn't care for you when nothing could have been further from the truth." I look away with a shake of my head. "When I started seeing you with Tara and realized your heart might be settling elsewhere, however, I could no longer deny my true feelings. But by then, it was too late. I was devastated to know I had missed my chance."

There's a long, intense pause. I shift my gaze back to Austin. He hasn't taken his eyes off of me. His chest is rising and falling a little faster. There's something searching in the way he's watching me that compels me to go on:

"Then, after the earthquake, when I thought I might be losing you—really losing you—that was when I knew how much I truly and completely loved you."

Austin stares for another long second, and then he takes a purposeful step forward to close the gap between us. I begin feeling the heat of his body, and the way he's studying me now is causing my insides to tingle with anticipation. Suddenly, he puts his arms around me and lifts me off the ground. I let out a laugh as he turns and sets me down so I'm sitting on the railing of the bridge, which brings me almost up to his eye level. Keeping one arm securely around my waist, Austin stands right in front of me. Our faces—our lips—are nearly touching.

"Rachel Nelson, I'm in love with you," he repeats. He uses his other hand to brush my cheek. His touch electrifies me. "I fell in love with you on the first day of medical school. I have fallen deeper in love with you every day since."

Tears of joy fill my eyes. "You truly mean that? I always thought you hated me."

Austin sighs, and his brows pull together. "Rachel, why do you think I was always trying so hard to impress you? It was because you're the most intelligent, caring, beautiful woman I have ever met. In every discussion group, on every hospital round, in every didactic session, and on every rotation, I was trying to impress you and keep up with you." He stops, his forehead creasing more deeply. "I thought you despised me, though, so I never told you how I felt." He exhales and peers off into the distance. "After three years of agonizing, I finally convinced myself I had to move on. But when I tried, I discovered I couldn't." He focuses on me once more. His expression softens as he reaches out and tucks a strand of my hair behind my ear. "Rachel, during the earthquake, your voice . . . the touch of your hand . . . your nearness . . . you were all I wanted. I knew that more than I had ever known it before. Still, however, I thought I had no chance with you, and I again told myself I needed to move on. But tonight, after ending things with Tara, I realized I had to tell you how I felt. I was actually leaving the pub to walk to your apartment, hoping to find you there. As futile as it seemed, I wanted you to at least hear what I had to say."

Exhilarating warmth fills my entire body. If this is a dream, it's a perfect, wonderful dream, and I never want to wake up.

"Austin," I whisper, "I—"

I don't even get to finish before Austin cups his free hand around the back of my head, bends down, and passionately presses his lips against mine.

Fireworks explode in my heart. Lightning shoots down my spine. Without hesitation, I wrap my arms around Austin's neck and begin returning his kisses with the same passion as he's kissing me. He tightens his hold around my back and lifts me off the railing as our mouths continue to intertwine, releasing all the desire, love, and angst that has built up over the past three years. I wrap my legs around his waist as we keep eagerly exploring one another's lips. I'm breathless. I'm soaring.

At last, yet far too soon, we pull our faces apart to gaze at each other once more. I can't stop smiling. Austin is smiling, too, as he carefully sets me back on the railing. He lets his hands run down my back as he holds me, which sends another thrill through my body. Closing his eyes, Austin leans forward and rests his forehead against mine.

"Rachel, next summer, our lives might change a lot. We don't even know where either of us will be going for residency training. But I'm willing to do whatever it takes to make this work, because I love you more than anything."

I allow my tears to fall freely. "We'll make it work, Austin. These past few weeks, I've learned that nothing matters more than being with the people you care about." I lift my hand and run it along his cheek, relishing how it feels to touch him. "It may have taken a massive earthquake to get that idea through my stubborn head, but I finally understand it now. As long as we've got each other, we'll figure things out as we enter the next chapters of our lives."

Austin says no more and begins kissing me again. His kisses are even more ardent, yet even more tender, than before. I grab hold of his shirt and kiss him fervently in return.

Slowly, Austin pulls back and smiles at me again. His smile is so warm. So loving. So sincere. "Since I messed up your original plans for the night, will you let me take you out to dinner?"

I giggle. "As long as it's somewhere quieter than an Irish pub. After all, you're still recovering from a concussion, and you never know what I might do when I hear that music."

He tips back his head and releases a carefree laugh. "True, we should probably avoid the pub. I might not be able to keep up with your disco fever this time."

Still chuckling, he helps me down from the railing, wraps an arm around my shoulders, and pulls me in close. I nearly melt as I let myself fall into his embrace.

"I know a quiet little French eatery that's not too far from your place," I hear him say.

I look up at him. "Funny you should mention that. I've always wanted to go there."

Austin smiles and takes my hand in his. For a moment, we gaze at our hands wrapped together—it's the most beautiful, perfect thing I've ever seen—and then we start walking back in the direction we came. I close my eyes and inhale the warm summertime air while the breeze caresses my face. I then reopen my eyes and gaze around at the park. Our park. Tonight, this place is just for Austin and me.

"You know this area well," I remark after a time, gazing up at Austin once more. "If you were always trying to study as much as I was, how come you're so familiar with it?"

The corners of his mouth curve upward. "Well, I actually don't live too far from here."

"Really?" I laugh, leaning into him as we keep walking. The way his thumb is stroking my hand is causing wonderful goosebumps to spread over me. "We've practically been neighbors all this time? I never knew that."

Austin looks my way again, his eyes shining alluringly in the lamplight. "I have a feeling there's a lot we have to catch up on."

"True." I sigh contentedly and lean against him. It feels so safe. So right. "Even though we've known each other for over three years, it seems like things for us are only just beginning."

Austin and I make our way through the park as the twilight deepens. Once we get close to the path that leads back to the restaurants,

Austin brings me to a stop. Keeping my hand in his, he raises it to his mouth and presses his lips against it.

"I love you," he says again.

I use my free hand to tug him down by his shirt so I can plant another kiss on his lips. "I love you, too."

And love, I realize, is the most important thing of all.

Epilogue

"Wait, wait, wait!"

Austin halts just before pulling open the door of the Italian restaurant we were about to enter. He turns around to face me. His brow furrows.

"What's the matter?"

"Nothing." I quickly use my teeth to pull the mitten off my right hand, and I start fishing around in the pocket of my huge winter parka to retrieve my cell phone. "I just want to read the email again. I want to be absolutely positive it says what I think it says."

Austin chuckles and steps out of the doorway. He gently brushes a few snowflakes from the tip of my nose. "Fair enough. Read it as many times as you would like."

I pull my phone from my pocket and use it to access my email account while my bare fingers rapidly grow cold in the freezing night air. This is the coldest March the region has seen in years, but I don't mind. I'm so ecstatic right now, I could be stranded in the middle of Antarctica and wouldn't care.

As soon as the email loads on the phone's screen, I clear my throat and begin reading it aloud:

Dear Ms. Nelson,
We're pleased to inform you that you have been accepted into Lakewood Medical Center's emergency medicine residency program.

I break off from reading and raise my eyes to Austin, overcome with as much delight and astonishment as the first time I read the email. I've probably re-read the message about a hundred times since receiving it this morning, but the pure joy and elation still hasn't worn off. With a smile I can't contain, I focus again on the email and resume reading the message I now practically know by heart:

As one of twelve residents who will be joining our program this July, you will become part of one of the most respected emergency medicine residency training programs in the country. This year's pool of applicants was the largest and most competitive yet, so you should be very proud of all you have accomplished to reach this point in your career.

I pause again to reread that paragraph to myself. It still doesn't quite seem real. It's too wonderful. It's a dream come true. I then resume reading aloud:

We look forward to seeing you in July, and we're excited to guide you through your three years of residency as you train to become a board-certified emergency medicine physician.
Sincerely,

Lakewood Medical Center's Emergency Medicine
Residency Committee.

I have to take yet another breath before I
put away my phone and look up at Austin once
more. "Can you believe it?"

"Yes, I can." Austin is smiling as he bends
down, uses a finger to tip up my chin, and kisses
me tenderly. "You're an incredible medical
student and a wonderful person. You earned this,
Rachel. Congratulations."

I squeal giddily and wrap my arms around
his neck.

Austin laughs, lifts me from the ground,
and spins me around. "I love you."

"I love you, too."

Austin gives me another kiss and sets me
back on my feet. Turning, he opens the
restaurant door. We exchange another smile that
sends a thrilling quiver through me before I pass
him to step inside.

I scan the restaurant, which is cozily
decorated with authentic Italian décor and lit
candles. Soft music is playing overhead. The
enticing aromas of pasta, rosemary, cheese,
tomato, and oregano are wafting through the air.

Scanning the room, I soon spot Savannah
Drake, Wes Kent, and the rest of our group of
friends seated at a table by the large front
window. Savannah gives me a wave when she
sees me. I smile, wave back, and begin stomping
the snow off my boots.

Austin shakes the snow from his coat and
then helps me remove mine. After hanging our

parkas on the rack near the door, he takes me by the hand, and we make our way across the restaurant to join the others.

"Congratulations, Rach!" Savannah gets up from her seat and comes around the table to greet me with a hug. "I'm so excited we'll both be doing our emergency medicine residency at Lakewood!"

"Me, too." I return her hug, and then I peer past her to smile playfully at Dr. Kent . . . I mean, Wes. "I'm guessing you were pretty glad to hear Sav is staying around for residency, too."

Wes chuckles. "Even I didn't know the residency committee's final decision until this morning. Needless to say, I was thrilled."

I give Wes another smile before returning my attention to Savannah. Her eyes are sparkling with happiness as she squeezes my hand and then goes back to her place next to Wes. Austin pulls out the chair across the table from Savannah for me, and then he sits to my right. Once we're situated, I look down the table and grin at the others in the group.

"Hi, everyone." I give them a wave.

"Hi, Rach! Happy Match Day! Sav told me you also got into residency at Lakewood!" Danielle Gillespie claps enthusiastically. "I got into the OBGYN program at University Hospital, which was my first choice, so I'll be staying in the area, too!"

I give her a thumbs-up. "That's wonderful."

Danielle's boyfriend, Joel, who's seated at her left, is smiling as much as she is—actually, maybe even more so. Leaning in close to her, he gives Danielle a kiss on the cheek and whispers something in her ear that causes her to blush and snuggle against him.

Savannah catches my attention with humorous roll of her eyes. I stifle my snicker. I know what she means: Danielle and Joel are ridiculously lovey-dovey in public, yet somehow they're still totally adorable.

I turn next to Tyler Warren, who's sitting beside Joel. "Tyler, please tell me . . ."

Tyler grins and adjusts his glasses. "Yup. I got into Lakewood's emergency medicine residency, too."

"I'm so glad," I tell him sincerely. Tyler is one of the best med students out there, and it will be great having him in the program with us.

As the server arrives and starts placing glasses of water in front of everyone, Savannah fixes a curious look on Austin.

"May I ask about you?" Savannah's gaze flicks my way before refocusing on him. Her expression is more serious now. "I'm assuming you found out about your internal medicine residency today?"

Austin and I exchange a glance, and then he concentrates on Savannah and nods. "I got into the program at Lakewood."

"That's fantastic." Savannah looks between Austin and me again as her smile reappears. "I'm so happy for you both."

"Thanks," I say, my own smile growing even wider when Austin takes my hand under the table.

Wes drapes one arm around the back of Savannah's chair and uses his other arm to raise his drink. "Well, we only have water at the moment, but I once heard that's about all Rachel should drink, anyway, so I say this is a good time to toast everyone for getting into their residency programs."

I laugh as I lift my water glass in the air like the others.

"To the future," Wes says with a tip of his head.

"To the future," I echo before taking a drink. I set my glass back on the table, and then I give Austin a nudge and lower my voice. "So how, exactly, did Wes Kent hear it's best for me to avoid alcoholic beverages?"

Austin snorts a laugh. "Let's just say, I think I might have uttered a few things I normally wouldn't have while I was concussed in the emergency department."

My eyes widen. "Oh no. What else did you say that I don't know about?"

"I have no idea, actually." Austin's shoulders are now shaking with his quiet laughter. "But I can't wait to find out."

I sigh. "Austin Cahill, if I wasn't so madly in love with you, I'd think you were the most infuriating man I had ever met."

He grins, but then his expression becomes more pensive as he keeps watching me.

"What is it?" I ask, searching his face.

"I'm thinking about the future," he says, still speaking so softly that only I can hear him.

"Oh? Anything in particular?"

He rests a hand on mine once more. "I'm thinking about how grateful I am that you'll be going on this journey of residency with me."

My chest warms with love for him, and I can't resist giving Austin a kiss. Then, while beautiful snow continues falling past the window, and friends laugh and converse around me, I sit back and smile in pure happiness.

With Austin at my side, I cannot wait to see what the future holds.

Acknowledgements

As always, I first want to thank you, dear readers. Thank you from the bottom of my heart. You're the reason I write, and you are the reason I continue to get to write. Thank you.

Bucket, thanks for your incredible insights into the world of gaming and the Flaming Sword of Death...

To two former colleagues, thanks for arguing about wood glue years ago. I still laugh about it to this day.

Thank you, Mary, Katherine, Stephanie, Renee, Madeline, Heather W, Christine, Teresa, and Nikki for voting on design ideas.

Thank you, Madeline, for your blurbage wisdom once again. Also, thanks for doing a fantastic copy edit. Your eagle eye is so appreciated.

To Kim H, a billion thanks for an awesome copy edit, and for your enthusiasm and support. You're amazing.

To Katie W, thank you for always being so supportive and encouraging. It has been a joy to reconnect over books!

Thank you to my family, always.

To Nick, my best supporter, advocate, idea bouncer-off-er, and friend, thank you. XO.

And to Cookie. Thanks, little buddy.

About the Author

TJ Amberson hails from the Pacific Northwest, where she lives with her husband, the most wonderful guy and best on-demand story advisor ever. When she's not writing, TJ might be found enjoying a hot chocolate, pretending to know how to garden, riding her bike, video editing, or playing the piano. She loves to travel. She adores all things cozy and holiday-themed. She cheers for happily-ever-afters. And she thinks there's no such thing as too much seasonal décor.

With a love of several genres, TJ Amberson writes sweet (clean) romance and romantic comedies, and clean fantasy adventures for teens and advanced tween readers.

www.tjamberson.com

Facebook: authortjamberson
Instagram: tjamberson
YouTube: realtjproductions
Pinterest: tjamberson

Made in United States
North Haven, CT
23 June 2022

20551749R00186